Someone

To Watch

Over Me

Two people died in the week before
I was supposed to turn in this book,
and I want to dedicate it to both of them.

My friend and carpool buddy of four years,
Laura Morrison, who fought bravely for
five years against breast cancer.
She would have endured anything to be here
to raise her two children, whom she loved
completely and of whom she was so proud.
I miss you, Laura. It's so odd to be in
a world without you.

And ten-year-old Jessica Harris, who played
on my daughter's and Laura's daughter's
soccer team, whose death is one of those
things I will never understand.
Soccer season is starting again, Jessica.
We miss you, too.

Someone To Watch Over Me

TERESA HILL

Steeple
Hill®

Published by Steeple Hill Books™

STEEPLE HILL BOOKS

Steeple
Hill®

ISBN-13: 978-0-373-78582-7
ISBN-10: 0-373-78582-8

SOMEONE TO WATCH OVER ME

Copyright © 2004 by Teresa Hill

www.SteepleHill.com

Printed in U.S.A.

Those of you who've read my work before
are probably thinking, This is weird and
You're writing what?

Yeah, it's weird to me, too, and definitely not
something I ever expected to be doing.

What can I say? Life is strange. We never
know what's coming or where life will lead us.
Mine has led me here.

The last few years have been scarier
and more difficult, more uncertain and
more humbling than any I ever imagined
experiencing, and through them all,
God has shown me unequivocally that He is
with me, helping me and guiding me in ways
I see as nothing short of a miracle.

He also sent many people to help me along
the way—my amazing children, John and
Laura, whom I love completely, my wonderful
husband, Bob, the kind of friends who can
get me through anything and did,
Barbara Samuel, Christie Ridgway,
Vicki Hinze, Gail Virardi, June Taylor
and most of all, my grandfather,
Joseph Haggard Jr. I wouldn't have made it
without all of you.

And—don't laugh—my dogs. (I was lonely and asked God for some more friends. He sent dogs.) Fletch, a beautiful Australian shepherd we found at the shelter, who was the inspiration for Romeo; and the love of his life, a sweet, little mixed-breed named Sophie, who showed up at our door during an ice storm.

Also, special thanks go out to all the wonderful writers at my workshop in New Zealand, who helped brainstorm ways to complicate this story.

Chapter One

William Jackson Cassidy had escorted this particular reprobate before, and it never failed. The two of them walking down the street side by side drew every female eye for a half a mile.

Heads turned. Slow, admiring smiles spread across faces of women young and old. A pretty, little curly-headed thing beamed at them from across the parking lot, and Romeo perked right up.

"Don't even think about it," Jax warned, giving a little tug on the line that held them together.

More than one woman had commented that they resembled one another, although Jax just didn't see it.

Oh, they both had hair that was a little longer and blonder than most. Jax's used to drag the top of his shoulders when it wasn't pulled back into a disreputable-looking ponytail that more than one woman had claimed made him look dangerous in a very interesting way. He now had what was, for him, a fairly short, neat trim, the ends barely brushing his collar in the back. Romeo, too, had gotten a trim, since spring was coming on strong already in north

Georgia, even though it was only March. Both he and Romeo were full through the shoulders and lean in the hips, and Jax wouldn't deny that they both probably had a little swagger to their walk.

But Jax wasn't nearly as conceited or as much of a flirt as Romeo, who was probably the most pathetic thing Jax had ever encountered. Jax chased criminals for a living. He'd seen "pathetic" before.

Romeo was a police academy dropout and now, a kept man. Kept, unfortunately, by Jax's softhearted, dying mother, who was completely blind to every fault Romeo had.

"She probably left you every dime she's got," Jax complained, just imagining the way Romeo would strut then.

For the moment, Romeo just kept on walking, oblivious, as ever, to any insult Jax slung his way.

The security guard at the hospital's employee entrance was an off-duty cop and a friend, who let them slip in the back way and up the stairs. Jax thanked the man and tried not to sound ungrateful for the patrolman's offer of sympathy. He wasn't ungrateful, not really, just trying as hard as he could to deny what was happening, which was hard when everybody he saw kept wanting to talk about it.

He knew they meant well, but it didn't help to know everyone else felt lousy about what was happening. He felt lousy, too. That bit about misery loving company just wasn't working for him. He thought he'd be better off if everyone in town would just let him wallow in his misery and pretended to be oblivious to the whole situation.

But they all knew his mother, and they all loved her. Most of them either had known his father or had fathers who'd known his father, through the job. A good number of them had dated one or more of his sisters, and the rest—the females—had dated Jax himself.

So everybody knew, and he supposed they all wanted to help, but the hard truth was, his mother was dying.

Nothing made that better, and he wasn't sure how much more he could stand, watching her suffer this way.

They got to the third floor, and Jax held up a hand to signal Romeo to stop.

"Remember, be quiet," he warned as he eased open the door, which led directly onto the hospice ward. "All right. Coast is clear."

The three nurses at the nurses' station obligingly looked the other way, feigning a sudden and unfailing interest in a splotch of paint on the ceiling of the hall. They were sweethearts. All of them. Any other time, and he would have been as charming to them as humanly possible, giving them one of the legendary smiles for which the Cassidy men were known.

He wasn't being conceited. His mother had told him all about the power of a Cassidy male's charm from the moment of his birth and sworn he wouldn't be getting away with anything with her because of it. Supposedly he'd gurgled and slobbered on her, waved his fists madly and smiled with every bit of the charm she feared a male child of Billy Cassidy's would have.

As his grandma Cassidy had told the story, his mother had promptly started praying that God would send her nothing but female children from then on, and she'd gotten her wish. Three times. Then she'd proceeded to try as hard as she could to raise her only son to think the ability to charm women was something of a burden, dangerous, unpredictable and a completely unfair advantage to wage against the women of this world.

It was the one thing she'd never convinced him of, despite the fact that they loved each other dearly.

Jax slipped out the door and into the hall. Romeo perked up as he spotted the women at the desk.

"You say a word to them, and you'll sleep outside for a week," Jax threatened.

He got nothing but a low growl in return.

Romeo had never met a woman he didn't like. He saw a pretty one and everything else went straight out of his head.

"Just remember where we are, and that you're not supposed to be here," Jax reminded him.

As hospitals went, this wasn't bad. It was in a nice, old, whitewashed stone building with a wide, elegant, wraparound porch and tall, white columns, which used to be the main hospital seventy years ago. Now, the real hospital lay off to the right, attached to the hospice unit by a pretty atrium.

They kept things quieter over here. It was dark and peaceful. The patients slept as long as they could in the morning and throughout the day, had as much medication as their systems could stand and as little pain as was humanly possible, although it was still too much.

Jax hated the place.

But his mother was in the room down the hall, and there was nothing on this earth that would keep him away from her now or at any other time in her life when she needed him.

His three little sisters were all exhausted from the battle they'd fought to keep their mother at home, where she'd asked to stay until the end. But in the middle of the night, forty-eight hours ago, her breathing had gotten so labored and the pain so bad and his sisters had cried so many tears and hurt so badly themselves, that maybe he'd just gotten too scared to let it end like that. Because he'd called 911, and they'd carted his mother off here, where, with the kind of strength she'd always possessed and he'd never understood, she still clung stubbornly to life.

She was one amazing woman. How could she do something as ordinary as die?

Pausing outside the door, he looked over to Romeo and shook his head in disgust. "Don't jump on her or hang all over her. She hurts just about everywhere," Jax said, then thought of one more thing. "And don't you dare cry."

Jax pushed open the door. The room was dim. His mother's body nothing but a faint impression under the pretty quilt stitched by his own grandma Jackson's hand, the woman whose family name he carried. William, for his father, although everybody had called his father Billy, and Jackson, for his mother's family. William Jackson Cassidy.

His mother had realized right away what a mouthful it was.

She was the one who'd given him the nickname Jax when he was still tiny, when she'd been young and absolutely stunning, from the pictures he'd seen, and had what everyone must have thought was a long, happy life ahead of her. A husband she loved dearly, one who clearly adored her, a son who adored her just as much, and three beautiful daughters.

"Didn't quite work out that way, did it, Mom?" he whispered.

Her pretty, honey-colored hair was long gone, her eyes sunk down into her face, dark circles under them, no color at all in her cheeks. She turned her head ever so slowly toward him and managed a weak smile.

Then she caught sight of Romeo and said, "Oh, baby. You made it."

Romeo stood there and grinned like a fool. His tail swished back and forth in a move that he seemed to think made women swoon. Of course, he thought everything he did made women swoon, and Jax couldn't deny it was pretty much true.

The dog had a way with women.

Especially Jax's mother.

"Come here, sweet thing," his mother said.

"I take it you mean the dog, and not me?" Jax said, taking the chair by her bedside and sitting down.

"You know I love you," she murmured weakly, turning her cheek for his kiss.

He gave her one, trying to make it seem like any other greeting he'd given her over the years. Casual and easy, as if he had ages to say hello to her this way. As if this might not be the last time.

How could that be? *The last time?*

What were they going to do without her?

"You love the dog more than any of us," he said, because it was a familiar argument, and he couldn't stand to talk about her dying.

"You're just jealous…because he's prettier than you…women like him better," his mother said, actually managing to make him grin when he wouldn't have thought anything could. She was one of those who claimed he and the dog were way too much alike. Another subject he was happy to talk about, instead of what was going on here.

Romeo whined and put his front paws up on the bed, then stuck his cold nose against his mother's cheek. She smiled and turned her face to him. "Come here, baby."

The dog leaped up onto the bed.

"Romeo, what did I just tell you?" Jax reminded him.

The dog gave him a look that he could swear said, *She does love me more than you, and I am prettier than you. So there.*

"It's all right," his mother said, the words coming slowly, her breathing labored. "…been at this for a long time. He knows…to be careful. Come right up here beside me, baby."

Her fifty-five-pound baby crept up very slowly, feeling his way, until he was as close to her as he could get, pressed against her side, all stretched out on the bed, his head on her right arm, his nose against her cheek. He whimpered softly.

"Yes. That's my good boy." His mother leaned her head against the dog's and gave a contented sigh, then turned back to Jax. "Thank you for bringing him."

"You know I'd do anything for you," he said and worried he might be the one to start to cry.

"Yes, I know."

"Sorry about bringing you here."

"It's fine…. Doesn't hurt much now. The medication is… They keep the really good stuff here. I needed it."

"If you want, we'll take you back home." And somehow they'd find the strength to see this through to the end. If she could do it, so could the rest of them.

"No…. Better this way," she said, lightly caressing the dog who'd been her pride and joy for the last year and a half. Romeo had flunked out of K-9 school and Jax had brought him to his mother after someone had broken into old Mrs. Watkins's house, three blocks down from his mother's place. Romeo was supposed to protect her, although if anyone ever broke in, the worthless dog would probably try to charm them to death.

Romeo was practically purring now. Female attention of any kind did that to him. He was the most ridiculous excuse for a dog Jax had ever seen.

"Don't worry," his mother said. "Won't be long now."

Jax stiffened. How did she know that? How could she sound so calm about it? How could he want so badly to get up and run away? She was his mother, and she was the one who was dying. If she could handle it with such dignity and grace, surely he could find a fraction of her courage and strength.

"Did you run the girls off?" she asked, about to drift off. It didn't take long to wear her out these days.

Jax nodded. "I told them you didn't want anyone but your two favorite boys tonight."

"Good. Done all they can. I know that. Make sure they do, too."

"I will."

She lifted her right hand off the blanket, a sign that he knew meant she wanted him to hold it. He did, wrapping both of his around hers, which was like ice. He thought it got colder every day.

"I know you'll take good care of them," she said. "You always have."

"No, you have. You've taken care of all of us."

He'd done what he could after his father died. Jax had been eleven, the girls eight, five and almost two. His mother hadn't had a paying job since before Jax was born. Raising four kids, his parents hadn't had any real savings to fall back on. Just living had taken everything his father made and then some. He'd moonlighted from his job as a policeman by working security at a furniture warehouse, and had been shot and killed after stopping late one night at a convenience store on his way home from his second job, killed by a stupid kid trying to clean out the till.

Just like that. *Boom. No more dad.*

Jax still remembered the way he'd screamed when they'd told him. Just for a minute. Then he'd pulled himself together for his sisters, who'd come running into the room to see what was wrong.

Life had changed in an instant.

It was like that.

You never knew when someone was going to snatch something you loved away from you, a lesson he'd learned young and taken to heart.

He really didn't need to go over this ground again, and neither did his sisters, and yet, it seemed, that's exactly what they were doing.

"Jax?" his mother said maybe twenty minutes later. She did that. Just drifted off without warning, scaring him every time she did it now. Because one time, it would happen and she wouldn't wake up again.

"We're right here," he said, Romeo on one side, him on the other.

"I just wanted you to know…I'm not scared."

Jax didn't see how that could possibly be. She was dying. But then, she was a religious woman. He wasn't a religious man, something she simply didn't understand, although she didn't pester him about it, either. She had complete faith that he'd come to his senses one day, as she put it.

"I'm glad you're not scared," he said, carefully skating around the whole religion thing. He wasn't lying. He *was* grateful. He wasn't sure he could have handled her being scared and facing something he couldn't stop or change in any way. Anything that brought her comfort right now was fine with him.

She closed her eyes and smiled dreamily. "Guess who I saw last night?"

"Who?" She'd had all kinds of people dropping by.

"Your father."

Jax stiffened. He doubted his dad had dropped by, since he'd been dead for nineteen years.

"He hasn't been far away today," his mother said as easily as she might have told him her cousin Ruth dropped by.

Okay. She was on a whole lot of morphine. The doctors had warned that it did funny things to people, that people said odd things and believed they saw odd things, too. The doctors had said not to be alarmed by it.

Sure. Jax could do that. He was not alarmed.

"So nice to see him," she said. "He looked so good. Like always. In his day, he was even prettier than you and Romeo."

"Oh," Jax said. What else could he say?

"He's waiting for me." She smiled at that.

Jax gave a little choking sound, couldn't stop it, and he really, really wanted to get up and run away. But obviously, it made her feel better to think his dad was there, waiting. *Fine.* She could see all the dead relatives she wanted if it made her feel better.

"But I'll still be with you," she said. "Always be with you. And the girls."

"I know, Mom."

"No, you don't. But…that's all right. You don't have to believe for it to happen, Jax."

"For what to happen?"

"For me to help you."

"Mom—"

"Girls will lean on you…you'll let them. But who'll take care of you? Have to be me."

He brought her hand to his lips and kissed it. "Whatever you say, Mom."

The dog started to make this pathetic, whining, crying sound that drove Jax absolutely crazy.

Take it like a man, Romeo, Jax wanted to say. He hadn't cried in years. Probably not since his father died.

"Want you to know…no regrets," she said. "Except not more time…with you and the girls. With my grandchildren. I wanted a dozen. But even that…doesn't sting the way it used to. No regrets…important to be able to say when you're where I am. I want you to be able to say it, too. No regrets."

"I'll say it now," he claimed. "I don't have any."

He lived his life exactly the way he wanted, and it suited him just fine.

"You don't even know," his mother said.

"Know what?"

"What's really important. You need to make some changes, Jax. It's time."

"What do you want me to do?" he asked, because he'd promise her anything and he hated so much to think that she was disappointed in him in any way.

"Believe."

"Believe in what?"

"Love."

"I love you," he said. "I love Kimmie and Kathie and Katie."

"You'll get it right. In time," she said, moving from one subject to another, as she tended to do of late. "I know you will."

"Get what right?"

"Try not to miss me too much. And don't worry. I'll be fine."

No, she wouldn't. She'd be gone. He didn't care what she believed, what she thought she'd seen. There was nothing else. She'd be nothing.

"One more thing," she whispered, her lips barely moving, the words slurring together. "One more favor."

"Anything," he said.

"Left you a job to take care of. In my will."

"Okay. I will. Promise."

"You know? Doesn't really hurt anymore," she said, and for a moment it was as if someone had taken the weight of the world off her emaciated body, eased all the stress lines on her face and put some color back into her cheeks. "Doesn't hurt at all."

"Good." He sure didn't want her to hurt.

"Billy," she said, the faintest of smiles on her face.

That was his father's name.

It was the last word she said.

She died with a smile on her face and his dead father's name on her lips, Jax's hand in one of hers, and the other buried in the dog's fur.

Jax froze for a moment, staring at the quilt over her chest, willing it to rise and fall as she took more air into her lungs. But nothing happened. There was no more of the wheezing, labored sound of her struggling for one more breath, that hideous, hideous sound.

Romeo seemed to know what had happened. He looked at Jax, as if to say, *Do something!*

"I can't," Jax said. "I already did too much bringing her here, and she signed all the papers weeks ago."

No one was coming to try to make her breathe again or get her heart going. Her choice, and he'd accepted it. No one would do anything.

Romeo whimpered pitifully. He licked her face frantically for a moment, until Jax got up and pulled him off. Romeo growled and showed his teeth. Jax swore and said, "She's gone. Let her be."

He thought for a minute, the two of them might go at it, right there in his mother's room, and he wouldn't have minded that. He was up for a good brawl right now. But all the fight went out of the dog. It was like his whole face just fell. He curled back up next to Jax's mom, his snout laid over her chest, and started whimpering again. Jax sat back down in his chair and buried his face against her other shoulder, because he still needed to touch her, to not let go yet.

A nurse came in sometime later to check on her, halted in the doorway at the sight of him and the dog leaning over her.

"Go away," Jax said, glancing at her briefly, and then pressing his face against his mother's shoulder again.

"I... Is she gone?"

"Just go away," Jax yelled.

Another nurse came in twenty minutes later, asking if she could do anything, if he'd like her to call anyone.

"Just go away," Jax said again.

The girls would be mad that he hadn't called, but what was the point? It was the middle of the night, and none of them had slept in days, and he'd screwed up and brought his mother here and sent the girls home.

"It wasn't supposed to happen like this," he said to no one but the dog.

Romeo whined, as if he agreed for once with something Jax said.

"And it wasn't supposed to happen yet," he yelled.

Romeo frowned, then laid his head back down on Jax's mother's chest, the two of them in complete accord. Neither one of them wanted to do anything but sit here and hang on to her and pretend she wasn't gone.

Chapter Two

Jax and the dog stayed until morning came and with it Jax's three sisters. Katie, the oldest, was twenty-seven, part owner of her own mortgage-finance company and a junior real estate mogul. She wore crisp, no-nonsense power suits with matching pumps, never a hair out of place, and she arrived issuing orders as usual.

"Jax! You haven't taken the dog home yet? It's seven! The place is full of people. The doctors will be making rounds soon—"

"Katie?" He stood up slowly, stiffly, every muscle in his body aching, and went to her, taking her by the arms.

"We promised we'd get him in and out without too many people seeing him—"

"Katie?" He looked her right in the eye. "It's over. She's gone."

"And they're about to serve breakfast. Romeo will want to know where his plate is, the beggar...."

Her voice finally trailed off. She looked to the bed, where the dog was still curled up next to their mother. Romeo whined and put his head down over her silent heart.

"But…we were going to take her home," Katie said.

"I know."

"She wanted to be home. We promised."

"I know."

Her expression shattered, mouth falling open, lips trembling, eyes blinking furiously at the tears overflowing, as she stepped back, away from Jax, and looked to the bed. He still hadn't let anyone do anything to her, hadn't been able to bear it.

Katie reached out and brushed her fingers over their mother's forehead. "She was supposed to be home."

As if their plans mattered in this. If they'd had any say in the matter, she wouldn't be dead.

"Look, I offered to take her last night," Jax said. "She said it was fine to stay, said the medication was better here, and she didn't hurt as much. She was ready to go, Katie."

"But we were all supposed to be here with her." She sobbed once more.

Order was very, very important to Katie. If she broke things down into a checklist, she could handle anything, and their mother hadn't died the way she was supposed to. This was a completely typical Katie response. Jax answered all her questions, accepted the blame for sending her and their other two sisters home to rest, for not calling immediately when their mother died, everything.

And when she started to cry harder, he held on to her until she got herself under control.

The middle one, Kathie, was the quietest of the three, and shy in the sweetest of ways. She had the same pretty, blond hair they all did, tended to wear hers long and loose. Her eyes were blue, and she dressed like a Gypsy, except without the bold colors. She liked pastels, long, gauzy skirts that blew in the wind like her hair and peasant tops. Everything about her was soft, including her heart.

She stepped into the room, realized what had happened and got very, very still, as if moving might break some spell, as if by freezing in place she could stop time and never move forward into the time when she had to accept what had happened and go on.

She sat by their mother's bedside and fussed over the dog, who snuggled against her and buried his nose in her sweater, as if he was hurting as much as the rest of them, and Jax stood behind her with his hands on her shoulders, wishing he could do more.

The last to arrive was Kim, the baby, who bounced into the room with the same enthusiasm she did everything else, her arms full this morning with flowers and the newspaper and another book of crossword puzzles, which their mother loved but couldn't concentrate enough to do anymore. Kim did them for her, talking through all the answers with her.

She was a tomboy, wore her hair in one, long braid, wore a comfortable pair of jeans and plain, cotton T-shirt. As a girl, she'd tagged along after Jax, trying to be as rough and tough as him or any of his friends, getting muddy, dusty and wet, with scraped knees, bruised shins and the occasional busted lip. A hockey puck had been the culprit, last time he remembered her bruised and bleeding.

"Kimmie, I'm so sorry," he said, when she slowed down enough to realize what had happened.

She fought not to cry then, to be a true tough-girl. But there was nothing of the tough-girl that morning. Her entire body racked with sobs, and she went from Jax's arms to Katie's to Kathie's and then back to Jax's.

They were a mess. No two ways about it. All of them heartbroken and lost in a way Jax didn't think grown-ups could ever be. He was thirty, after all. Surely a man knew who he was by then and knew that he could take care of himself and his family. Surely he didn't panic at the loss of his mommy when he was thirty.

But she'd been one amazing woman. A rock. Funny, happy, even bubbly at times. Open, honest, trusting as could be. Generous, hardworking, a woman who would have done anything for them.

Life had been hard for her. She'd worked so hard once his father was gone, and she hadn't had any particular job skills to fall back on, except a mountain of pride. Tons of people had offered to help, but she hadn't taken a dime from anyone.

It had been him and her, trying to hold things together. Mostly her, he feared, although he'd done what he could.

And now it was just him.

Him and the girls.

They were still crying. One of them would stop and then two, and he'd think the worst was over. Then in trying to get the last one to stop, the other two would start. Or the dog would, and then everyone would get going again.

"Look, we've got to go," he said, feeling like someone had kicked out every tooth he had, broken every bone in his face, in his entire body. He felt like a lump of putty about to fall, and he couldn't look at the bed anymore, at the woman he loved so much who was in it. "We have to let the hospital do whatever it has to do, and we have all that stuff on Katie's list to take care of. Staying here…it's not going to change anything."

"But I'm not ready to let her go," Kim cried.

"She's already gone, Kimmie."

They hadn't been able to hang on to her tightly enough to keep her. There was something so wrong in that idea. If you loved someone, and you hung on as tightly as you could, you should be able to keep her safely by your side.

Jax felt a stinging in his eyes, felt raw and weak and uneasy in a way he never had before. He felt alone, even with his sisters clustered around him, wasn't feeling all that confident in his abilities to even take care of himself, much less them, something he'd never doubted before.

He drew in a deep breath, then another, reminded himself that he never, ever cried, and that it sure wouldn't do any good even if he did. Look how much his sisters had cried. They didn't feel any better.

"We have to go," he said again, thinking that surely they did. There had to be a funeral. They had to put their mother in the ground.

His stomach churned.

The girls started talking about what they had to do, what their mother would want done, what she'd wear. He bit back a curse, along with something like, *Who cared what she'd be buried in?* They debated it with enough honest interest and concern that he knew what he'd hear if he said anything.

A woman thing.

He'd grown up outnumbered and badly misunderstood.

Fine. He let them debate her wardrobe, right down to earrings and shoes. *Shoes? It wasn't like she'd be walking anywhere.*

They were almost together again. They had a plan, Katie's, and her lists. Everyone had been assigned jobs to do.

His sisters fussed over their mother one more time. Touching her cheek, holding her cold, cold hand, straightening the quilt covering her body. Kim put her head over their mother's chest, as if she had to make absolutely sure her heart had stopped beating.

They gave him forlorn looks like the ones they'd worn when stupid boys had broken their hearts over the years, or when they'd had a falling-out with each other and vowed never to speak to each other again. Like the ones they'd had when their mother was first diagnosed with cancer. When she heard that it had come back. When she and the doctors agreed it was pointless to fight anymore. When their father's friend and partner had come to tell them their dad was gone.

They'd huddled around Jax then, little stair-step girls, all blond and blue-eyed and innocent. Kim had sucked her thumb. Kathie had taken to hiding in Jax's closet at night until she thought he was asleep and then creeping over to sleep on the floor by his bed. Katie started making lists.

So this was all familiar territory. Dreaded, but familiar.

He got the girls on their feet and by his side, and then there was just the dog. Jax was afraid he'd have a fight on his hands, but Romeo seemed to understand. He took his turn nuzzling her cheek and whining over her, and then jumped off the bed and stood quietly by Jax's side.

"Good dog," Kim said, stooping over to hug Romeo and then wrapping her arm around Jax's waist.

He took the dog's leash. Kathie leaned into his other side, her head on his shoulder, and Katie linked her arm with Kathie's.

"Okay. Ready?" he asked.

"We should say a little prayer," Kathie said. "Mom would like that."

"Okay," Jax said.

They could say anything they wanted, as long as they left. He bowed his head with the rest of them, and Kim did it. She started off by thanking God for their mother and ended with something that sounded vaguely like a threat, a take-good-care-of-her-or-else thing.

Or else what?

Katie raised her head and gave her sister an odd look.

"Well, He'd better take care of her," Kim said. "All those prayers she said. All the ones people said on her behalf. And she's still gone."

"It's okay," Jax said. None of them were particularly religious, except their mother, and he understood exactly how Kim felt. "Now we go."

They pivoted around as best they could without letting go of each other and trooped out.

Two of their mother's friends were outside the door, one crying. One of her neighbors was standing there holding fresh flowers. At the nurses' station, three women stood staring, sad, understanding expressions on their faces. Jax looked down at the floor, and then looked away. He just didn't have anything left, not for anyone.

The girls pulled themselves together and thanked their mother's friends for all their kindness during her illness and over the years. They thanked each and every one of the nurses on the floor, showing all the graciousness and kindness their mother had taught them. She would have been proud. His sisters could be a little flaky, each in her own way, but they were strong, smart women, good down to the core.

Their mother had loved them well.

She'd loved Jax, too. Completely. Powerfully. Joyously. But she'd been disappointed in him, too. He knew that.

She'd said it, right there at the end, in that jumble of thoughts where she'd believed she'd seen his father again.

And it wasn't as if it was a surprise that she was disappointed in him. She thought he was playing at life, wasting it, letting it slip through his fingers. That he had no faith. Not just in the God she trusted so completely, but in other people as well.

In life and in love.

Losing his father hadn't weakened her faith in either of those things. Nothing had.

So where had it come from? he wondered. The trust? The faith? The hope?

He trusted that life would hurt him sooner or later, that people would disappoint him and disappear, had faith that there was nothing more to this world than what he could see with his eyes and touch with his hands.

And yet he wanted to believe what she'd said, that she'd watch over him, even now. That his father had been waiting for her, even after all this time, and God had come for her, taken her by the hand and led her.... Wherever it was that people went. That nothing hurt her anymore, and she'd never even be sad or miss him and his sisters or her silly dog.

That's what he wanted to believe.

But he didn't.

So once more, he gathered up his poor, brokenhearted sisters and the dog. Arm in arm, they walked out of the place where they'd lost their mother.

Gwendolyn Moss dragged herself out into the midday sunshine in the town park across from Petal Pushers, the bright, cheery flower shop where she worked.

On the north end of the park, on a bench beneath a huge, sprawling oak and a cluster of magnolias, she sat and ate the sandwich she'd packed that morning, all the while trying her best not to be afraid.

It was high noon, sunshine raining down through the branches of the trees, dappling the ground with spots of light among the lazy shadows. The temperature was a perfect, balmy seventy degrees with an ever-so-slight breeze, and the park was smack-dab in the middle of a small picturesque, Southern town.

No one was going to grab her and drag her off into a dark corner because there were no dark corners here. Gwen had made sure of that. Otherwise, she wouldn't have come outside.

She sat off on the fringes of the park, keeping to herself but careful not to stray too far from the crowds, even in broad daylight.

There was a playground a little off to the right, where mothers gathered to gossip while their children pushed each other on the swings and climbed into the tree fort, athletic fields to the south where adults and children alike played and friends clustered around to watch them.

Magnolia Falls Park was shaped like a crescent moon that ran from the north to the south end of town, all along the west side, following the path of and surrounding Falls Creek. For the most part, the creek was not much more than a wide, shallow stream of water rushing over a slick, smooth, sloping rock face. But to the south, still surrounded by parkland, the creek bed dropped all of thirty feet over a quarter of a mile, into a wide, rounded pool of water surrounded by a dozen magnolia trees, forming Magnolia Falls, for which the park and the town was named.

It was especially pretty there, and Gwen liked the soothing noise the rushing water made, but for now she preferred her little corner on the fringes of the park. It was farther than she'd have come just a month or so ago. So this was progress of sorts.

There was sunshine on her face and her bare arms, heat when for so long she'd been so cold, light when for so long she'd hidden in darkness, air when at times she'd found it hard to even breathe.

As she munched on her sandwich, she eyed a bench closer to the playground. Maybe next week or next month, when the sun was even hotter and more pleasant, she'd lunch there and not be afraid.

Finishing her lunch, she crumpled up her napkin, put it in her little brown bag and tossed the whole thing into a nearby garbage can, then set off around the far western perimeter of the park, toward the flower shop where she'd worked for the past three months.

There were towering trees, oaks, pines, a willow here and there, in addition to the magnolias, walking paths, playing fields, a playground, an amphitheater and just about anything else anyone had been able to think of. The park hosted outdoor arts festivals, music festivals, kids' festivals, garden shows, town celebrations, all sorts of things. It seemed any excuse to fill the park with people was welcomed.

Gwen was going to attend one of those festivals one day. For now, she watched a baby in a stroller throw a fit and fling her rattle onto the sidewalk, then cry and pout when she didn't get the toy back after the mother picked it up.

Pretty, yellow tulips edged the sidewalk that must have just burst into bloom, and there were leaves in that brand-new green of spring slowly unfurling on the trees. Tiny baby squirrels chattered and scampered about. Birds were raising a ruckus in the trees.

Two kids squabbled loudly and vehemently over a ball, a disagreement that quickly led to shoving and parental intervention. Gwen actually grinned at that.

Fight back. Don't let anyone walk all over you like that.

The parents would be horrified. Her parents certainly would have been. She'd been raised never to lift her hand to anyone, never to raise a fuss. It certainly wasn't the reason for what had happened to her, but still, she had to wonder what would have happened if she'd screamed long and loud. If she'd struck out with her fists or her knee.

Not that it really mattered. She hadn't.

People said attackers could pick out someone born to be a victim just by the way she walked, that attitude alone could dissuade a criminal from going after one woman and targeting another one instead.

She didn't want to be a victim anymore.

Feeling bolder by the minute, Gwen, born a follower of all rules great and small, stepped off the sidewalk that skirted the park and trudged toward the creek, walked along its banks and then crossed it on one of the pretty, arching, stone-and-wood footbridges that crossed it at various points throughout the town.

Looking around, she saw there were power walkers, arms pumping energetically, making a trek around the fringes of the park, a vendor selling ice cream from a cart, little boys shrieking and trampling some of the new spring flowers as they played a wild game of chase. No victims there.

Walking on, she lifted her head high, threw her shoulders back and tried to strut confidently, not at all sure if she was succeeding or not. The motion felt awkward at best. She hoped no one was laughing or even paying her the least bit of attention.

Now that she looked about, she realized no one was.

In fact... How odd. It seemed nearly every eye was on something or someone else at the opposite end of the park.

At least, every female eye. She turned, thinking something might be wrong, and that's when she saw them.

"Oh, my," Gwen said, stopping altogether and staring.

Runners, a man and a dog, both impossibly masculine, with dark blond hair, broad through the shoulder, narrow at the waist, and just so pretty it was impossible not to look. Sunlight caught in their hair and haloed around them. They were moving quickly, at a grueling pace that would have defeated her within a half mile. But they looked like they'd been at it forever.

The allover tan of the man, the leanness of his muscles and the rhythm in which he moved said he did this often. The look on his face said he was completely oblivious to the attention he was receiving.

Women were all but falling at his feet. If he stopped running long enough, surely they would.

The dog pranced. There was simply no other word. Nose stuck high in the air, as if he were king of all he surveyed, tail twitching proudly. He wasn't even looking where he was going. He was too busy soaking up the attention of all the women.

"It has been too long since that man graced us with his presence," a woman Gwen passed said to her friend. "He certainly brightens up the atmosphere in the park, doesn't he?"

"Oh, yeah. We could sell tickets for his run," her friend said. "People would pay just to watch."

Gwen's mouth started to twitch into something that might have been an honest-to-goodness smile. What a pair. The gorgeous man and the equally gorgeous dog. No reason a woman couldn't appreciate the sight. There were all sorts of nice things to look at here in the park in the soft, spring sunshine today.

She decided to circle back to the ice-cream vendor and have a scoop of chocolate. Why not? She could use it.

She was still savoring the last bite when she came across the man and the dog again at the edge of the park. He was swiping at the sweat on his forehead, still breathing hard, power positively radiating from him.

Gwen had never been that comfortable with men like him. Very pretty men. Confident ones. Powerful ones. He was probably pushy, probably expected all sorts of things from a woman, just because he bought her a nice dinner. She wasn't that kind of girl.

Not that he'd ever pay attention to a mouse like Gwen.

At the moment, three little boys were clustered around the dog, who was breathing hard, tongue lolling out. He seemed to be grinning, if that were possible, in between showing his appreciation for their attention and lapping at a cup filled with water, provided by the man standing at his side.

"Come on," said the first kid, on his knees in the dirt beside the dog. "What's his name?"

"Killer," the man claimed with a straight face.

The dog looked at the man and gave a low growl, then whined sympathetically to the kid, as if to say he was completely misunderstood and unappreciated.

The kids giggled, and the next one took up the cause. "No it's not. Tell us his name."

"Butch," the man said, glancing for the first time at Gwen, who quickly looked away.

The dog whined once more, laid himself flat on the ground, his tail wagging enthusiastically, as if begging the kids to play with him.

"Is not," the biggest kid said.

"No, it's not. But you can just call her Sweetpea. She loves that."

The dog gave the man a look of pure disgust, and then turned puppy-dog eyes onto the boys, begging them to save him from such humiliating treatment.

Gwen couldn't help it. She grinned.

"Mister, I don't think your dog likes you very much," one of the boys said.

"She's just a little upset because she lost her pink bow on our run."

"Uh-uh," the littlest kid said. "She's a boy dog."

"Oh, I guess so. How about that. He just acts like a girl."

Gwen had a feeling the dog might just turn around and take a hunk out of the man who'd insulted him so, but instead, the dog caught sight of her and forgot the little boys completely.

He made a little purring sound. Beautiful, blue eyes gazed up at her with a kind of interest she seldom inspired in males, and yes, he could do something with his expression that looked distinctly like a smile.

He swished his bushy tail back and forth for a moment, and then walked over to her, nuzzled his snout against her shins for a moment, then dropped to the ground and rolled over onto his back, presenting her with his soft, furry belly for her to rub.

"That's it, boys," the man said. "That dog won't even remember you're alive when there's a woman nearby to impress."

The boys grumbled, tried to get the dog's attention again, but to no avail. The dog didn't so much as look at them. They finally gave up and walked off in a sulk, and the gorgeous man came closer.

"Romeo, believe it or not, not everyone falls in love with you at first sight," the man said, shaking his head, looking both mussed and disreputable.

Gwen tried very hard not to look at him anymore. The dog grinned some more at her, waiting, as if he definitely believed he was irresistible and was sure she would, too.

It wasn't so bad, being the focus of his admiration, Gwen decided.

She grinned back at the dog, thinking he probably made friends so much more easily than she did. Just walk up and grin at someone and fall onto his back in the grass, inviting her to pet him.

"What a sweet thing you are," she said, forgetting all about the dirt or the dampness of the grass and her favorite, mousy-colored skirt as she got down on her knees and rubbed a hand through the luxuriously soft fur of the dog's belly.

He whimpered. His tongue lolled out of his mouth, and then he started licking her knee, a wet, silly touch that nearly had her laughing out loud. Her entire day had brightened.

"Romeo, you are such a dog," the man said.

"Romeo?" Gwen said, daring a quick look up at the man whose hair sparkled like gold in the sun.

"Yes."

"That's really his name?"

The man nodded. "Believe me, he earns it every day."

She let her hand linger on the dog, thinking it had been a long time since'd she touched any living thing, surprised at how pleasurable something as simple as rubbing the dog's fur could be.

The detective who'd handled her case had wanted her to get a dog. For protection and for company. She'd never really considered it, but maybe that was a mistake. Maybe she should. If she could find one as sweet as this one.

"You're so pretty," she told him.

Romeo licked her knee one more time, and then gave the man a smug-looking smile, as if to say, *So there.*

And then Gwen started to worry about the dog. "You really do like him, don't you?" Gwen asked the man.

"I tolerate him. That's it."

"Oh." Gwen puzzled over that, then thought she'd figured out what was going on. "So, he's not your dog?"

"No," the man said, all the light, all the gold and sunshine, fading away in an instant.

What had she said? The dog was such a sore spot?

"But you know him?" Gwen tried. "I mean…he has a home? Because if he doesn't… He seems so sweet, and I was supposed to get a dog."

"Believe me, sweetheart, I'd love to give him to you, but I'm stuck with him for the moment."

"Oh."

So…maybe it was his wife's dog? His girlfriend's? His son or daughter's? A man like this wouldn't be all alone in the world.

"Come on, Romeo. Let's go home," he said, nodding tightly in her direction, and then turned around, leaving.

The dog was more polite, rolling to his feet and nuzzling his wet, cold nose against her hand before trotting off behind the man, who didn't give Gwen so much as a backward glance.

Chapter Three

Jax broke into a light jog, then a flat-out run, wanting to leave everything behind. How far would he have to go to do that?

He wore himself out before he got past the falls. Giving up, he collapsed onto his back in the soft, spring grass, close enough that the swish of the water sliding over the falls was just about the only sound he could hear.

Romeo caught up with him and gave a little, confused whine by Jax's right ear, and when Jax didn't answer, Romeo licked the side of his face.

"Get back." Jax shoved him, and stayed where he was, flat on the grass.

Romeo snarled at first, then whined pitifully.

"Give me a break, Romeo."

Gazing up into the branches of the tree, Jax recognized where he was. Beneath the oldest tree in the park. His mother had picnicked here as a girl. His father had fallen out of this tree and broken his arm in two places, and twelve years later, Billy Cassidy had proposed to Ellen Jackson, right under this tree. They'd sneaked off one night after she was supposed to be home safe in her bed, to come here. As his father told the story, he'd barely gotten the proposal out when Grandpa Jackson had come along looking for his little girl, and he hadn't been happy at all with their engagement. Billy Cassidy had a reputation with the ladies, after all, and Ellen had only been eighteen at the time, to Billy's twenty-two.

But nothing Grandpa Jackson said had swayed Jax's mother from her decision that Billy Cassidy was the man for her. Eventually her father had given in and walked her down the aisle of a little church two blocks away.

From everything Jax had ever seen or heard of their marriage, neither one of them had ever regretted it, until the day his father died.

Restless and angry and lost, Jax sat up and watched the water come over the falls and swirl and churn into the wide pool waiting below. No matter what, the water just kept moving, just the way the world insisted that it had to keep turning and changing.

He'd seen children playing and arguing this morning on his run, mothers pushing baby strollers, the team from the Elm Street firehouse playing a fierce game of softball against a bunch of city policemen, many of whom he knew.

He'd stared at them, wondering how things could go on in such a completely normal way, just like the water coming over the falls.

Didn't they know? His mother had died last night. She was gone. Everything had changed.

One minute, she'd been talking to him about the husband who'd proposed to her under this tree, and the next, she'd been gone.

How could someone be here one minute and just gone the next?

How did that work?

It seemed like too great a change to happen so imperceptibly.

Here and gone.

Gone.

Shouldn't the world stop for something like that? Shouldn't everyone take note of the fact that a wonderful woman like his mother was no longer a part of this earth? He fought the urge to go stop the softball game and tell them all what had happened. He'd stop cars in the street, shout the news from the rooftops.

And they'd all think he was crazy.

Glancing up, he saw that the sky was still blue. The sun was shining. Water was flowing. Cops were playing softball. Kids were arguing. Babies crying. The whole world was moving, and he was left standing still, still trying to figure out what had actually happened.

He still couldn't quite believe it.

She was gone.

Working at the flower shop, Gwen heard all the town news, both good and bad. That afternoon, she heard that the nice lady who lived around the corner from her had finally died following a long, hard battle with cancer.

Gwen hadn't actually met Ellen Cassidy, but Gwen's aunt considered her a good friend, and judging by the number of flowers and plants sent to Mrs. Cassidy from the shop where Gwen worked, so did many people in town.

As she drove herself home that night, Gwen saw that Mrs. Cassidy's house was overrun with visitors. Which meant people might like something to eat and drink, which meant Gwen had been right when she'd walked three doors down from the flower shop after work and purchased a quiche to take to Mrs. Cassidy's family.

The closest parking space she could find was nearly a block away. She'd probably have been closer parked in her own driveway. But this street was well lit, with lots of people coming and going. She felt safer here.

She walked briskly to the front door, stood up straight and tall, and rang the bell. When the door opened, she found herself face-to-face with the gorgeous man from the park.

"Hi," he said, looking somber yet still very pretty all in black, his blond hair slicked back and still kind of wet.

"Hi." Gwen's mouth was hanging open, as if she were incapable of even talking to such an attractive man. Funny, she hadn't had any trouble earlier in the park. Of course, they'd had the dog between them then. The man just looked at her, waiting, and finally she remembered why she'd come and held up the dish. "I brought a quiche."

"Thank you." He stepped back to give her room. "Come in, please."

"Oh, I don't need to do that. I didn't even know your…Mrs. Cassidy. Was she your mother?"

He nodded, looking like he had when she'd asked about the dog.

"I didn't really know her," Gwen said. "I just heard about her from so many people. I work at the flower shop on the edge of the park—"

"Joanie Graham's place?"

"Yes. So many people came by to send things to her. And my aunt spoke highly of her. She must have been a very special woman."

"She was," he said. "Please. Come in."

"All right. Just for a moment." She stepped across the threshold, saw the house was packed with people.

"This way." He closed the door and then fell into step beside her, guiding her through the crush of friends and neighbors with a polite hand at her back, down the hall.

She felt a little tremble shoot down her spine, a little spooked at his touch, a little…well, *pleased* was the only word that seemed to fit. Honestly, she wasn't sure which feeling was stronger. She wasn't scared of him. Not here in the middle of a house full of people. No one was going to hurt her here. But the thought of finding it pleasant to have him touch her was just as unsettling.

She'd thought for a while after the attack that she would be happy if no one ever touched her again, but her therapist had warned her that touch was something the human body craved, much in the same way it needed food to eat and air to breathe. Not necessarily a romantic touch, but any kind of touch. A hug. A hand in hers. A friendly shoulder to cry on. Anything.

No one touched her anymore.

It was one of the saddest realizations she'd had in months. What in the world was she going to do about that?

Gwen glanced guiltily up at the good-looking man at her side. He would not be helping her with that particular problem.

She started babbling, as she tended to do when she was nervous.

"I saw the cars on my way home…. I live just around the block. My aunt was Charlotte, and when she moved to Florida a few months ago, she offered me the use of her house." Aunt Charlotte had admitted to being in a terrible rut after her husband died and very, very lonely. Her two sons, their wives and children had settled in Florida four years ago, and she missed them terribly. Now that her husband was gone, there was nothing keeping her here. She'd leased a furnished condo, left all her things behind and gone to Florida to try out living there. If she liked it, she was moving permanently. "She spoke very highly of your mother," Gwen said. "And…well, when I saw that you had a crowd of people dropping by, I thought someone might be hungry…."

Her voice trailed off at the end. They'd gotten to the kitchen where the counters were already overflowing with culinary offerings.

"I guess everyone else had the same idea," she said, feeling both foolish and intrusive now.

"No, it's good." He took the quiche from her and found a place for it on the counter. "My sisters were in a panic this afternoon, claiming the house would be full and that we didn't have anything to offer anyone. They were about to call the deli on the corner and beg them for an emergency delivery of some trays of food, when friends and neighbors started arriving, bringing things. People have been very kind."

Gwen nodded, seeing clearly that no matter how kind anyone had been, this man was still sad and tired. And she'd been having entirely inappropriate thoughts about him at a time like this.

He'd probably been exhausted before he'd set out to run today, maybe intent on exhausting himself even more to forget for a little while what had happened.

"I'm sorry you lost her," she said. "I know how hard that is."

He nodded. "Thanks…. Uh. Sorry. I didn't even ask your name."

"Gwen," she said. "Gwen Moss."

He held out his hand, gripped hers for a moment and said, "Jackson Cassidy. Most people call me Jax."

"If there's anything I can do…" she said.

He nodded. "I guess we'll need flowers. I forgot. I want her to have lots of them. Pretty, colorful ones. Not funeral-ish stuff. She liked big, bold colors."

"Whatever you want," Gwen promised, although she hated doing funeral arrangements.

"I'll come in. Soon. My sisters and I have about a million things to do, and I think flowers ended up on my list of things to take care of."

She wanted to tell him they'd make it as quick and pain-less as possible for him, but doubted anything about this would be painless. Life was so difficult at times.

She'd been completely unprepared for that. Somehow, she'd gotten the idea that life was supposed to be a breeze, that bad things would somehow simply not touch her.

Was that the way it was supposed to be? Or had she just gotten unlucky, been in the wrong place at the wrong time?

That's what the detective had said to her. Wrong place, wrong time. While she'd sat shivering on a darkened curb near an even darker alley, on a cold, dreary night that still had the power to send her shooting out of bed screaming.

Gwen looked up to find Jack Cassidy staring down at her. She wondered exactly how his mother had died. In a warm, safe bed surrounded by the people who loved her and not feeling any pain? The kind of death a person saw coming from miles away, which gave her all the time she needed to say her goodbyes and tell the people she loved how important they were to her?

Gwen hoped Mrs. Cassidy went just like that, then won-dered if it really mattered at all. If anything could lessen the pain of losing someone you loved. The woman was still gone, after all.

"Are you all right?" he asked.

Gwen nodded. "I just… It's been a tough year. I should go."

She turned to do just that, and then saw the dog. Romeo, if possible, looked even more solemn than Jackson Cassidy had. His head hung low as he moped into the kitchen and whined pitifully.

"Oh, you poor baby," Gwen said.

He looked up at her with sad, puppy-dog eyes, and she bent down and fussed over him, taking his snout between her two hands and touching her nose to his wet one. She kissed his face, then released him and stood back up.

Romeo brushed up against her, leaning into her side, and she rubbed the soft fur on his equally soft head.

"He was your mother's dog?" she asked.

"Yes."

"I remember my aunt talking about what a gorgeous dog your mother had, but I hadn't seen him since I came to the neighborhood."

"My mother hadn't been out much in the last few months, and Romeo didn't want to leave her side."

"Oh." It made her even sadder for the dog. He was sitting at her feet, and she leaned down and hugged him. He gave a little whine and stuck out his bottom lip, as if to show the depths of his misery.

One of these sad, lost males was going to make her cry tonight if she didn't watch out.

She stood up one more time, determined to go. "I'd be happy to help with the dog. Or with anything. Honestly. Just give me a call. I'm at—"

"I know the house," he said. "I grew up here, and Mrs. Moss has been there ever since I can remember. I'll come see you about the flowers tomorrow…. Wait. That's Sunday, isn't it? I guess Monday morning."

"We can do them tomorrow afternoon, if you're having visitation on Monday."

"We will. I guess." He frowned. "Sorry, it's just—"

"I know. All a jumble."

"I hate to ask someone to come in on a Sunday," he began.

"We deal with this sort of thing all the time at the shop." People just kept dying. She hadn't expected to be in the middle of it, in a flower shop, although she supposed she would have known, if she'd just given it some thought. Flowers didn't only mark happy times. "It's no problem."

Gwen would go to Sunday-morning services at church and to the shop afterward.

"Thanks," Jax said.

She nodded. "I should go now. The front door is this way?"

"Yes, but your house is just three houses down, if you use the back alley." His hand was back, resting in the small of her back. He must be used to leading women around, because he did it with a certain amount of grace and effortlessness she couldn't help but admire.

He probably did everything that way. Some people were just born with an incredible sense of confidence.

"I think Romeo needs to go out, anyway," he said. "We'll walk you."

"Oh, no." She panicked a little, in spite of herself, trying to save herself by adding in a much friendlier tone, "You don't have to do that."

He stopped right there in the middle of the kitchen, his gaze narrowing on her face. She wondered exactly what he saw in her expression. For the most part, she thought she managed to keep the worst of it fairly well hidden. She'd just been surprised, and it was dark out and she really didn't know him. She didn't want to be in a dark alley with anyone, let alone a big, powerful man she really didn't know.

"It's all right," he said, still watching her more closely than she would have liked. "You're in good hands. I'm a cop and Romeo's a K-9-school dropout. Between the two of us, I think we can handle any trouble that could possibly come along in the alley. Although, I have to tell you, I've been traveling it since I was five, and the only trouble I've ever met with there was skinned knees from bicycle wrecks and a bloody lip here and there, if we really crashed or another kid threw a punch at me."

Gwen was afraid she was trapped. That she'd have to go with him or look foolish for not going. She stalled instead. "You...uh. You get into fights in the alley?"

He grinned. "Not since I was nine. But I think I could handle myself if someone happened to jump us tonight."

Gwen could feel the blood draining from her face. It was as if her whole being sagged, all the strength going out of her, a paralyzing fear moving in, in its wake.

He saw it all, too. She could imagine exactly what she must look like to him as he watched her turn into a pathetically fearful creature, a grown woman afraid of the dark.

She thought she might actually have swayed on her feet. His hands shot out to steady her. "It's all right."

But it wasn't, and maybe it never would be, and she really hated it when people saw that. How much she truly was not "all right."

"I have to go," she said in a shaky voice she despised, as well.

"Okay."

"That way." She pointed toward what she thought was the direction of the front door, then added, "By myself."

"Okay," he said quietly, using a tone she imagined he might on a spooked child. "Did you drive?"

She nodded, not caring how foolish that seemed. She didn't walk down dark streets at night.

"Can I watch from the front porch, until you get to your car?"

She nodded again, so very foolish. He was either afraid she'd fall apart before she even made it to her car or afraid she'd freak out if he followed her to the door, because she thought he meant to follow her out onto the street. And she might have. She fought not to cry. It would have been the final humiliation.

"I'm sorry," she said.

"It's all right. Whatever you need to do to feel safe, you do it."

He made it not sound so foolish after all, and she was grateful enough for the understanding that it alone might make her cry.

Maybe it was one of those nights when tears were inevitable.

Just not here, she begged. *Please, not here.*

She put a hand in her pocket and came up with her keys. She knew to have them in her hand, her thumb on the panic button that had come along with the alarm system on the new car she'd bought just for that safety feature. And so she could be reasonably assured that she wouldn't be breaking down anytime soon on any dark roads alone at night, and that if she did and someone tried to get close to her, the alarm would shriek and, hopefully, scare them away.

So many things she did differently these days.

She put her head down, forgetting all about not looking like a victim, and made it down the hall and past all those people in the living room without speaking to anyone. Jackson Cassidy followed her, keeping his distance so he wouldn't scare her.

He opened the door for her and stood back to let her pass through alone. Romeo waited there by his side, looking concerned for her, as well.

"Sorry," she said again.

"No problem," he claimed. Maybe he was used to paranoid, frightened women from his job.

She made it down the stairs and up the sidewalk. Her car was halfway down the block, probably farther away than the walk in the alley would have been. But here she was on a brightly lit street and not alone with a man she really didn't know. She felt foolish but safer.

As he'd said, seeing so clearly, whatever she had to do to feel safe....

That was a problem she wasn't about to explain to him.

She wasn't sure if she'd ever feel safe again.

Jax watched her all the way, Romeo by his side. She sat in the car for a few minutes before turning on the lights and pulling onto the street.

"Let's go to the backyard," Jax told the dog.

He headed around the house and climbed the steps to the back porch. He could see old Mrs. Moss's house from there, waited and watched as the car turned into the driveway, as Gwen got out, opened the door and started flicking on lights in the house. Until she was inside, safe and sound.

Romeo stood beside him, watching every bit as intently.

"Wonder what the story is there," Jax said.

One thing was certain, it wasn't the normal reticence a woman would show at the idea of walking down a dark alley in a small town with a man she barely knew. It was fear, pure and simple, the kind that came not in imagining what bad things might happen, but in knowing, firsthand.

Someone, at some point, had attacked Gwen Moss.

"You know, Romeo. Some days, life is rotten."

Chapter Four

Standing safely in her own driveway, her car locked, house keys in her hand and ready, Gwen glanced back at Mrs. Cassidy's house. On the back porch, watching her, stood a tall, shadowy figure. She couldn't see his face, not at that distance and in the dark, but she was certain it was Jax.

Was he worried about her? Or simply wondering if she was capable of getting herself home without falling apart?

Not that it mattered in the least what Jackson Cassidy or any other man thought of her.

But she was caught up in the idea of him waiting and watching to see that she got safely inside, feeling for a moment like it wasn't all up to her. That if something happened on her way home, he would have helped her.

Gwen turned and unlocked the back door. Inside, she punched her code into the security system she'd had installed and then turned on lights. All of them. Gwen liked lights. Bright ones. Especially at night.

She clicked on the TV, which was usually set to one of the music channels because she didn't like a completely quiet house any more than she liked a dark one. It was too easy to hear the normal things that went bump in the night and wonder if they were actually normal or something she should be concerned about.

So she let the music drown out the little sounds.

She'd do anything she could to make it easier on herself, and she didn't care if that made her a coward or weak. She just didn't care.

She went into the kitchen, automatically checking to see that everything was in its place, just as she'd left it, reassured to see that it was. Then she made herself a plate with chicken salad and some apple slices, which she ate at the breakfast bar in the kitchen while glancing at a magazine.

She'd look at the pretty pictures of happy people and try to think about whether her skirts were the right length or whether lemon-colored or chartreuse shirts were going to be in this spring. Not that she cared in the least, but it did keep her mind occupied.

Sunday loomed, long and lonely, before her. Usually, she went to church in the morning, more out of habit than anything else. Sometimes she shook up her schedule by trying to sleep in, then going to Sunday-evening services. Either way, the day was long.

Maybe she should join one of the volunteer groups at church. There was one that built or repaired houses for the elderly. That might work. She'd be outside and surrounded by a lot of people. She could whack a nail with a hammer every now and then. That might feel good—to hit something.

Gwen had that urge from time to time, and it didn't shock her anymore, the way it had at first. It was simply how she felt, and it wasn't like she was going to actually hurt anyone. She'd be helping, pounding nails into boards in someone's house.

Maybe next week she'd find the name and number of the project leader and volunteer.

Gwen finished her dinner, eating no more than half of it, and quickly cleaned her plate and utensils and then faced her tidy, empty house.

She felt safe inside its walls most of the time.

Relatively safe. She might actually be getting better. Oh, she got impatient with herself and just plain mad at the whole world sometimes, but that's just the way life was. Things happened.

Bad things.

People got hurt. They got scared. They got mad. They ran away. They got lost.

Why was that? Gwen just didn't know.

She sat down on the sofa, curling up on one end, her head against the left arm, her feet tucked under her. Her eyes wandered around the house that still didn't feel like her own, and she happened to glance at a figurine on the mantel, one her aunt had left behind. It was an angel.

A woman in a beautiful, long, flowing gown with something that looked like wings. She had the kindest expression on her face.

Gwen was at something of a standoff with God ever since the attack—she didn't think she really believed anymore—but she liked having her angel on the mantel, liked to imagine a real angel sent by God watching over her. There was something motherly about the idea, and Gwen had been missing her mother since she moved here.

Her mother hadn't quite understood what had happened to Gwen. Gwen understood not wanting to believe awful things could just happen to people. But when that

led to people thinking she was somehow responsible…
That's when she stopped understanding and was just
plain hurt.

Plus, there was that whole mad-at-God thing Gwen had
going on, which her mother really disapproved of. The attack had somehow become a test of faith that Gwen had
failed, at least in her mother's eyes.

Things had gone from bad to worse at home, and Gwen
had just wanted to get away. So when her aunt had decided
to move, Gwen had jumped at the chance to come to Magnolia Falls.

She curled up on her couch, her head on a pillow tucked
into one end, all the lights still burning, the music still
playing softly to cover all those pesky little night sounds,
her little figurine seeming to watch over her in a way she
found comforting beyond any kind of logic, and in that
moment, the day didn't seem so horrible or overwhelming.

She needed someone to listen, to say that yes, sometimes life was really scary and so very difficult, and that
people on Earth really didn't quite understand why; she
needed someone to even be a little angry on her behalf.

As if what had happened to her had been so bad, it
could make God mad? It hadn't been. Not in the grand
scheme of things.

It had just shaken her to the core, left her feeling vulnerable and alone. It was like being dropped in a deep, dark
hole and not knowing how to get out.

So she'd come here, to a place where no one really
knew her, a place she'd visited a few times and always
felt safe. To a place where the man who'd attacked her
wouldn't be able to find her once he got out of prison.
That had been important to her—that he wouldn't know
where she was.

She'd told herself she'd rebuild her life here, that she'd get better.

Maybe she would.

In the meantime, she curled up almost in a ball and miserably poured out her troubles to an empty room and wondered if anyone was listening.

I'm so tired, Gwen said. *Everything seems so hard, like such an effort. Sometimes, I don't know how I'll be able to go on, if things are always this hard. Help me. Please. Couldn't you just help me? Couldn't you just take all the pain away?*

And when she was done, she cried a little bit, closed her eyes and imagined someone stroking her hair, telling her everything was going to be okay.

Jax woke disoriented, with the sun blazing into his eyes. He groaned and rolled over, to get away from the light, then realized he was on the sofa in his mother's living room.

Wincing at the pain in his head, he stared at the clock, and saw that it was six-thirty. Late for him.

He rolled up and onto his feet, shrugging out the kinks as he walked down the hall, had the bedroom door open and actually stared at the empty bed for at least fifteen seconds before he remembered his mother was gone.

It hit him once more, as if it were happening all over again. He'd counted on this day being a tiny bit easier, but it didn't seem to be working that way. He didn't know how to do this, how to say goodbye to the woman who'd taken care of him his entire life, how to be without her.

The bedsprings creaked ever so slightly, and his heart gave a lurch, thinking maybe it had all been some horrible dream. He rushed over to the bed and started digging through the covers.

And uncovered the dog.

"Romeo?" he yelled. "What are you doing?"

The dog whined and laid his head down on the pillow. Big, sad puppy eyes seemed to ask where Jax's mother was, why she wasn't in her bed where she belonged and when she'd be coming home.

"She's not coming back," Jax said. "She's gone."

How would he ever make this ridiculous creature understand, when Jax didn't understand himself?

Romeo made a pitiful squeaking sound and buried his nose in the pillow, as if he might find Jax's mother there.

Jax was getting ready to yell at the dog again, when he heard a sound behind him. His sisters, all three of them, standing in a row like the little stair-step girls he remembered, crowded into the doorway watching him with the dog.

They'd spent the night, not wanting to be alone any more than he had, and now they looked bleak, exhausted, angry, as surprised as he'd been to see that today might even be harder than the day before and probably wondering how they, too, would get through it.

There was nothing to say. The reality of the situation said it all.

Romeo started whining again, low, heartbroken sounds, something like Jax might have made himself, if he'd allowed himself the luxury.

He was getting ready to yell once more, but Kim got to Romeo first. She knelt by the side of the bed, fussing over the dog and hugging him and crying.

Fine.

She could comfort the canine, offer him something Jax denied himself. He looked back at his other two sisters, who gave him a look that said plainly, *What else is there to do?*

Katie finally offered to go make coffee. Kathie said she was getting dressed because they had so much to do. Jax walked out onto the back porch, just to get out of the house and all the misery that seemed to be contained inside it. He stood there and listened to the birds making a racket, a car being started down the block, a siren blaring in the distance.

Day One without his mother.

It had to get better, because if it didn't, he wouldn't be able to stand it.

Jax got elected to go to the funeral home, something that made cutting off his right arm sound not so bad. He shoved open the door and marched down the hall, determined to get it over with as quickly as possible. He didn't care what the funeral cost, and he really didn't care what the service was like.

Sorry, Mom, he whispered, as if she might hear.

Jax knew the director, John Williams, who also served as the county coroner. How in the world did he handle those two jobs day after day?

John met him at the door and tried to put him at ease with small talk, but Jax cut him off.

"I need to do this and get out of here," he said, taking a seat in John's office.

"Sure," John said, opening up a file on his desk. "I understand. And I have some…well, relatively good news. Your mother wanted to spare you and the girls as much as possible, so she came to see me a few months back and took care of all the planning herself."

"She did?" Jax asked.

"Yes."

"Thank you, Mother," he said aloud, sagging into the chair, thinking he might just slide right out of it if he wasn't careful. Then found himself near tears thinking about her, able to think clearly enough and unselfishly enough to do this herself to make things easier for him and his sisters. "She tried to make the whole thing as easy on us as possible. I mean, there she was, dying, and still trying to take care of us."

"I know. That's the kind of woman she was." He went over all the details of the service, then said, "That's it, really. Unless there's something else I can do?"

Bring her back to life? Jax thought.

Wasn't going to happen.

Explain to him why it was that people had to die?

He doubted that was in the funeral-home instruction manual.

Tell him how people got through this?

That was an idea. This man faced death every day. He had to know so much more about it than Jax did.

Tell him what was left of his mother was nothing but flesh and bones. That it wasn't really her. That she wasn't here and she wasn't dead? That she never would be?

That would help. But Jax didn't think he believed that, either, although right now, he very much wanted to. He wanted something to hang on to, and it just didn't feel as if there was anything.

"I wish there were more I could say." John shook his head. "But the only real thing I've learned in this business is that life is precious. Every day is. A lot of people spend so much time worrying about silly, inconsequential things or chasing after things that, in the end, really don't mean a thing."

"The make-every-day-count stuff?" Jax asked.

"Yeah. Something like that. Your mother did that. She was a happy woman, walked in here with a smile on her face while she made all the arrangements. She brought two of her favorite blouses—a pink one and a yellow one—and asked me which one I thought she'd looked better in. She went with the pink because she thought it was the cheeriest color, nothing dark or gloomy or anything like that. And a pretty, matching scarf for her head. I guess she hated all the wigs she tried."

"Yeah. She said they were all too hot and itchy." She'd used the most brightly colored scarves she could find. They'd turned it into a joke, all of her friends and family trying to outdo each other in finding the loudest, funniest scarves they could for her, and she'd worn them all with a smile on her face, refusing to feel sorry for herself.

"That reminds me," John said. "She wanted you to spread the word for her—no black at the funeral. Her request."

"Okay." He could do that and he even managed not to blurt out, *Like that's going to help?*

He found tears welling up in his eyes once again. What a horrible day.

"I have to go," he said abruptly, getting to his feet.

"Sure. Take this," John said, handing him a piece of paper. "Everything's written down. Call me if you have any questions. We'll take good care of her, Jax."

"I know. Thanks."

He drove back to his mother's house, but it was empty except for the dog, who looked up hopefully when the door opened, only to be severely disappointed when he realized it was only Jax.

Jax went to the refrigerator and found neat, precise notes from his sisters, all of whom had set off to take care of their assigned tasks, plus a note that Gwen Moss called, saying she'd be at the flower shop anytime after 1:00 p.m.

Flowers were the only thing left on his list, and it just

so happened that the flower shop was on the edge of the park where he and Romeo ran.

Jax changed into a pair of running shorts and shoes and a ratty T-shirt, and ran until his legs absolutely burned and even Romeo looked exhausted. He stopped, dripping with sweat and dying for about a gallon of water, near the edge of the park not far from the flower shop, frowning. He hadn't planned to run quite that far or to be this much of a mess when he got done. Did he have to go home to shower and change, or would Gwen take pity on him and let him into the shop this way? He thought she probably would.

"All right, Romeo. Time to turn on the charm, and we can probably get in the door. What do you say?"

Romeo had plopped down beside him, sprawled on the grass, panting heavily. He gave Jax a look that said, *You expect me to move? Now?*

"She's a nice lady. Look sad and she'll fuss over you, like she did yesterday."

He took off toward the shop, urging the dog to follow. The flower shop was in a row of old, brick buildings, renovated completely about fifteen years ago and now prime town real estate. A few doors down, the café had built a tree-shaded patio overlooking the park, and people had taken to eating outside on nice days. The sidewalks were wide and prettily landscaped, the shop owners often setting up merchandise outside, too, on nice days. People lingered here and chatted with neighbors and enjoyed the view. His mother had loved coming here, when she wasn't sick.

Petal Pushers was an eccentric little place, its windows decorated with cartoon girls and boys playing with flowers, something new every couple of weeks drawn by its owner, Joanie Graham. Today, there was a tiny, stick-figured girl holding a bouquet behind her back, shyly ready to present it to a stick-figured boy on the windows.

Jax should own stock in the place, with as much money as he'd dropped at Joanie's over the years, but he'd never come to pick out flowers for a funeral before.

He tried the door but found it was locked. When he knocked on the glass, Gwen appeared out of the back room and came to let him in.

"Romeo, too? Is that okay?" Jax asked, halting in the open doorway. "He won't bother anything."

"Of course." They came inside, and Gwen knelt down to talk to Romeo. "Hi, baby. Did you have a good run?"

Romeo made sad-puppy eyes at her and touched his nose to her cheeks, first the left then the right. Gwen grinned at him.

"His version of a kiss." Jax rolled his eyes. "My sister Kim taught him that trick."

"What a sweet thing." Gwen fussed over him some more, petting him and kissing his snout. "He looks tired. Is he thirsty, too?"

"Oh, yeah. We're both kind of a mess. Sorry about that."

Gwen glanced up at Jax. He'd wiped himself off as best he could.

"It's okay. Come on into the back. We'll see what we can do."

Romeo trotted after her, taking only a moment to sniff at a few of the more outlandishly bright sprays of flowers in big, bright pink containers spread around the room. Joanie often mixed her bouquets right out here in front of her customers, letting them point and choose what they wanted and her filling in with whatever it took to finish an arrangement.

The shop was done in a wildly bright palette of colors—teal, lime green, pinks and purples. It positively shouted cheerfulness and made the woman who stood before him stand out all the more in contrast to the attitude and color of the shop.

He wondered why Joanie had hired her, because she definitely didn't seem to fit in. Gwen was a study in browns. Brown hair, brown eyes, khaki slacks and a plain, loose, chocolate-colored T-shirt beneath a trademark green Petal Pushers apron with more stick kids and flowers on it, a very plain, tentative woman in a shop that was anything but plain or tentative. She stood in the back room looking serious and uneasy, as if Jax might do just about anything in the next few moments. He stopped where he was, a quick glance telling him they were alone among the refrigerated compartments and industrial-size sinks.

He didn't want to spook her, as he had last night.

She found a bowl that was probably meant to hold flowers and filled it up with water and sat it on the floor, for the dog, then handed Jax a small, white towel and a bottle of water from one of the big refrigerators in back.

"Thanks," he said.

"You're welcome."

"And thanks for meeting here today."

"It's no problem. I didn't have anything to do and…" She frowned, looking away. "It's fine."

Scared and at loose ends, in a town where she probably didn't know a lot of people, Jax figured. And kindhearted, just as he'd suspected.

He took a long drink of water and then started dabbing at the sweat on his arms and face with the towel.

She glanced at him, and then just as quickly looked away.

Shy, scared and lonely, he corrected himself. Not at all his type. "I'll hurry," he promised.

"Okay. I'll be uh…I'll be out front. Whenever you're ready."

Jax wiped off the worst of the sweat. When he came back to the front of the shop, with Romeo trotting after him, Gwen had her head stuck in a cooler full of flowers by the front window.

"Gwen, is it okay for me to be here with you?" He hesitated five feet away once again. "Last night…I didn't mean to make you uncomfortable."

She whirled around to face him. He saw heat blooming in her cheeks. She closed her eyes for a moment, then managed to give him the barest of smiles. "It's all right. And it's not you. Not your fault."

Yeah, but it was some man's.

"So…" She put a determined smile on her sad face. "Did your mother have a favorite flower? Do you have any idea what she would have wanted?"

Which meant she didn't want to talk about this with him, which was fine too. Her right. He was just curious, thinking there might be something he could do to help. But he'd leave that for another day.

Not one when he was planning his mother's funeral.

"She liked anything bright and cheery," he said, frowning at the flower case, full to overflowing. "You know, I just thought of something. She made her own funeral arrangements, and she might have specified something in her instructions. Which I just left on the refrigerator at home." He frowned yet again. "Sorry."

"It's all right. I know how difficult this is. I mean, I don't really know. My mother's… She's fine. But we do a lot of flowers for funerals, so I've seen a lot of people trying to handle this and…I understand. You're welcome to use the phone by the cash register, if you think anyone's home."

"Sure. I'll try that." He found the phone, made the call. Kim was there, and he frowned as she read the arrangements his mother had made.

"Couldn't find it?" Gwen asked once he hung up.

"No. We did. She didn't want any flowers. She said people had already spent a fortune on flowers for her, while she was sick—"

"They had. She had a lot of people who cared about her."

"Yeah. And she was really into her cancer support group, said the group needed money for their programs a lot more than she needed more flowers, so she asked everyone to make a donation instead."

"Lots of people make requests like that. If you'll leave a name and address for the support group, we'll keep it here, in case people call to order flowers."

"Okay. Thanks." He rubbed his hands against his forehead, which absolutely ached, and then remembered. "I'm sorry. I took up your Sunday afternoon for nothing."

"No," she said. "It's fine. I didn't have anything planned; and honestly, it's… Well, sometimes the days are so long, you know?"

"Oh, yeah. I know. Cancer time, we called it, like the regular rules of time didn't even apply." Days could creep along so that every minute was agony.

"You miss her terribly, don't you?"

He nodded. "And it's selfish of me, that I'd wish one more day like that on her, but…I guess everybody thinks they're going to have time to say everything they wanted to say, and now I wonder if anyone ever gets enough time to say it all or to do everything they always thought they'd do."

Jax looked up self-consciously, realizing he'd said a lot more than he intended. Judging from the look on

Gwen's face, he'd either said way too much or something terribly wrong.

"I'm sorry. Did you lose someone recently?"

"No." She hesitated. "Not really. I just… I almost lost myself."

Chapter Five

She said it with a sad, apologetic smile, as if that wouldn't really count, losing herself. And he wondered if she meant it literally—if she'd nearly died—or if she was talking figuratively.

How out of line would he be to ask that question? Not that they seemed to be observing any of the boundaries of what ordinarily constituted polite conversation. He supposed having someone die did that to people.

"Gwen, just so you know, I'm going to be staying at my mother's for a while. The lease on my apartment was up two months ago, and she really didn't need to be alone then, so I moved back in. I haven't even started to think about finding my own place again. So if you need someone to talk to or if anything happens, anytime at all, just give me a call or come knock on the door. Or you can always call the police department and ask for me. I'm off this week and maybe next week, but I'll be back there soon."

"Thank you," she said. "It's good to know there's someone I can call. Especially someone around the corner."

"Anything I should know about this situation?" he tried. "I mean, if I were keeping an eye on the place, watching out for trouble, it would help to know what to look for."

"You don't have to do that," she offered.

"Sure I do. It's my job."

"Oh. Okay. It's… It's a man.…" She turned pale and hugged her arms around her own waist. "But then, you probably guessed that much."

Jax nodded. "What does the guy look like?"

"White. Five-ten, a hundred and eighty pounds, short brown hair, brown eyes, nineteen years old. I could get you a picture."

"Okay." Sounded like she'd given out that description more than once. "Is this guy on the loose or locked up?"

"Locked up. In Virginia."

"Good. Is he going to stay that way?"

She looked truly frightened then. Her eyes got so big, and she looked like he'd just knocked the breath out of her. "He's supposed to."

"I mean, has he been convicted and sentenced already?" She nodded.

"Okay. No reason to think he wouldn't stay locked up. I know that's easy for me to say, when I'm not the one he hurt or whatever it was that he did to you." Jax really didn't want to know exactly what the guy had done. "He'll stay there, Gwen. Trust that. And I'll keep an eye out for you."

"Thank you," she said.

Romeo came up to her and nudged her hand until it was resting against his head. He looked up at her with something that bore a remarkable resemblance to a smile and made silly dog noises at her that Romeo probably thought were both soothing and charming, and she just ate it up.

His mother swore Jax could do the same thing in a heartbeat with a skittish female crime victim and that his father could, too. Jax was highly skeptical of that notion, and offended, too. He didn't flirt with women who'd just been traumatized by crime. That would be crass, and he tried never to be that. And he wasn't nearly as shameless as Romeo.

Gwen rubbed the dog's ears and hugged him to her side for a moment. Romeo gave her his poor-misunderstood-hound-dog look. He got a lot of affection out of that expression, too.

Shameless. The dog was absolutely shameless.

And women were never skittish around Romeo.

Not that Jax was jealous of a dog.

"Give it a break, Romeo," he said finally.

Romeo made a face at him, then turned back to Gwen and most likely laid his poor-misunderstood-hound-dog look on her again.

"He really is the sweetest thing," Gwen said.

"Oh, yeah. He's a prince. He'll help watch your house, too."

"Thank you, sweet boy," she said, fussing over him some more.

"I'll get you the name and address of my mother's cancer support group. And you bring me the photograph, Gwen."

"I will."

"Thanks for today."

"You're welcome."

He took a long, slow breath and escaped, one more thing taken care of.

Fighting off an odd, restless energy, Gwen watched Jax and the dog leave. Hearing him talk about how he wished so much for just one more day with his mother made Gwen think she'd squandered the past year, like a woman who had all the time in the world to pull her life back together. Or a woman waiting for things to magically get better on their own.

How often did that happen?

Impatient with herself and her fears, she locked up the shop, marched off through the park, across Falls Creek and to her aunt's house, suddenly impatient with everything.

It was an absolutely beautiful spring day, with plenty of sunshine and a perfect temperature, birds chirping, flowers blooming, the whole world seeming welcoming. And she was going to lock herself away inside her aunt's dreary house again? Surely not.

Although her aunt had assured Gwen that she was free to make any changes she liked, Gwen hadn't done anything, and the house was truly dark and dreary. No wonder Aunt Charlotte had wanted to get away.

In the meantime, she was happy to have Gwen here, so her house wouldn't be empty.

That was how Gwen had come to run away to Magnolia Falls.

It had seemed like a smart move, an easy move, a furnished house just waiting for her, in a little town where she'd always felt safe, a chance to start over. Except she hadn't started over. She hadn't really done anything.

What if things weren't going to get better unless she did something to make them better? What if she couldn't afford to wallow in her own misery anymore?

Gwen went to the picture window at the back of the living room and pulled open the curtains she'd always left shut tight to keep anyone from seeing inside. Afternoon sunshine poured in, and bits of dust flew off the curtains and a nearby table, floating freely on a ray of light.

She went and found a feather duster and got rid of all the dust she could find in every room in the house. Then she pulled open all the curtains and shades, then the windows themselves. The spring breeze was strong and felt as if it was capable of stirring up all sorts of things, which surely wouldn't be a bad thing.

She pulled open the big, solid wooden back door, leaving only the screen door, just to see if she could stand having nothing but a thin wire mesh between her and the outside world.

Her aunt's house and every one else's on the block backed up to the alley, including Jax's mother's. So she had at least eight little old ladies that she knew of and one really cute cop who could see her backyard and back door. It wasn't exactly a prime spot for crime, and this did happen to be a bright, sunny, spring day.

Surely she could risk airing out the house.

The light changed the house so much, made it feel so much more alive. There were blinds hung at most of the windows, she saw now that she'd pulled the curtains aside, which meant she could put up pretty, light-colored sheers instead of the curtains and just close the blinds at night. That sounded like a good change and certainly not a dangerous one.

She could pack up some of her aunt's things and unpack some of her own, but that could wait for another day. She wanted to be in the sunshine today.

Gwen ended up pulling weeds in her mess of a yard. She pulled until her hands ached, uncovering what must have once been a well-planned yard, with neat, tidy bushes and a multitude of flowers. Some of them had survived being smothered, and she decided she wanted more. Some color here and there. Something bright and decidedly cheery. A quick trip to the market down the street, and she had three flats of bedding plants, all of which she managed to install before dinnertime.

By then, she was pleasantly tired, even a little achy, but it felt good. The house looked so much better.

She'd brought some daffodils and crocuses inside with her. They were in a pretty, green vase in the kitchen. She liked them so much, she went out and picked a few more and set them on the mantel next to her angel.

Maybe she'd stumbled upon an answer to feeling better. Maybe she just had to plow ahead, back into life, stay as busy as possible. The yard could certainly use the work.

Some of the ladies on this street had beautiful gardens and so many flowers were in bloom now. Which made her think of Jax when he'd told her his mother didn't want any flowers at her funeral. It seemed to make him so sad, and Gwen really didn't want him to be. There were too many sad people in the world already, and he should not be one of them.

Then she had an idea, one little thing she could do to help. He'd made her feel better today, and she wanted to return the favor.

The first thing Jax and his sisters noticed when they walked into the visitation room was the huge spray of flowers draped across their mother's casket. A bright, cheery, full-of-life bouquet of colors.

Jax was glad someone had ignored her wishes.

Sorry, Mother, he said to himself.

He'd developed a habit of talking to her in his head, and why shouldn't he? He'd talked to her nearly every day of his life, and he feared it was going to be a hard habit to break. So he'd just keep doing it.

"She said no flowers!" Katie hovered in the doorway with the other two. None of them had wanted to walk into this room.

"But they're so lively," said Kim, who was hanging on to Jax's arm, Kathie on his other one.

"It doesn't matter. She said no flowers," said Katie, who'd probably never broken a rule in her life.

"Let's see who dared flout the no-flower rule." Jax disentangled himself from his sisters and went just far enough into the room to grab the small card tucked into the arrangement. He pulled it out and read, *Hope you don't mind. They came from the gardens of her neighbors, who were very happy to give them up for her. Gwen.*

Jax actually grinned.

How 'bout that, Mom? Nice, huh? He'd wanted her to have them. He didn't care what she'd asked everyone to do. They hadn't cost anything, and they'd distracted him in that first awful moment when he'd had to walk into the visitation room, something he'd been dreading all day.

Thank you, Gwen.

"Well?" Katie demanded, from her spot in the doorway.

"It's all right." Jax went back to where he'd left his sisters. "They're from Gwen."

"Who's Gwen?"

"One of Mom's neighbors," Jax said. "Mrs. Moss's niece. She moved in a few months ago, when Mrs. Moss left for Florida. She works at Joanie Graham's flower shop."

"The woman who came by the house with a quiche the day Mom died?" Katie frowned. "Do you know this woman?"

"Not really. I just met her that night. Well, no… Romeo

and I met her earlier that day. We went running, and she was having lunch in the park."

"You picked up a woman the day Mom died?" Katie asked.

"No," he insisted. "It wasn't like that."

"Honestly, Jax. What is wrong with you?"

"I didn't pick her up. I didn't do anything with her. She's a nice woman."

"*Oh.*"

"What does that mean?" Jax asked.

"That you're not interested? That she's not your type? A *nice* woman?"

"Hey, that was mean," Jax said. "And I never said I wasn't interested because she's nice. I've dated lots of nice women. I just mean, she's a nice person. You'd like her if you got to know her."

Katie looked chagrined, and then she looked like she might cry.

"Whoa," he said. "Sorry. Bad day."

"I know. I'm sorry. I just thought…"

"That I'd hit on somebody at my own mother's funeral?" he asked.

"Maybe."

Okay. If he was honest with himself, he'd admit that he might. It would beat crying in front of half the town or feeling so lousy he wished he could die, too, which seemed like his main options at the moment.

"I just don't want to walk into that room," Katie said. "That's all."

"That's no reason to pick on Jax," Kim said, leaning in closer to his side and taking his arm once again.

"I know," Katie admitted.

"Okay," he said. "If we needed to, we could critique my relationships with women, all the way from grade school to the present, if we really needed to. That would take some time."

"All day," Kim said.

"All week," Kathie claimed.

"No," Katie said. "At least a month."

Jax glared at them, more than happy for a good sibling brawl to take his mind off everything else.

"I just don't want to do this," Kathie said, turning her face into his shoulder. She was the most tenderhearted one of them all. And one least likely to give him a hard time about anything.

He wrapped his arm around her and pulled her close. "I know."

"And I feel like such a baby."

"Yeah," he teased. "Almost twenty-four, and all grown up. You and Kim probably think you know everything."

"I don't think I know anything anymore," Kim cried.

"Me neither," Kathie said, snuggling closer to him.

Katie just stood there, stubbornly on her own and fighting back tears, looking worriedly at him and her sisters.

We'll figure this out, all of us together, won't we? her look said.

He nodded and hoped he wouldn't make a liar of himself one day soon.

Gwen dropped the flowers off at the funeral home well before the service began. She arranged them herself, then put her palm flat against the polished surface of the casket. She thought about her squandering time and Mrs. Cassidy watching it crawl by in what had to have been agony, wondered if she'd ever understand life and death and everything that fell in between.

Your son seems very nice, she told Mrs. Cassidy just in case the woman could hear her.

And Romeo is absolutely adorable.

Now what?

I hope you like the flowers. I hope it was okay to bring them.

She wondered if Mrs. Cassidy had been afraid, if she'd gotten mad at God, too. If she'd felt betrayed by her illness and all the pain and being separated from everyone she loved. She wondered if the woman had any answers now.

When Gwen got home, she made a tray of vegetables, which she took to the Cassidy house. Gwen suspected it was one of Jax's sisters who answered the door, giving Gwen a look that she couldn't quite decipher, but it hadn't exactly been welcoming. Gwen left as quickly as she'd come, then went outside to her still untidy front yard.

She was on her knees in the dirt, pulling weeds, later that evening when Jax and Romeo came walking down the street.

Romeo had a brightly colored scarf tied around his neck, which he seemed to be enduring with much good humor, and Jax was wearing a pair of khaki pants and a wild, Hawaiian-print shirt in turquoise and maroon.

"Romeo and I are making a run for it," he said. "We couldn't take one more person telling us my mother's in a better place and that we shouldn't even be sad. If we'd stayed in that house, we'd have screamed at somebody, and my mother wouldn't have liked that. So we left. We thought you might take pity on us."

Romeo whined pitifully, as if to help plead their case, and then reached out and licked Gwen's hand through the fence.

"Think we could hide out here for a few minutes?" Jax asked.

"Sure." She walked to the front gate and opened it for them.

Romeo came trotting through, eyeing the pile of weeds she'd pulled and left discarded in the yard for the moment.

"Romeo?" Jax waited until the dog turned and looked at him. "No."

Romeo whined again and sidled up to Gwen, until she found her open palm under his head. He sat down by her side and waited, for her to fuss over him, she supposed.

Gwen laughed. "He really is a flirt."

"Yeah. He got kicked out of police academy for it."

"You've got to be kidding."

"No. He really was. He was in training to be part of the K-9 squad, and he was great, really intelligent, willing to do the work, capable of understanding and remembering a great deal—until a woman walked by. Lost all concentration every time that happened."

Gwen laughed again. Romeo gave her his poor-misunderstood-pup look, but he was grinning, too. She could see it.

"Yeah, if all crime victims and cops were men, Romeo would have been the greatest K-9 cop ever."

"That is the most ridiculous thing I've ever heard."

"It's true. Ask anybody at the station. The guys were all so sure they could break him of the habit, but nobody could. He could be in the middle of taking down a suspect and a good-looking woman would walk by, and off he'd go, trailing after her, like that was more important than anything else he could think of."

Romeo gave a halfhearted growl at Jax, and then turned back to Gwen and grinned. She scratched behind his ears. "You sweet baby."

Jax rolled his eyes and made a disgusted sound.

"And he looks so nice today," Gwen said, straightening his bandanna, which was actually a silk scarf. Wrong thing

to say, she figured out as she looked up at Jax, who wa
grinning anymore. "Your mother's?"

He nodded.

Romeo looked sad again.

Gwen wondered which one of them missed her more.

"Thanks for the flowers," Jax said. "They were beautiful."

"You're welcome. I was worried I might have over-
stepped, going against her wishes. But they didn't cost
anything, and it sounded like that was her only objection."

"I wanted her to have flowers," he said. "Wanted her to
have everything, including beating this disease, but… Sorry."

"It's all right."

He stood there with his hands shoved deeply in his
pockets and moisture glistening in his eyes. She'd heard
people say that they knew his sisters would be fine because
Jax would take care of them, that Jax would take care of
everything. They'd even talked about how good he'd been
with the girls when their father had died, when Jax was
only eleven.

But Gwen had wondered, if he was so busy taking care
of his sisters and everything else and had been since he was
eleven, who took care of him? His mother probably had.
He obviously loved her very much. But now she was gone,
and he seemed so alone.

A very strong, capable man, but so alone.

People had always thought Gwen was so strong, too, so
capable. She had thought so herself, but the truth was, she
wasn't. Life had gotten really hard, and she'd crumbled like
a stale, dry cookie.

But surely Jax wasn't as weak as her.

Still, she was starting to wonder about this thing called
strength. If she'd stumbled through her whole life thinking she had it in abundance—until things got hard—she

wondered if other people did, too. Or if anyone was really that strong. If everyone didn't need someone at one time or another.

"Want to have a seat on my front steps?" she asked. "I'd offer you a chair, but I don't have one out here, and it's too nice a day to be inside."

"Sure." He took the right side of the porch, easing himself down to sit on the base of the porch, his long legs stretching down the three steps to the ground from there.

Gwen sat down opposite him, her back against one of the beams holding up the porch, dusting the dirt off her knees and hands as best she could. Romeo flopped down belly-first onto the porch, his legs seeming to just go out from beneath him. With what sounded remarkably like a long-suffering sigh, he laid his soft head on her right thigh and gazed up at her with blue eyes, almost a perfect match for Jax's.

"Why don't you relax a bit, Romeo?" Jax said. "Make yourself at home."

"He's fine." Gwen laughed and scratched the dog's head and wondered if Jax ever let anyone fuss over him at all. Surely there would have been any number of women willing to take on the task. The other thing she'd heard about him over the last few days was that Jackson Cassidy had a way with women, that they just adored him. Given the way he looked, his easy manner and the ease with which he carried himself, Gwen was sure it was true.

So where was the current woman in his life? She should be here by his side, keeping Gwen from wanting to take care of Jax, too.

"Oh, I meant to tell you—great shirt," she said.

He grinned. "My mother's orders. No black. You should have seen the crowd. Even the guys I work with on the police force and all those guys who knew my dad showed en masse with no uniforms, just one loud shirt after another. We looked like we were gathering for a luau. I'd have brought leis if I'd thought of it in time."

"Did it help?" she couldn't help but ask. "The colors, I mean."

"I don't know." He shrugged. "I'm sure it didn't hurt that we at least didn't look grim. Which reminds me—you've done some work around here."

"Not so grim?" she asked.

"That's not what I said."

"I know, but it's true. The place looked neglected. I finally noticed and did something about it." She'd brought some light and color into her home at least.

Which made her think of Jax's mother. Which would be worse? she wondered. Mourning someone who'd been completely in love with life and very happily living it, or someone who'd closed herself off from everyone and was barely living at all? One had lost so much more than the other, but the latter seemed like such a waste.

She still worried about the wasted time, the way she'd seemed to just give up. To hear Jax tell the story, his mother had never given up. Not that it had made a difference in the end. She'd still died.

And Gwen hadn't. She'd just lived for a while as if she had.

"You know," Jax said, "you look about as sad as I feel."

Chapter Six

Gwen didn't know what to say. She wouldn't have wished this kind of sadness on her worst enemy, but it was certainly nice to think there was someone else in the world who understood how she felt. She believed he did.

"What did you mean the other day, when you said you'd almost lost yourself?" he asked. "If you don't mind my asking. Because I don't want to upset you—"

"I meant that, until the attack, nothing really bad had ever happened to me," she blurted out. It wasn't easy to talk about, but if he was in the same place she was, maybe there was something about her story that would help him, and she wanted to help. "My life was ordinary as could be. I mean, my father's never really been around, but my mom and I were fine. We had lots of friends and life was good. I went to college, got a degree in business and a job handling corporate travel accounts. One of the perks was great deals on trips, and you won't believe it, but I wasn't scared of anything. I was going to see the whole world, just for fun, and when I was done, I'd get married, have my children, maybe do some writing on the side about all the places I'd been. I had it all planned out, and I thought life would be a breeze, that nothing really bad would ever happen to me. You know?"

And then she remembered who she was talking to.

"Sorry. Of course you don't know about that. You lost your father when you were so young."

"Yeah, but after that, I thought I'd paid my dues. Bad times were over. Then my mom got cancer."

"Oh. So you do know." Gwen frowned. "Now I feel bad for having only one awful thing happen to me."

"Yeah, guilt is a wonderful thing, isn't it?" He almost grinned. "The gift that keeps on giving. I didn't mean to make you feel bad, comparing my life to yours. I just feel like—"

"Like you've lost yourself?"

"Yeah."

"Like the whole world shifted, and so many things you'd assumed about your life, you were wrong about, and you just want your old life back?"

"Exactly," he said. "I have to go back to work. They've been really generous with leave time, but I can't be out forever, and I have to find a new apartment, and wrap everything up with my mom and just…live. I have to get my life back. How do I do that?"

"I don't know."

"It seems different than when I lost my father. Harder, but how can that be?"

"You were a child. Nobody expected you to handle it well when you lost your father. But now… How old are you?"

"Thirty, just last month."

Gwen nodded. "You're not a child anymore. I wasn't, either. I was all grown up, and I never thought anything would come along that could shake me up so completely."

He nodded. "Yeah."

"This changes the way you look at yourself as an adult. It shows you that you're not as strong as you thought you were. That maybe things will come along in this life that you can't handle. At least, it was like that for me. I always thought I was so sensible and capable and strong, even. Last year showed me I didn't even know I could be so afraid."

She realized she was crying and hastily scrubbed away her tears with the back of her hands. But they were dirty. She saw the dirt on her fingers a second after she touched her hand to her face.

"Here," Jax said, brushing her hands away before she could even try to fix the mess. "Let me."

She gave up on doing it herself. She'd only get his hands dirty as well if she tried. He tugged on the ends of his shirt and used it to wipe away the tears and smears of dirt on her cheeks.

"I'm sorry. It's just awful. I wish no one else in the world would ever have to feel like this."

"Me, neither," Jax said, his hands on her cheeks so gentle, he might well make her cry again.

He was close, too, probably closer than she'd been to any man since the attack, and she waited, wondering if that would scare her, the way it had when other men had gotten anywhere near her.

Not that there was anything remotely threatening in his presence, and it wasn't even dark outside. Darkness was the worst.

"Okay, give me your hands," Jax said, easing away ever so slightly.

"You don't have to do that," she said, looking straight ahead and finding her gaze on the open V of his shirt, staring at his throat and a bit of sun-browned skin, waiting again for nerves to take over.

"Hands, Gwen," he demanded.

Obediently, she held out one.

He cupped the back of her hand in one of his, and she made herself stare at that same spot on his throat, not quite sure how she'd come to be in this place, sitting so close to him, talking to him about how horrible things could be and him cleaning her face and hands.

Life was so strange sometimes, but that shouldn't surprise her anymore.

"Can you tell me about what happened to you?" he asked, as if he might have wanted to know what the weather was supposed to be like, and he didn't look at her. He seemed completely absorbed in the task he'd set for himself.

The gentleness of his touch, of his voice, the way his presence was somehow soothing and unsettling at the same time… She didn't know what to make of this man.

She'd met him three days ago, and already she felt as if he'd turned her life upside down. Her house was different. Her life was different. She'd been so alone, and now there was a warm, flesh-and-blood man sitting on her front steps cradling her hand in his, wiping away her tears and asking her to spill her soul out to him.

Gwen was thinking, *Do I really have to do this? Do I have to tell him every awful thing?* While another part of her was thinking that he was a policeman, after all. It wasn't as if anything she had to say would come as a shock to him.

"I'll start for you," he offered. "It was a year ago."

"Nearly."

"And it was dark."

"Yes." If she closed her eyes, she could see the darkness again. The rain. The blur of the city streetlight, so far away. She wanted to tell Jax to stop, to go away. To not be kind or understanding or sad for her. To give up on this idea of pushing her out of her shell, whether she was ready or not.

She felt like she was losing control of her life again, this time to a kind, terribly handsome, brokenhearted man and a flirtatious dog. It was one thing to do things because she'd decided she was ready, another to have him pushing this way and making her want to push herself.

"Come on, Gwen. It was a man," Jax said, gently stroking her hand with his shirt. "I know it was a man."

"Yes." Gwen risked a glance up into his face. Kind, beautifully blue eyes stared back at her. Bleak eyes with sad, little, crinkly lines at the corners that spoke of sleepless nights and heartfelt pain, way too much understanding in his expression.

"And he hurt you. With his fists?"

"And a knife. He had a knife." She didn't really have to say it. She just turned her head to the right, and this close he could see the scar there on the side of her neck, where that man had cut her. "I thought he'd cut my throat. I mean… You know what I mean. He did, but it wasn't deep. I didn't know that, because I couldn't see it. I just knew that it hurt, and I was bleeding, and… He was just trying to scare me. That's what the policeman said later. I was hysterical and thought I couldn't breathe and that I was bleeding to death, but…it wasn't that bad."

"Sounds pretty bad," Jax said, his jaw gone tight. He put down one of her hands and she held out the other. If anything, his touch was even gentler than before as he bent over her hand and went to work cleaning it. "Gwen, did he rape you?"

"Not quite," she said, still wondering whether it really mattered. The *not quite* part.

"You got away?"

"No, I got…lucky." That's what so many people had said. *Lucky.* "Someone came along."

A couple of kids had walked into the dark alley. She'd heard them but never seen them. They hadn't come to help her, but they had scared her attacker away. She'd stayed there, frozen, in the alley. Lying on the cold, wet pavement, bleeding, the rain running down her face and all down her body, and she'd kept hoping it would somehow wash everything away. That she'd wake up and nothing would have happened to her.

She looked up at Jax's angry face, hoping he didn't pity her and determined to finish this and never talk to him about it again.

"I was on a date," she said. "A second date with a man I'd just met. We were downtown at the arts center. When we left, he wanted me to come home with him. When I told him that I wouldn't, he got mad. I told him I'd find my own way home, didn't think a thing about it. I planned just to get in a taxi. We hadn't come that far from the theater, and there had been so many people there. But when I got out, it was so quiet. I guess I got turned around in the dark. Next thing I knew, somebody grabbed me and pulled me into a dark alley. It all happened so fast and I was so shocked, I didn't even make a sound. It was all I could do to breathe. Can you imagine that? A woman about to be raped, and she can't even make a sound."

"It happens when people get scared. It's not unusual at all."

"I hated myself for not even making a sound. When the prosecutor started talking to me about what it would be like at the trial, she said his attorney would say, 'Did you tell him no? Did you tell him to stop?' And I thought, how could anyone think a woman wanted a stranger to grab her off the streets and drag her into an alley and hold a knife to her throat? Was it only wrong if I told him I didn't want him to do that?"

"I'm sorry, Gwen. I'm so sorry."

She shrugged as best she could and blinked back fresh tears and looked off into the sky, because she couldn't look at him.

"They convicted him of attempted rape?" Jax asked.

"Aggravated assault. We didn't push on the attempted-rape charge," she admitted. "The prosecutor said it could have gone either way. I never really got a clear look at his face, and the kids who stumbled into the alley ran right back out, so there were no witnesses, and he hadn't really raped me."

There had been bruises, torn clothes, a nick here and there from the knife, but even the cut on her neck hadn't required more than a dozen stitches. She'd been *lucky*, after all.

Gwen looked up at Jax once again. "You think I'm a coward for not pressing on the attempted-rape charge?"

"No. The prosecutor was right. Could have gone either way, and with the knife wound, aggravated assault was a lock."

"Yeah, I was lucky he cut my throat." She tried not to sound so bitter. "The prosecutor said that. The guy pled guilty to the assault. We dropped the attempted-rape thing, and I never had to come face-to-face with him in court."

"That's understandable."

"Well, some people didn't understand." They thought if it had really happened the way she said, the guy should have been convicted of attempted rape.

"Some people are idiots. You didn't do anything wrong, Gwen."

"I must have. Because if I didn't… If this was just one of those things that happen, like a roll of the dice. My number just came up…. That's crazy. What kind of world are we living in? Something just as lousy could be right around the next corner, and who wants to live in a world like that?"

She paused long enough to take a breath, and felt more tears streaming down her face. Romeo made sympathetic sounds and nudged his nose against her shoulder, then her cheek, sniffing at her tears.

"Romeo, stop it," Jax said.

"No, it's okay. He's sweet." Gwen put her arm around the dog, buried her face in his warm neck and let more tears fall.

Jax's arm settled, warm and soothing, around her shoulder. His hand pressed against the side of her face, urging it down against his shoulder, and then she somehow found her face buried against his neck, tears falling unchecked onto that crazy shirt he wore.

She curled her body into his, one hand slipping around his back and the other clutching his shirt. His hand stroked her hair, and the dog whined and tried to get closer, too.

"Romeo, give it a break," Jax said. "I've got her."

The dog obviously didn't like that. He growled at Jax, and somehow Gwen started to laugh, surrounded by a big, warm, furry dog and a nice, broad-shouldered cop.

Much too soon, she forced herself to ease away from him, but he caught her with his arms, stopping her when they were nearly nose-to-nose.

When any man had gotten too close, something inside of her had curled up in fear. People had told her time would fix that, but she hadn't believed that, either.

Was it time?

Or this man in particular?

It couldn't be him, Gwen thought. Not the completely self-assured, completely comfortable around women, completely charming and gorgeous Jackson Cassidy.

He leaned in even closer, tilting his head to one side. His warm, soft lips settled ever so gently against her cheek, and one of his hands cupped her other cheek, brushing at the moisture there with his thumb.

It was the sweetest kiss, the kindest touch.

Part of her wanted to cry again, at feeling so alive. If she was the kind of woman who could be casually intimate with a man, he'd be great. But she wasn't that kind of woman.

"I'm sorry," he said, backing away. "No one deserves to be treated like that, Gwen. Don't let anyone make you feel like you did anything wrong. And I'm sorry I made you talk about the attack."

"No. It's okay," she insisted. "Maybe I need to. Not saying anything sure hasn't done me any good. I think I'm still as much of a mess now as I was when it first happened."

Jax was still close. She thought that maybe—just maybe—curled up in his arms, she wouldn't be afraid at all.

What an amazing gift that would be.

She'd come to a point where she tried to stay on alert at all times, watching and waiting and fighting off the panic that someone was going to hurt her again, and she didn't know how much longer she could do that. It took too much out of her, and yet she didn't know how she could stop, either.

Was a man the answer? She'd never even considered that.

He was a nice man. If she asked, he'd probably just sit here and hold her for as long as she needed him to. Gwen wondered if any length of time would be enough. But she couldn't ask him to do that.

Jax smiled at her and pushed a strand of hair back from her face and tucked it behind her right ear. He kissed the tip of her nose—which made her smile—and maybe he was going to actually touch his lips to hers. Maybe. How would that be?

But before he could, someone called his name. A woman. He turned his head, and Gwen did, too.

Standing outside the gate to Gwen's aunt's house was a very angry-looking woman in a bright pink dress with a lovely scarf around her neck, obviously a funeral attendee and obviously very unhappy.

"Jackson Cassidy!" she roared. "Honestly, at your own mother's funeral!"

Gwen straightened guiltily. Her cheeks positively burned. Jax moved more slowly, easing himself away and getting to his feet. He looked down at Gwen and said, "Sorry. My sister, Katie. She's been thinking I still need a mother, and she may have to take on the job."

"No, I'm sorry."

"I'd introduce you, but let's save that for another day, when she's not so wound up."

"Jax, I swear," the woman began again. "Even for you, this is low."

"Katie, enough," he said sternly. He looked at Gwen one more time, mouthing, *Sorry,* then turned to the dog. "Let's go, Romeo."

Gwen sat there and watched them go, the woman stalking off ahead of them, the dog whining and trying to get her to play, to somehow make amends, Jax in his silly purple-flowered shirt, hands buried deep in his pockets looking as if he had the weight of the world on his weary shoulders.

Jax set a leisurely pace, refusing to hurry to catch his fuming sister.

She stalked ahead of him, muttering as she went. Romeo was trying to fix things by trotting beside her, licking her hand every now and then. Katie was having none of that. You'd think she'd caught Jax half-naked, the way she'd carried on.

He'd had enough of her whole attitude toward him, but he really didn't want to get into it with her today. He didn't want to get into anything today. Because he really didn't want to yell at his poor sad sister today, but he wasn't going to take garbage off of her, either.

Katie finally stopped about ten feet ahead of him, turned around and planted her hands on her hips, glaring at him. *Great.*

"You just buried your mother four hours ago," she said.

"I know. I was there." He glanced down the block to their mother's place, five houses away. Thank goodness no one was outside on the porch. Maybe no one would hear.

"Ahhhh!" she growled, no words seeming adequate for her in her state.

"Katie, I swear, you're going to blow a fuse one day if you don't tone it down."

"She was our mother!" Katie said. "And you sneak out of the house after the funeral to go pick up some girl?"

"I walked out of the house because I couldn't stand to be there any longer. Can you understand that? Would you rather I stayed and screamed my fool head off at the lady in Mom's cancer support group who was bawling and saying she didn't know how she'd get along without Mom because she took such good care of all of them. I was thinking, Lady, she was my mother. I need her. My sisters need her. This stupid dog needs her. Don't think you need her any more than we do. And then the minister started telling me how much better off she is now than she was here on earth, and I'm thinking, What does that mean? That we're selfish for wanting her to live? To be with us? I don't want her to hurt the way she did the last two awful years. I'm the last person who'd want that for her. But I still want her with us."

"Me, too," Katie said.

"So I walked out of the house rather than growl at somebody and make a scene. Big deal, Katie."

"But you didn't have to go see a woman."

"You're saying I should swear off women out of respect for my dead mother?" he asked. Not that he hadn't. He hadn't been out on a date in months, hadn't had a minute to himself.

"On the day you bury her, I would think you could keep your lips to yourself," Katie said.

Jax scowled at her. "It wasn't a big romantic moment. She was upset, Katie. She's had a lousy year. I've had a lousy year. She was telling me about hers, and the next thing I knew, she was crying. What was I supposed to do? Be insensitive and do nothing while she cried her eyes out? What does that have to do with losing our mother?"

"You were kissing that woman," Katie said. "I saw you. Anyone walking down the street would have seen you."

"Well, you know what? I really don't care. Let 'em say what they want. Let 'em think what they want. If they don't know us well enough to know I loved my mother and that losing her was one of the hardest things I've ever had to face, then I don't care what they think."

"I do."

"That would be your problem."

He was nearly shouting at the end, frustration and the exhaustion of the past few days getting the better of him. His sister stood there on the street, looking smaller and sadder every moment. She could be fierce when she tore into someone, laying down the law or defending someone she loved, and right now, to her, she was defending someone she loved. Jax got that. He knew why she was the way she was. He just didn't have the strength or the patience to deal with her right now.

But before he could say anything else, she lost every bit of anger inside of her. It drained away in a moment, leaving her as weary-looking as he felt, every bit as defeated and every bit as sad.

Tears filled her eyes and rolled down her cheeks. Romeo whined and licked her hand, then glared at Jax.

Inside, Jax was roaring, railing against fate and cancer and near to weeping himself. But for his sister, he didn't let any of those things show. He slowly walked to her, took her gently by the arms and pulled her to him. She clung to him, just as Gwen had only moments before, and he just let her cry it out. Jax was an expert at tears. With three sisters, he'd had to be.

Too bad none of their problems of late had involved skinned knees or bad grades or a boy who'd pulled their hair on the bus to school.

"I'm sorry," Katie said finally. "I shouldn't have yelled at you."

"It's okay," he insisted.

"It's just that when I saw the two of you, I thought…I know he loved her, too. I know he loved her as much as I did."

"You know I did."

"It looked like you'd forgotten her. Like it wasn't hurting you at all."

"Believe me, Katie, it hurts."

"That woman—"

"Gwen," he said. "Her name is Gwen. Someone jumped her in an alley last year and nearly raped her, and she's still a mess. The night Mom died, she brought over a plate of food. When I offered to walk her home down the back alley, she nearly broke down. She was terrified to be alone with me, and I wanted some details about the attack, in case anything else happened. You know, so I'd know what to look for. When she was telling me about it, she started to cry. That's all."

"Oh."

"And I'm telling you not because you have a right to know, but because if you see her, I don't want you saying anything about me and her kissing on her porch the day we buried our mother."

"Okay. I'm sorry," she said, genuine regret in her sad, watery eyes.

"It was a peck on the cheek, Katie, because she looked so sad."

"Okay." Katie sniffled and looked chagrined as he dried her tears as best he could.

"Be nice to her. She could use all the friends she can get."

"Okay."

"And she brought those pretty flowers for Mom, because I told her I wanted Mom to have them but I didn't want to go against her wishes. So Gwen gathered the flowers out of the neighbors' gardens."

"That was nice," Katie admitted.

"She is nice. And shy and scared and definitely not my type. I mean, come on. You know me. I want someone easy and fun. No strings."

"You don't really want that, Jax."

"Yeah, I do. I like it just fine."

"You're going to see how wrong you are about that someday."

Which was way too close to what his mother had said with her dying breath. *Mom... God, please. Please.* He didn't really believe. Losing his mother made him want to, because if all that stuff she believed was true, then she wasn't really gone. She was in a much better place, and nothing hurt her anymore, and he had a shot of seeing her again sometime, somewhere, and that's what he wanted for him and for her.

But he didn't really believe.

He looked over at his sister, who seemed just as heart-broken.

"The cars are gone. Looks like everyone's left," she said.

"Good." They were all nice people, and they all loved his mother. But he just wanted to lock himself into a room and hide, not letting anyone get near him, not even his sisters. He loved them, but they needed so much from him right now, and he wasn't sure how much more he had to give.

What do I do about that, Mom?

Of course, she didn't answer. She was gone.

Chapter Seven

The next morning, Gwen found herself walking ever so slowly past Jax's mother's house, just in case he came outside and one thing might lead to another, and then, there she'd be, back in his arms.

Just as a test, of course.

She hadn't been afraid when he'd touched her. It was the most amazing thing, and she needed him to hold her again, to be sure it wasn't a fluke or something. If it was just him or if she'd be okay with other people being that close to her.

The twelve-year-old girl inside of her had come up with the brilliant plan of creeping past Jax's house—in hopes that he might see her and—

"Hello, dear."

Gwen yelped. There was no other word for it. It sounded like something Romeo might say. She whipped her head around, cheeks burning, to find Mrs. Altman, who lived next door to Jax's mother, standing by her mailbox and smiling at her.

"Hello, Mrs. Altman," Gwen called out, hoping against hope that the sweet old lady hadn't noticed her stalking Jax.

From the look Mrs. Altman was giving her, kind of like Gwen might have sprouted antlers or something, she had. *Great.*

But raised in the South in a gentler era, Mrs. Altman didn't mention it. Instead, she smiled kindly and said, "That was a lovely thing you did for Ellen. The flowers were just beautiful."

"It was no trouble at all," Gwen said. And done with what she thought were completely pure motives at the time, but maybe she'd been wrong about that, too. Maybe she'd been after Jax even then.

"You look troubled, dear," Mrs. Altman said. "Has anything happened?"

"Oh…. No. I'm fine," Gwen stammered.

"Do you need to speak to one of Ellen's children? Because I'm fairly certain they're inside. You can just go up there and knock on the door."

"No. No. It's nothing like that. I was just…thinking about some things…on my way to work." That was it. *Work.* "And I really have to hurry or I'll be late. Joanie really doesn't like it when anyone's late. So, I have to run. Bye, Mrs. Altman."

And with that, the odd, sprouted-antlers look was back on the kind older lady's face.

Gwen escaped and hurried to the flower shop, afraid of other blunders she might commit along the way. Plus, she *was* nearly late. She rushed into the shop at eight fifty-five, five minutes shy of opening time.

Joanie arrived at nine-thirty, and Gwen managed not to do anything silly until all of 10:07, when out the front window of the shop, she caught sight of a man and a dog running through the park.

She'd have known that pair anywhere. Jax was running shirtless in the bright spring sunshine, his gorgeous flirt of a dog right next to him on this exceptionally beautiful day. Did the sky truly look bluer than ever, or was it Gwen's imagination?

It was like a disease she'd never had before. *Man sickness.* She could not get him off her mind. She could not pry her eyes away from him, as he ran past the store window.

Maybe that was why it had felt so good when Jax held her.

He and the dog ran down a small hill, nearly disappearing from her view. Gwen stood up on her toes, leaning into the window for balance, and—

"Ahhh!" She nearly upset a huge bucket of gladiolas at her feet.

"Gwen?" Joanie came flying out of the back room. At five feet tall and maybe a hundred pounds, she was like a tiny cyclone, always busy and always stirring things up. "Are you all right?"

"Yes. Fine. Sorry I scared you. I was just…" She righted the gladiolas and then glanced guiltily at the window, thinking she was safe, her crime hidden. But just her luck, Jax ran back into view.

"Oh, I see," Joanie said, a whole new tone coming into her voice.

"No. Really. It's not that—" The flat-out lie stopped Gwen cold. She really tried hard not to lie.

"Oh, honey, don't apologize. I appreciate the sights as much as any woman. Don't you just want to go up to him and thank him for being kind enough to run past our window?"

Gwen just whimpered in another Romeo-like communication.

"You know what my mama always said?" Joanie continued. "If God wanted him to be ugly, he would be. But he's not, and I happen to think that beauty is a thing to be admired, whether it's a pretty flower or a tree or the sky or a man."

"Oh. Okay."

"Besides, I've known him forever. Believe me, he wouldn't mind."

"I believe you about that," Gwen said. "How do you know him?"

"Every woman in town knows Jax. If they weren't friends with his mother, they knew his sisters or they dated him or had a daughter who dated him or a friend who dated him. But everybody knows him."

Gwen grinned. "But how do you know him?"

"I've known his mother for years. And he also dated my two younger sisters. That man has a way with women."

"I know."

"You do?" Joanie sounded so shocked, it was funny.

"I mean… I didn't mean it like that. Really." She tried to backtrack.

"No, it's okay. I didn't mean it like that, either. It's just that you haven't shown any interest in men since you came here, so I was surprised."

"He's been kind to me, and I guess he can't help but be charming."

"Oh, he can't. It's in his genes. His father, Billy Cassidy, was the best-looking man I ever saw. The funniest. The happiest. He never met a stranger. Never hurt anybody."

"What happened to him?" Gwen asked.

"Somebody shot him almost twenty years ago. He was a cop, too. Walked into a convenience store one night when he was off duty, and stumbled into a robbery. There were a half-dozen people in the store, and he put himself between all of them and the guy's gun, trying to talk the guy into giving up, and the guy shot him dead, just like that. It was just one of those things, you know?"

"Yeah. I know."

"Jax was only eleven, I think, and the oldest, the only boy. He grew up fast. I mean, he still knew how to have a good time and everything, but underneath all that… He was a big help to his mother and really good with his sisters. They could have fallen apart, but the whole family just kind of pulled together and kept going. You've got to admire people who can get through something like that and still find a way to be happy."

Oh, yes. Gwen was just starting to see how hard that was—to pick up and keep going. To be anything close to happy.

And yet, Jax and his family had done it.

So…maybe he could show her how.

Sure. She could just walk up to the man and tell him she was a wreck and that being in his arms had been the nicest moments she'd had in almost a year, and could he please just do it again? He'd think she was pathetic, but he'd probably do as she asked because he was a nice man.

Gwen frowned. Would it be worth it? Baring her soul this way?

Maybe it would.

"Oh, honey," Joanie said, "I have to tell you, he's one man you don't want to fall for. He never stays with anyone for long."

"I know. It's not about that. Really."

Then what was it? Gwen waited for the question that never came.

Joanie studied her with an even more worried look.

"That reminds me," Gwen said. "How did he manage to date both your little sisters?"

"That part was easy for him. The real question is how he did it and still managed to have them both liking him in the end. I mean, the man manages to stay friends with just about every woman he ever goes out with. It's like women just can't get mad at him or they can't stay that way."

"Is he…seeing anyone now?" she thought to ask. Just in case. Really.

"I was gonna say he's always seeing someone, but honestly, I don't remember the last time I saw him around town with anyone. The last few months, I think it's all he and his sisters could do to take care of their mother. She really wanted to stay at home instead of in the hospital, and they managed, right up until the end. They were really good to her."

So, Jax was tired and lonely and sad, and Gwen was thinking of using him to try to make herself feel better?

Maybe she'd have to go for the completely honest, straightforward approach or nothing at all. She'd march right up to him and explain the situation. He was a reasonable man. He'd understand.

Besides, she needed to know if she was truly over her fear of men. How could she possibly make plans for her future if she didn't know? And he probably hugged a dozen different women a day. It was probably his favorite way of saying hello. What was one more woman to hug?

There. She'd made it sound practically noble and necessary to her entire future that she get herself back into Jax's arms.

After they got back from their run, Romeo started crying. He searched the house, inch by inch, sniffing all the corners, nosing things aside, pawing at closed doors until Jax opened them.

"What?" Jax said.

Romeo practically howled, and then he went into Jax's mother's bedroom and came back with the scarf he'd worn to the funeral in his mouth. He dropped it at Jax's feet and then barked out what sounded like a demand for answers.

"Don't do this, Romeo. Not today."

Romeo growled and pawed at the scarf.

"Look, the lawyer's coming, okay? Remember? Alicia. You like her." One of Jax's ex-girlfriends, actually. She and his mother thought it was so funny, how his mother kept running into women he used to date. She said it was proof he'd dated too many women. "It's time for the reading of the will. You'll probably be the richest dog in town."

Romeo howled once more. Obviously, he wasn't after Jax's mother's money.

"Okay, I know. Not funny." Jax actually sat down in front of the dog and tried one more time to explain. "Mom would just love seeing me do this, you know."

Was he really going to have a conversation with the dog?

Romeo scratched at the scarf again, more insistent than the last time, and barked like he could cheerily tear Jax apart if he didn't produce his mother ASAP.

"Okay. Here we go," Jax said very slowly, as if the dog read lips or something. "She's not coming back. I'm sorry. I miss her, too, but there's nothing I can do, and if you keep wandering through the house, crying all day, I don't know what I'll do to you."

And then the crying sound came back. It was just awful. A squeaky, pitiful sound that went on and on and on.

"I don't understand it myself," Jax said. "How can I possibly explain it to a dog?"

Romeo just cried.

"How about a muzzle?" Jax suggested. "Could we get you a muzzle? I know it keeps dogs from biting, but does it keep them quiet, too?"

Jax didn't know. He didn't know anything.

Except that he was actually talking to the dog.

How do you like that, Mom?

"Okay, just go ahead and cry," Jax said, getting to his feet. He glanced at the clock and saw that he was running late. He headed for the back bedroom, which was his, and started pulling on jeans and a T-shirt because he'd just gotten out of the shower when Romeo started fussing.

Romeo followed, sniffing through Jax's closet and his dresser drawers.

"I didn't hide her in the bureau, I swear," Jax said, then nearly tripped over the dog, who was sniffing under Jax's bed.

Jax closed his eyes and sank down to the floor. Romeo sat up and they were eye-to-eye again.

"Look, I just can't do this," Jax said. "Do you understand? I can't listen to this. I can't watch you search the house for her or wait at the door for her or look at me like you want to know why I can't bring her back. She's gone."

Romeo whined again and looked out the window, still hopeful.

How had he gotten the job of breaking the news to the dog? He wanted to sit down and whine along with Romeo, and then someone else could come along and explain everything to both of them, especially why they couldn't be with her now.

Great. His mother always said he and the dog were just alike. *I'm finally starting to see the resemblance, Mom.*

Jax wondered if it was the pressure of losing his mother and being stuck with her constantly whining, fussing, crying, heartbroken dog that had him losing it.

At least Alicia Campbell was coming this morning with the will. If Jax knew his mother, and he did, she'd laid out everything, all nice and neat, down to the smallest details. Custody of Romeo would be high on her list. She'd loved the silly creature too much not to put a lot of thought into who would raise him.

So, this was a turning point. They'd see the will. He and his sisters would find all the things she'd promised to everyone, deliver them, clean out the house, put it on the market, and then, maybe, things would slowly get back to normal. Jax would go back to work, find an apartment, pick up with his old life. Somehow, he'd take care of the girls, and he'd forget all about the dog. *Sorry, Mom. I need to do it. All of it. It won't be the same without you, but I can't stay in this limbo much longer. It's too hard, too painful.*

She'd understand.

So, Jax had a plan. Divide up her stuff, sell the house, get on with his life. He hoped it worked, that it gave him some small measure of relief, because he still couldn't imagine being without her.

Jax's sisters arrived an hour later, looking solemn and teary-eyed. Alicia showed up right on time, ten minutes later. She was wearing a beautifully cut, dark blue suit and heels, briefcase in hand, looking impossibly grown up compared to the girl he'd dated sophomore year of high school.

"Hi, Jax," she said, kissing him softly on the cheek, then greeting his sisters one by one and the dog.

Jax's mother had gotten a real kick out of hiring Alicia. Thanks to her, his mother knew more about his life in high school than Jax remembered sometimes. She'd offered to hire another lawyer, but said if she tried to avoid every woman Jax had dated at one time or another, she'd have to move to another town. Either that or give up eating out, getting her teeth cleaned, buying a car, buying insurance, banking, gardening, going to the gym and having chemo. One of his exes had been a chemo nurse.

Jax had told her she was welcome to see any of his former girlfriends anytime she wanted and talk about anything she liked. She'd laughed and told him she was going to laugh the loudest on his wedding day.

Except now she wouldn't be around to see it.

Jax pushed the thought aside and offered Alicia a chair. "Thanks for coming to the house."

"No problem," she said, settling into his mother's favorite chair by the window.

Romeo, looking greatly offended, plopped down in his usual spot beside that chair and glared at Jax, as if it was all his fault that his mother was gone and this other woman was sitting in her chair.

Jax stood behind his sisters seated on the sofa, hands braced on its back for support.

"I'm so sorry about this." Alicia opened her briefcase and pulled out a file. "She was an amazing woman."

One of Jax's sisters started sniffling, clutching a tissue and dabbing at her eyes, and then the next one started and then the next. It was as if they were all hooked up to the same faucet. Turn it on and the tears started flowing.

Jax grimaced, but didn't say a thing. The waterworks had to stop eventually, and until it did, he'd handle their tears the way he'd handled everything else.

"Is there anything I can do?" Alicia began.

"Let's just get this over with," Jax cut in, then worked to soften his tone. "Please?"

"Of course. It's all very straightforward. I've brought copies for each of you that I'll leave here, and I'll read through the entire document word for word, if you like—"

"Not necessary," Jax assured her.

Alicia looked at each of the girls in turn, to see if any of them objected, and they all shook their heads to indicate they agreed with Jax.

"All right. Well, I suspect parts of this will come as a surprise to the four of you. I was surprised myself when your mother made these changes, but I can assure you, she was absolutely lucid and clear about them."

"We're fine with whatever she wanted," Jax said. No way they were going to squabble amongst themselves over their own mother's possessions. They just weren't that kind of people.

"Good, because I can assure you, there was no question in my mind about her competency."

Jax had an odd feeling that he might want to sit down, which was silly. His mother had been perfectly comfortable with her life, but she was also a woman who'd raised four children on her own and a cop's pension. There really wasn't anything to her estate for anyone to fight over, nothing she had that he could imagine him and his sisters fighting over.

So why did he feel as if he really wasn't going to like what he was about to hear? As long as she hadn't left him the dog, he'd be fine.

"First," Alicia said, "you should know that it was her intention that the bulk of her estate be divided into roughly five equal parts. One for each of you and—"

Jax held his breath, thinking for a moment his mother really had left the dog money. He missed the next part of what Alicia said and had to ask, "Wait. What?"

"Her favorite charities," Alicia repeated.

"Nothing for the dog?" Jax asked.

Alicia frowned at him. So did all three of his sisters. Romeo lifted his head and whined, as if to ask what he'd missed.

"Nothing. Go back to sleep," Jax said, then looked at the four women. "Sorry. Go ahead. Please."

They all still looked annoyed.

"Bad joke," he said, trying to make amends.

Alicia used to have a sense of humor, but that might have disappeared with her divorce, although the women he knew said it was more likely the part about raising four children alone that had done it. "Sorry. Really."

Alicia took a breath and let it out slowly. "As I said, a guideline—five roughly equal parts. She didn't specify charities, except to say to please remember her church. She also mentioned putting away money for the girls' weddings or perhaps down payments on homes for each of you some-day. Katie, I know you already have a home, but your mother said you'd discussed several ideas about renova-tions and she thought you might use the money for that. But, as I said, all of those are suggestions only.

"She wanted me to say one more time, for her, that she was as proud of you as she could possibly be and loved you all dearly. She asked that you try your best not to miss her too much and to know that she'll be watching over you all, even now. She felt extremely blessed in the life she led."

The girls' tears started again. Jax stared at the ceiling and thought, *Just let it be over. Please.*

"That's really it. There's not a lot of money to the estate. The house, a little life insurance, but those are all offset by medical bills and a few other expenses," Alicia said. "Jax, she named you executor of the estate. There'll be some paper-work, but I'll do my best to make that as painless as possible for you. But really, she's left everything in your hands."

"All right," Jax said warily, then waited for the rest of it.

The lawyer didn't say anything.

Jax must have missed something again. "So," he said, "do you have a list or something?"

"Yes. Her bank accounts, credit cards, household bills that will still be coming in. It'll be months before the medical bills are settled, of course. She paid for her own funeral months ago, so you don't have to worry about that."

She handed Jax the lists.

"Okay," Jax said blankly. "What about all of her stuff?"

Alicia took a breath and smiled a tad mischievously, a smile that showed that dimple and reminded him of all the trouble he'd gotten into with her ages ago. "As executor of the estate," she said, "it's yours to disperse as you wish."

"Huh?" Jax said.

"She gave you complete discretion to dispose of all her possessions."

Romeo chose that moment to start sniffing around Alicia's briefcase and whining, as if Alicia might have hidden Jax's mother inside. "Oh, and I almost forgot. That includes the dog, of course."

"Okay, wait," Jax said. "This isn't funny. Not at all."

"I'm sorry. You're right. It's not." But the dimple in her cheek didn't disappear, no matter how hard Alicia struggled to keep a straight face.

"She wanted me to divide up everything?"

"Everything," Alicia repeated.

He stared blankly at her and waited. She didn't squirm or start babbling, two things most people did when confronted with a prolonged silence. It was no fun at all, trying to intimidate her with cop tricks.

"Is this a joke?" Jax asked finally.

"No. Really. I wouldn't do that. Not with a will."

Jax scratched his head and tried to ignore the soft sniffling sounds his sisters were making. They were a morose-looking group, and he could imagine his mother wanting them all to smile today and cooking up something with Alicia to do just that.

Except, he didn't think this was funny at all.

The dog part, maybe.

He could see where his sisters would think it was funny, but the rest really wasn't.

"Alicia, explain this to me. Now. Please."

"I don't know that there's really any more I can tell you," she claimed.

"So, she was tired and just didn't have the strength to handle all this?" Jax could understand that, although he was surprised she'd waited that long to take care of everything. She was a very well-organized, responsible woman.

"No, I don't think it was that," Alicia said.

"What was it?"

"I don't know."

Which had Jax fantasizing about strangling Alicia.

"What do you mean, you don't know? You were her lawyer."

"Yes. *Hers*. I've told you everything she asked me to. The bottom line is, everything she had is yours, Jax. Even the bit about dividing the estate five ways isn't binding. You can do whatever you like with everything she had."

Jax gave up on getting anything else out of Alicia, who still seemed to be enjoying this too much. He looked back to his sisters, still sniffling and looking tragic, not making any move to help him. They didn't seem inclined to do anything at all. Even Katie, Miss List-Maker-Maniac, Miss I-Can-Organize-Anything, just sat there, looking to him to make it all better.

This was a perfect job for Katie, so why hadn't she gotten it?

"Well, if that's everything, I should be going," Alicia said, getting to her feet.

The girls sniffled some more and tried to smile and thank her.

What did she mean, *That's everything?*

That was definitely not everything.

Jax did not want to take care of anything else. He wanted his life back. He wanted back out on the streets, saving his little town from what little crime there was.

He followed Alicia to the front door, then went outside with her, closing the door behind them, not wanting his sisters to hear.

"Wait a minute," he said when they were on the front porch together. "You can't just leave it at that."

"I didn't," Alicia said. "Your mother did. She trusted you, Jax. She said there'd never been a time in her life when she honestly needed you to take care of something for her that you'd refused. And she was sure you'd do this for her."

Jax's shoulders sagged, any other words of protest he might have stuck in his now too-tight throat.

Never refused her anything?

Surely he had.

But honestly, he couldn't remember a single time. They'd always needed so much cooperation just to keep the family going, and he'd always thought she worked so hard and that everyone needed so much from her. He'd tried to take as much of the burden off her as he could.

"It'll be fine," Alicia said, taking him in her arms for a brief hug and giving him a little smile. "The house is paid for, so you won't have to rush to get it on the market, right?"

Jax nodded. *No rush.*

"That means you can take your time about going through her things and dispersing them. And I'll be in touch about all the paperwork."

Alicia turned and climbed into a sparkly, champagne-colored car, all sleek and fast-looking.

Maybe he could ask her for a ride, just to get away from here.

But Jax waited too long to ask, and before he knew it, Alicia had roared away. He was stuck outside in the cool of the porch, not wanting to go back inside, still feeling kind of shell-shocked.

What had just happened?

He glared up at the pale blue sky, which had the nerve to look as peaceful as could be and said, *Mother!* but felt nothing more than a calm, cool breeze in response.

His head hurt. His heart hurt. And he was so tired.

He went back inside, to find his sisters chattering away about the most inconsequential things. Their mother's perfume. Her favorite flowers. The door to the basement that stuck, which used to make her so mad.

Jax didn't say anything. He was trying not to shout, waiting for them to notice that while they might be perfectly fine with the details of their mother's will, he was not.

But they didn't notice, and he thought maybe he didn't want to talk about this today after all. Memories were too close to the surface, too many frustrations threatening to erupt and overflow.

He let them chatter on, until they were talked out. Katie finally said she had to go—something about an appointment that was set weeks ago and couldn't be changed. One by one, they hugged him and told him goodbye, and then they hugged the dog, as if he was a bereaved relative, too.

He couldn't believe his mother had left him the dog to get rid of!

It would have been a perfect joke if she stuck her head in the door, grinning, right about now, and said, *Gotcha.*

But she loved him and the dog, and she knew Romeo didn't like Jax any more than Jax liked Romeo. So he couldn't imagine why his mother would ever do this.

"I'm so glad that's over," his sister Katie said right before she walked out the door. "I was dreading it."

Well, it wasn't over for him, and he was dreading what was left.

"Don't worry," she said. "We'll all help. We just need some time to be ready to take this on and to actually do something with all her things. Jax, are you all right?"

No, he was not all right.

What would she say if he told her that? He didn't think he ever had, not in all the years they'd spent together, not in all the times she'd ever asked had Jax ever been anything but okay.

If he said it now? Katie would probably call Kim and Kathie back, and they'd cry, and talk about how hard this was and how bad they all felt, and he absolutely could not handle that. So he shrugged and said he was as good as could be expected.

He remembered Alicia saying he'd never failed his mother before, and he sure didn't want to start now.

But he really didn't know if he could do this.

Chapter Eight

Once they were alone, Romeo started grumbling and whining and pawing at the door, as if he was demanding, *Where is she?*

"You're going to be the first thing to go," Jax threatened.

Romeo would normally have snarled at him and showed his teeth, but he must have been as confused as Jax, because there was no snarl. Not much of anything. Romeo looked all done-in, like he might pitch a fit if he had the energy, but he was too confused and too tired to do much more than fuss pitifully.

"No," Jax said. "Don't do that."

It was like having a crying baby. There was no reasoning with the dog when one of these spells hit.

"I mean it, Romeo. Not tonight."

Romeo stretched out on the floor, flat as a pancake, a big frown on his face.

"Go hide in her closet," Jax said. "Come on. I'll open up the door for you, and you can root around to your silly heart's content in all that stuff that smells like her. You can sleep there tonight if you want."

As opposed to sleeping in the middle of her bed, which was what Romeo had been doing.

But even the closet couldn't tempt Romeo.

He stayed on the floor, doing his best imitation of crying, which was really quite good. Maybe the dog could do commercials. He knew a lot of tricks. Maybe Jax could pawn him off on a trainer who got dogs into the movies. Romeo would eat up all that attention.

How did Jax go about finding a dog trainer/agent? Did they have casting calls or something?

It sounded like a lot of work. More work than he felt capable of managing at the moment.

Okay, maybe the dog wouldn't be the first to go.

But something had to.

He had to get started, just for the psychological boost alone. Taking action always made a man feel better, like he had some control, like he could change things, even really bad ones.

There. Jax had a plan.

He'd get rid of all the stuff, get rid of the house and the dog. Pick up his old life, and he'd feel better. It was a great plan.

He took a slow turn around the living room. There were tons of framed photos. Couldn't get rid of photos. The sofa was old and worn, but really, really comfortable. He'd fallen asleep on it so many nights, he should know.

He had a sofa of his own stored in the basement, but honestly, if he had a choice between comfort and how the thing looked, he'd much rather go for comfort. Maybe he'd keep this old sofa of his mother's and get rid of his.

He turned to the beat-up old recliner. Again, a marvel of comfort, and a man needed to be comfortable. Maybe he'd keep that, too.

There was a really ugly clock on the wall that Jax had made in eighth-grade shop class. Cut it out of a block of wood, very ineptly, in a shape that somewhat resembled an old-fashioned cottage, the kind a cuckoo bird would normally fly out of to announce the hour. Jax's didn't have a cuckoo bird, and the clock was certainly no marvel of beauty, but it hung proudly on his mother's wall, even to this day.

Why hadn't he ever bought her a new one?

He grabbed the clock off the wall, frowning at the mark it left on the wallpaper. It had faded all around the clock, leaving an outline where it had been. So, if he got rid of the stupid clock, he'd have to paint or put up new wallpaper, and more work was the last thing he needed now.

Maybe the clock wasn't the right place to start.

Jax opened the back door and walked out onto the porch. Mrs. Altman was next door in her backyard shooing a stray cat away from her garbage can. He remembered his mother saying that she worried about Mrs. Altman getting by financially. Apparently, her social security wasn't much, and she really struggled to make ends meet.

"Hello, Mrs. Altman," he called out.

She straightened up and squinted into the light of the setting sun, which was behind Jax. "Oh, hello, young man. How are you and your sisters holding up?"

"We'll manage. Somehow," he said, unable to mumble something as simple and as much a lie as *Fine, thanks.*

"If there's anything I can do, you just let me know. Your mother was one of the kindest women I've ever known."

Perfect. There it was. That so-often-repeated phrase, *If there's anything I can do…* "Actually, there is."

"What would that be, dear?"

"I have to get started cleaning out the house, and… Well…" His mother said the old lady lived at the pawnshop in winter, when her gas payments were high, getting rid of her things one by one, to try to cover the bills. What did his mother have that Mrs. Altman could pawn? He didn't want to hurt the woman's feelings, but if she needed it, his mother would have been happy to have her take whatever would pay her bills.

"Is there anything you need?" he finally said.

"Oh, dear. Those are your mother's things."

"I know, but—"

"You need to talk with your sisters first, and you'll want to keep some of her things yourself, of course. If you're not ready to do that now, it's okay. Why, I didn't get rid of any of Mr. Altman's things until he'd been gone for four years. So don't you feel like you have to hurry, dear. No need to rush."

But he wanted to rush. He wanted his life back.

"Isn't there something you'd like?" he tried again.

"I'm sure there are some little things that I could see and be instantly reminded of your mother—"

"Like what?" he asked.

"Oh, I don't know. But I'll give it some thought. And bless you for thinking of me, dear. You wait until your sisters are ready, and all of you go through the house together, and when you've done that, if you still want me to have something of hers, I will."

Something?

Not what he had in mind.

"Has that silly cat been in your mother's garbage, too?" Mrs. Altman asked, shooing the thing away one more time. "It makes the worst messes, and for some reason, it just loves my garbage. It makes such a racket at night trying to get in there."

Jax frowned. Mrs. Altman still had metal garbage cans, the 1950s variety, if he was any judge. Maybe he could give her his mother's nice, wheeled, plastic garbage cans. The old lady shouldn't be trying to drag those heavy metal cans to the curb, anyway.

Of course, he'd never be able to convince Mrs. Altman that they didn't need garbage cans at his mother's house, especially now that they had so much stuff to get rid of.

Okay. He'd thought of four different things he could begin to clear out of his mother's house, and had failed miserably to dispose of even one.

At this rate, he'd grow old and die here himself, surrounded by his mother's things.

Mrs. Altman kept fussing at the cat for another moment, then went inside and shut the door behind her. Jax stood there on the back porch, thinking just one, little thing. *One*.

He walked into the garage, which was probably the worst spot in the house. Stuff practically multiplied overnight in here. His mother cleaned out the house and put everything here, but it never made it any farther.

He peered into dark, dusty corners, thought of actually climbing the makeshift ladder and going into the attic above the garage. But right before he resorted to climbing, his gaze landed on the golf clubs shoved into a corner.

His mother had taken up golf five years ago, a phase that hadn't lasted much longer than six months. She loved being outside on the course, but she was a lousy golfer. After that, when a friend wanted to go play, his mother packed a picnic lunch, and she went along purely for the ride and the company. She and her friends had a grand time.

There was Jax's answer. Golf clubs.

His sister Katie played with the grim determination found only in people who took up the game purely for the networking opportunities it provided. She made nice to real estate guys, trying to get referrals to her fledgling mortgage company, and she did it wearing beautiful designer golf togs and playing with a really nice set of clubs that he and his sisters had bought her last year for her birthday. So she didn't need their mother's clubs. Neither of his other sisters played. He couldn't imagine them developing a sudden passion for the game.

Surely giving away the clubs wouldn't be a problem.

He just needed to find the right person for them.

Come on. There had to be someone.

Then he thought of Mrs. Baker, who went to his mother's church. Hadn't his mother told him that the last time she'd golfed with Geraldine Baker, Mrs. Baker had thrown one of her clubs into a tree in frustration, and they hadn't been able to get it down?

Yeah. He remembered that.

He went inside for the phone, found her number and called, accepting her condolences once again and then moving as quickly as he could to the real reason he'd called.

"I heard you had some trouble on that little par 3 on the Magnolia Valley course recently," he said.

"Oh, dear. Did your mother tell you about that?"

"Yes, she did, Mrs. Baker. And please don't be embarrassed. I don't think anyone plays the game for any length of time without giving a club a toss every now and then. It's a really frustrating game."

"It's horrible," she said. "I was mortified. Your mother and I made up a foursome with two old goats from that nice Methodist church across town, and they laughed so hard they nearly fell over. And then they wanted to try to climb that tree and get my club down."

"But they didn't, did they?"

"No. They're seventy, if they're a day. I was afraid one of them would have a heart attack and the other would break his neck. The silly club was still up there when your mother and I gave up and left. I suppose someone who works on that course got it down eventually, but I've been too embarrassed to go back and get it. Honestly, a woman of my age losing her temper that way. My little granddaughter even heard the story. I'll never live this down."

Jax plastered his palm over the receiver so she wouldn't hear him laughing at her. He just couldn't help it. Mrs. Baker was the last person on earth he'd have ever believed would have a smidgen of a temper.

"Ma'am, I was just starting to go through my mother's things, and I found her set of clubs and thought you might like to have them. She hardly used them at all, but she did enjoy the time she spent on the course with you and some of her other friends. I know she'd be happy to have you use them."

"Darling, I'm not ever hitting one of those ridiculous little balls again, thank you very much. I think I'll limit my golf days to riding around in the cart, like your mother did. She had the right idea about the game."

"Oh. Okay. You're sure?"

"I'm sure. It's the most frustration I've ever had, and to think we pay them to do that to us. It just doesn't make any sense at all."

Jax closed his eyes and bit back a groan. He was striking out again. He got off the phone with Mrs. Baker, defeated once more.

No clock.

No garbage can.

No golf clubs.

Surely there was something he could get rid of.

Maybe he could find a nice burglar to haul some stuff away. He knew quite a few, and they never stayed in jail for long. Surely one of them was out roaming the streets, casing a house or something.

But that would scare the neighbors, and most of them were little old ladies living alone. He couldn't scare little old ladies just to help get rid of his mother's stuff.

He wandered through the house a bit more and then found himself out on the back porch again. He looked up the alley, seeing no one, but glancing down the street, he saw Gwen working in her backyard.

She looked up and waved at him.

"Hi," he yelled back. "Got a minute?"

"Sure."

"Then come see me. I need some help."

"Okay." She started dusting off her jeans at the knees from where she'd been kneeling in the dirt. "Be right there."

Gwen showed up at the back door a few minutes later, her cheeks tinted a happy pink from the sun.

"You look good," he said, grinning at her.

She stopped right where she was and stared at him. "What?"

"You. You've got some sun on your cheeks. And your nose. Some color in your face." Some life in her pretty, brown eyes. "It looks good on you."

"O-oh." She stammered and left her mouth hanging open.

Was it so unusual for a man to pay her the slightest compliment? "Come on in. The lawyer who handled my mother's will just left, and my sisters did, too. You're completely safe. No one's going to come looking for me and yelling."

"Oh… That." She still looked uneasy.

"Everything okay?" he asked Gwen, just in case.

"Yes. Are you okay?"

He tried to shrug like a man who didn't feel as if he was carrying the weight of the world on his shoulders. "I've been better. You really want to help?"

"Sure. What can I do?"

"Walk through this house until you find one thing—any one thing—that you like or you think might be useful and take it home with you."

"Jax, these are your mother's things..."

"And she's gone."

"I know, but surely you don't have to do this right this minute."

"Yes. Right now," he insisted. "This is what I need."

"Why?" Gwen asked.

Leave it to her to find the one question he didn't want to answer.

"I have to get started. I have to think that I can do this— that I can get rid of all her things and pack up this house and sell it and then..."

"Forget her?" Gwen asked softly.

"I'll never do that. But having this house and all these things sitting here waiting for her won't bring her back."

"No. But I'm afraid getting rid of all her things won't make it hurt any less that she's gone, either."

Which made Jax want to throw something.

Of course, if he broke it, he could sweep up the pieces and put them in the nice wheeled plastic garbage can, and at least one thing would be gone.

"I just have to take one step toward getting this done," he said. "Can you understand that?"

"Yes." She gave him a sad smile. "*That* I understand perfectly."

Relief washed over him. He didn't think he'd ever been so grateful to another human being in his entire life. He very nearly picked her up and swung her around the living room. If he thought she'd laugh and like it, he would have. But a part of him was scared to touch her and bring back bad memories for her.

Sobering instantly, Jax gave her a small smile and settled for brushing the hair back from her face and tucking it behind her right ear. "You know something? You're a really nice woman."

She bore it fairly well, all things considered, and stared up at him with eyes that were huge and might have been telling him that she was frightened or that she might actually have been pleased by the compliment. He was usually so good with women and compliments, so smooth. He knew just what to say.

"You understand. You said so yourself. That you'd almost lost yourself, and it feels good to have someone who understands."

"You're not lost, Jax. You're just tired and angry, but you're still exactly who you were before you lost your mother."

"I'm not so sure about that," he said. After all, he'd never thought she'd been disappointed in him. He'd known she hadn't liked the way he went through women, but that was a completely different thing than being disappointed in him.

He wasn't sure he could bear to know he'd disappointed her.

Jax looked up to find Gwen staring at him.

"Did something happen today?"

He shrugged and shoved his hands into the front pockets of his jeans. "Reading of the will."

"And you didn't like something in your mother's will?"

"Oh, it was great. She left everything up to me, just threw the whole thing into my lap. How do you like that?"

Gwen frowned and said, "Why?"

"I don't know. It's not like her to do that. She tried the whole time she was sick to make things easier on all of us, and this... I would have sworn she'd made a list of everything she owned and who she wanted to have it."

"Maybe it just got to be too much for her. I mean, maybe she kept putting doing a real will off or she thought she'd have more time...."

"No, Gwen. It wasn't like that. Her death was a painfully slow, dreadful slide. We saw the end coming a mile away. In fact, she lasted longer than anyone expected."

"Maybe she just didn't want to spend her last bit of time dividing up her possessions."

"Maybe," he admitted. "It just seems out of character for her not to have taken care of it. I mean, the woman planned her own funeral, right down to what color blouse she wanted to wear and which Bible verses she wanted read. I just think there had to be a reason she did this."

"She never said anything to you about it?"

"No." Just like she'd never before said she was disappointed in him. "I just want to know why. I need to know."

"There's no one you can ask? No one she would have confided in?"

"I'm not sure." He ran through a list of her closest friends in his head. Who would she talk to about what she'd done with her will? Or why she was disappointed in Jax?

Gwen put her hand on his arm. "Well, you don't have to figure it all out tonight."

He looked down at that hand, thinking he liked having her touch him. He liked it a lot. She felt like an anchor on a strange and bewildering day. He had to fight the urge to grab on to her and just not let go.

He thought he'd feel better if he did and couldn't remember a single time in his life when he'd leaned on the strength of a woman. Except for his mother.

"Is there something else?" Gwen asked. "Something more than her asking you to divide up all her things?"

Jax frowned. "Figured that out, did you?"

"Just a hunch."

"Yeah, there's something else. But I don't even want to think about it, much less talk about it," he admitted, looking around at the walls of this house, at all her things surrounding him. "Of course, I can always concentrate on getting rid of my mother's stuff piece by piece. That should eat up a good bit of my time and maybe keep me from thinking too much about anything. Which reminds me— what are you going to take?"

"I don't know," Gwen said. "I haven't made up my mind."

"Dog's included in the list of available items, by the way."

"She left you the dog?"

"I'm telling you, she left me absolutely everything and just said to divide it up. It's bizarre. Especially when it comes to Romeo. I mean, she loved that dog. She was crazy about him, and she knew he drove me nuts. Why wouldn't she even name someone to take the dog?"

Romeo padded into the room, his head downcast, his big sad-eyed look on. He sidled over to Gwen and she just ate it up.

"Hi, baby," she said, going down on her haunches to ruffle the fur on his head. "Did you have a bad day, too?"

Romeo whined pathetically.

"Guess he figured out that his fate is entirely in my

hands," Jax said. "I should be grateful my mother didn't leave everything to him."

Romeo and Gwen both gave him unhappy looks at that.

"I'm sorry," he said to Gwen. "Bad day. How long do you figure I can get away with that as an excuse?"

"Please tell me you like this dog more than you let anyone know?" Gwen asked. "Because I really like Romeo and I want to know he'll be okay."

"I don't like the dog. And my mother knew that. She knew it."

"So, she was counting on you. She trusted you to do the right thing with him and with everything else. She showed complete faith in you—"

"No. Not that," he said much more sharply than he intended.

Gwen stared at him once again. "Sure you don't want to tell me the rest of it? The part that's eating away at you?"

"I'm sure." He closed his eyes, wishing he could take back everything he'd said.

When he looked down at her again, she had dropped to her knees with her arms around the dog. He had his head resting on her shoulder, snuggling against her, and Gwen had tears in her eyes.

She was trying to soothe the silly dog, petting him and telling him everything was going to be okay. Jax had the craziest thought. He wished he could be in the dog's position. That he could whine and fuss and cry, and some nice woman like Gwen would wrap her arms around him and just hang on, telling him everything was going to be okay. That he didn't have to do anything but fuss and whine and mourn his mother. No holding anyone together. No decisions to make. No one counting on him.

"I'm sorry," he said finally.

Gwen got to her feet, and she didn't quite look at him when she said, "You'll figure it out, Jax. All of it."

"I hope so." If he didn't, it would haunt him forever.

"You will. Just give it some time," she said, obviously ready to go. "You'll be okay?"

"Sure," he lied.

What else could he do? Fall apart?

Jax stood there and watched her go, wondering what it was about her that had words falling out of his mouth with things he'd had no intention of sharing with anyone. He thought about her when he was here alone and when he was surrounded by his weeping sisters and his mother's miserably lonely dog.

Somehow, Gwen Moss made it better. He thought about her when he shouldn't, and he'd been quite happy to call her over just a few minutes ago to—

Jax muttered under his breath as he remembered why he'd asked her to come over—to beg her to take something from this house.

But Gwen was gone, and she hadn't taken a single thing.

He was batting 0–6 that day at getting rid of things, and he was starting to think his mother's possessions were going to haunt him every bit as much as her words.

Well, that had gone really well.

Gwen felt guilty for deserting him that way, but she'd gotten all flustered. All she could think about was getting him to hold her again, this after the poor man just lost his mother.

How selfish can you possibly be, Gwen?

She hurried home, hoping he had no idea what she'd been thinking, then feeling even more guilty because she was still thinking of no one but herself. She hadn't cornered the market on suffering. Jax and his whole family were suffering, too.

She got home and noticed how different things were. The shades were pulled up. Afternoon sunshine danced across the pretty table by the window and the polished wooden floors. Flowers from the garden rested in a vase on the table and another on the kitchen counter. The world around her didn't look like such a scary place, and maybe—just maybe—she was getting better.

Jax had been a part of that.

Maybe instead of thinking of herself, she should be thinking of how she might help him. That sounded smart, maybe even kind.

Even if a part of her just really wanted to see him again?

Gwen wrestled with her own conscience over that one. In the end, she went with something her aunt Charlotte always said. That a woman could never go wrong acting out of kindness.

So, she would be kind.

She would try to help Jax.

And she knew just the kind of help he needed.

Gwen picked up the phone and the local phone book—a tiny thing—and found his mother's number. She dialed before she could think too hard about what she was about to do.

Jax answered, not sounding too happy at all.

"Hi," Gwen said. "It's me. I just wanted to tell you that I have a lot of spare time, and… Well, it's easier for me if I have something to do and I'm not here in this house all alone worrying and thinking about everything that's happened. The counselor I see told me I needed to get out more and to be around other people. So…well, I was thinking… You need help, right? And I need something to do. Maybe I could help you with your mother's things. It would be like therapy for me. It would be like you were doing me a favor."

She added that last part because she felt sure that Jackson Cassidy was much more comfortable helping other people than letting anyone help him. And it wasn't a lie at all. It would be helpful to her.

"So… What do you say? Can I come over sometime and help pack things? Or sort them? Or deliver them? Anything like that?"

He was silent for a long time, long enough to make her nervous and self-conscious. She wasn't one to invite herself to a man's house.

"Besides," she added, "I miss Romeo, and I think he misses me. I have to make sure you're taking proper care of him and not grumbling at him too much."

"Oh, sure." he said. "It's all about the dog."

"You're right. It's the dog I really want to see."

"You should know, he flirts with anything that moves, and he never met a female he didn't like."

She laughed. "I've heard the same thing about you."

"Yeah, well… That would be true, too. You need to understand that, Gwen. I wouldn't want you to get hurt."

"Jax, I always knew that was true. And I know I'm not… Well, I hear you have pretty varied tastes, but I doubt they run to mousy brunettes who are afraid of their own shadow."

"You're not a mouse," he said.

"Yes, I am, and I'm afraid of my own shadow most days, but I think I'm getting better. You will, too. I know right now it feels like you won't, but you will."

"I don't know about that."

"Just consider the possibility, okay? Maybe it doesn't seem likely that one day you'll feel better, but you've got to admit, it's possible." He stayed silent, and she added, "Come on. How about remotely possible?"

"Okay. Remotely."

"Good. So, I can come over sometime and help you?"

"Sure."

"How about tomorrow?" Now that she'd learned how to push, she was getting really good at it.

"Okay. Tomorrow."

"I'm done with work at six."

"I'll be here," he said.

Chapter Nine

Gwen got more and more nervous as the day went on. She'd practically forced her company upon this man, this really, really beautiful, sad, lost man.

And it wasn't as if she was being selfless here.

She was going to see him because she wanted to see him. She liked being around him. She felt safe with him, and she really hoped she wasn't going to try to push her way into his arms again, to see how that felt.

Bad Gwen. Bad, bad Gwen.

She'd told him she wanted to see the dog, and that was nearly an out-and-out lie. Gwen really didn't lie. She wanted to see the dog, but she wanted to see Jax more.

So she felt guilty and nervous, but excited, too.

Bad, bad Gwen.

She was trying very hard not to think of what she might wear. She was Gwen the mouse, after all, and mouse brown was her favorite color. She must look so dull to him. If he ever noticed how she looked.

Gwen stood in front of her closet and frowned. Had brown been *in* at some point in the last few years? How had she possibly managed to acquire so much of it?

She wanted to look like a normal woman with Jax. Not one who'd been traumatized and was still hiding from the world, but not one that was flirting or out to pick up a man, either.

What did one wear to help a newly made friend pack up his dead mother's things? Were there books about this stuff?

Jeans sounded right. She had jeans somewhere. She found them in the bottom of a drawer, pulled them out and tried them on, surprised to find them a bit snug. Her appetite had been stronger of late, but Aunt Charlotte's dryer did get awfully hot. Maybe they'd shrunk.

She turned around and studied her reflection in the mirror, trying to figure out how she'd look to a guy.

Bad, bad Gwen.

She made herself stop looking at the mirror and rummaged through her closet for a shirt. Brown, brown, black, gray. *Good grief, Gwen.*

It looked as if white was the best she could do, a truly bold fashion step, but maybe she was ready for it.

Gwen pulled off the blouse she wore to work and slipped the white thing over her head. It was simple as could be. Just a plain, white, short-sleeved, cotton thing.

Was it a little tight, too?

Gwen frowned again, thinking once more about Jax looking at her. He wasn't even interested in her. He was nearly sick with grief over losing his mother.

Maybe she should call and cancel.

Maybe she should call her therapist.

And say what? *I think I like a man. Isn't that awful? I need to come see you right away.*

Gwen sat down on the side of her bed, frustrated and nervous.

Okay, she liked him.

That wasn't so horrible, was it? Women were supposed to like men, not fear them. She'd always imagined she'd find a man to marry someday and have children with him. That would be hard if she didn't even like men. So this was not a bad thing.

Not that she was imagining sharing her life with Jackson Cassidy.

She could like him, couldn't she? And she'd certainly be safe with him, because he wasn't the least bit interested in her as a woman. So this was perfectly fine, perfectly reasonable.

He could be like a practice guy. A get-your-feet-wet-in-the-dating-world kind of guy.

"Okay," she told herself, looking at her own reflection once again, as if she'd suddenly sprouted wings or a tail or something.

She did look different in her jeans and bright white top. Her hair was halfway falling down from the way she'd had it piled on her head, and on sheer impulse she pulled out all the pins and let it fall to her shoulders.

Instantly, she lost that librarianish look she seemed to cultivate lately, and it was too much, too fast. She scraped her hair back into a high, tight ponytail, which, if she was not mistaken, did things that were okay for her face, maybe even nice. She didn't have that pale, hollowed-out, dark-circles-under-the-eyes, maybe-I've-been-seriously-ill look anymore that she'd acquired after the attack.

All that yard work wore her out but in a good way. She had been sleeping better, and there was some color in her cheeks, which was kind of nice, too. She dabbed on some lip gloss, but only because her lips were dry. Really, that was the only reason.

And then before she could get scared all over again, she rushed out the door and took off through the alley toward his house.

"Gwen?" Jax nearly didn't recognize her as she stood at the back door.

She gave him an odd look, then quickly glanced down at herself, frowning when she eyed him once again. "Is something wrong?"

"No. No. Of course not." He was afraid he still had that blank stare on his face. Either that, or a stunned one. *Gwen?*

"I thought we might be moving things or digging through dusty basement things or… I don't know what, really. So I pulled out an old pair of jeans."

"Great," he said, standing aside and motioning her to come in, doing a real double take at the way she looked.

He felt a very unwelcome spark of interest and immediately felt guilty for it. She was here to go through his dead mother's things, and she was a mouse. A little, brown scared-of-her-own-shadow mouse. He'd just told her she didn't act as shy and quiet as a mouse, but he was used to her dressing like one.

Well, she didn't look like one now.

Her vulnerability was still there. He suspected it always would be, and he'd never really found vulnerability all that interesting before… And he really had no business changing his mind about that right now, either.

She just…well, she was one nice-looking woman. Well, a man couldn't help but notice, could he? It wasn't like he was going to do anything about it.

"So?" she asked. "Where do you want to start?"

He got lost for a second, thinking of starting something he definitely couldn't start.

"I don't know," he said.

He'd been here all day and hadn't accomplished a thing, except to wonder some more about why his mother had done this to him. She had to have a reason. Maybe there was a letter somewhere in this house for him to find, a message, another rip-your-heart-out kind of thing, like that little zinger she'd thrown in there at the end about being disappointed in him.

He couldn't wait for that.

"Okay," Gwen said. "Do you know of anything in particular that she'd want someone to have? Say, your sisters? We could start there."

"They won't even talk to me about it," he admitted. "I barely get the words out, and they start to cry or change the subject or just leave. They don't want anything except her."

"Well, I'm sure they believe that now. But it's always nice to have something you can touch or hold, to remind you of someone who's gone. My grandmother died last year, and I have a quilt that used to be on the bed in her house where I slept. It reminds me of the dozens of days and nights I spent with her, and I think of her every time I see it. It's like having a little piece of her still with me. Your sisters will see that. You'll want some of her things, too. Can you think of anything you'd like?"

Jax shook his head.

"Well, we could always start with really impersonal things. Linens, little kitchen gadgets, stuff in the attic or the basement that no one's touched it in years."

"That sounds good." How broken up could anyone be over towels and sheets?

At least, that's what he thought. But once he'd gotten out the empty boxes to put things in and a garbage bag and was ready to go to work, and the only thing left to do was open the linen-closet door, he wasn't so sure.

He stood in front of that door long enough that he felt like a complete fool, until Gwen, who was behind him, put her hand on his shoulder and said, "Want me to start?"

"No." He sighed heavily. "It's crazy, I know. She doesn't need towels or sheets anymore. She can't use any of this stuff, and it's not like we need to have this house sitting here, like a shrine to her. It's not her. It's not her life. But doing this feels like taking her life apart, piece by piece, and I don't want to do that."

"Well, we don't have to. Not now. You can wait until you're ready—"

"What if I'm never going to be ready?"

"You'll get it done. One day," she said, that soft hand back on his shoulder.

Jax closed his eyes and took a breath. She could slide her arms around him right now, and that would be fine with him. If she would just hold on tight and not let him go, because he needed someone to hold him together. He was afraid he was going to come apart completely, that pieces of him would just start to fall to the floor until he was nothing but a pile of dust.

Over a stupid linen closet!

"Gwen?"

"Hmm?"

He couldn't quite get the words out. *Hold me. Please.*

But he could and did put his hand on hers and draw it around him. She resisted only for a moment and then he felt her coming closer, felt her soft curves settle against his back. Her other arm slid around him, locking around his waist, and her head rested against his shoulder, and it was so nice to have someone close. Maybe so nice to have *her* close.

"Just give me a few minutes," he said raggedly. "Okay?"

"Sure." She snuggled a bit against his back, settling in.

He let his head fall forward until his forehead rested against the door he couldn't open, and let himself lean on her, as much as he'd ever leaned on a woman in his entire life. His breathing was uneven and he couldn't even have said exactly what was wrong now, just that he felt as if he was choking again and had felt so alone he couldn't stand it, until she put her arms completely around him and held him until the worst of the emotions passed.

When it was over, he eased around in her arms, until they were face-to-face and he was holding her, too.

That was nice. He couldn't help but notice the way she fit into his arms. He stared down at her, her long, dark hair pulled back in that little-girl ponytail that showed off the bones in her face, her cheeks kissed by the sun and stained the prettiest shade of pink, her eyes big and wide. And then he noticed a solitary tear spilling out of the corner of her eye.

He brought up one hand to cup the side of her face. His thumb caught that tear, and he asked, "Is that for me?"

"For both of us, I guess. For everyone in the world who's hurting right now and sad and lonely. I get so lonely sometimes."

"Me, too," he said, then he touched his lips to her cheek, brushing the moisture away.

He heard her catch her breath and slowly raised his head, nuzzling the tip of his nose against hers for a moment before asking, "Too much?"

"No," she whispered.

If she'd been anyone else, he'd have kissed her like crazy, right then, but this was Gwen who was afraid of her own shadow, and all she'd been trying to do was get him through a bad moment. She was not the kind of woman who'd consider going any further as a reasonable remedy for making him feel better. But she was here, and she was in his arms, and he didn't feel so lost or so much like he was drowning with her there.

So he leaned back against the wall himself and brought her along with him, letting her lean against him, and covered her mouth with his. He tried his best not to frighten her, touching her as softly and slowly as he could.

Her arms went slack for a moment, and then they latched on to him once again, pulling him closer. He had to fight not to plaster her against him with his arms.

Gwen, he kept telling himself. *It's Gwen. Don't scare her.*

She stood up on her toes to get closer to him, and he grinned. She was so sweet. He finally lifted his head once again and saw a real smile on her face.

How had he ever thought she was a mouse?

Her face had a little glow to it, and it held none of the worry and sadness he'd always seen in it. She looked so happy, like she'd won a prize.

And he was definitely not a prize to a woman like her.

"Gwen?" he began, knowing he had to say this now. *I am not the man for you.*

"I didn't get scared," she said in the same way she might tell him she'd won the lottery.

"Good," he said.

"I mean, not at all!" That beautiful smile came back again.

"Well, I guess you are getting better."

She nodded, beaming. "Can you believe it? I wasn't sure if I even believed I'd be better someday."

"Hey, you were the one who was preaching possibilities to me just yesterday, remember?"

"Yes."

"You didn't even believe what you were telling me? Because I've gotta say, I found it pretty convincing, Gwen."

"I believed that you'd be better, but I had my doubts about me. Especially when it came to the man-woman stuff...." She blushed furiously and took a step back from him. He let his arms go lax, but he didn't let her go. She stared fixedly at his chest and frowned. "But I was okay. Wasn't I?"

"You were perfect," he said, and she smiled up at him again.

"You, too. I think you could turn kissing into an art form."

"You mean, it's not?"

She laughed out loud then, and for a moment, the whole world seemed brighter. That sound was like the sun, dazzling with light as it broke through the clouds on a miserable, gloomy day.

Gwen was happy, and he'd forgotten all about how lousy he felt, at least for a moment, and all things seemed possible.

He pulled her back into his arms, and she came quite willingly, snuggling against his chest this time. He let his chin rest against the top of her head and closed his eyes, giving himself a few more moments of bliss.

"You know, everyone I asked about you said the same thing—that you're the nicest man, and I kept thinking, how nice could he be if he goes through women that fast? But then, they said you always managed to stay friends with all those women."

Jax wasn't sure he understood how, but it didn't really matter right now. She knew what he was like, so he didn't have to worry that she'd go and get the wrong idea, and that was a relief. Because he really didn't want to hurt her.

"I could really use a friend, Jax."

"Well, you got one," he said.

"And it sure seems like you could use one, too," she said.

"Yeah. That would be good. Does that mean I can't kiss you anymore?"

She frowned, puzzling it out. "Not exactly."

"Can I hold you sometimes?"

"Yes. When you're sad."

"Just when I'm sad? What about when I'm very, very happy?"

"I guess that would be okay," she conceded.

"Lonely?"

"Definitely."

"Tired? Frustrated? Angry? Maybe when I just want to scream?"

"Or maybe whenever you want to?" She laughed. "It seems like you're trying to cover every possible emotion."

"I am," he admitted.

"But you have to understand, it's not going any further between us," she insisted, still in his arms.

"Okay."

"Don't say it like that. If you really want to know, I'll tell you exactly what you'd have to do."

"Done," he said, and he meant it.

"I don't think so."

"What do you want? Name it."

"All you have to do is fall in love with me and then you have to marry me," she said.

Jax stood there dumbfounded.

She laughed some more.

"You're kidding, right?" he asked finally.

"No, I'm not."

He kept waiting for the punch line, but none was forthcoming. "Are you telling me that you're actually saving yourself for the man you marry?"

"Not for him. For me. And, in case you didn't know, you're looking at me like I just grew a second head."

"You mean you've never…?

"Never," she said.

"And you're how old?"

"Twenty-four."

"Wow."

"And out popped a third head?" She laughed.

"I just…I don't know if I've ever—"

"I know. Whole new way of thinking, right?"

"Is this a religious thing?"

"That's part of it."

He nodded. "Okay. What else? Why are you doing this?"

"Why wouldn't I? I mean, just because it seems like everyone else is, doesn't mean it's the right thing for me. It's my life."

"But…why?"

"Because I think it's something most people do all too easily, like it doesn't mean anything at all, and it means something to me, Jax. It means a lot to me. And I have to admit, I've never been seriously tested… I mean, I've never really been in love, just…curious, and really, what kind of reason is that to give yourself to a man? Because you're curious? I want to be in love. I want to find someone to share the rest of my life with and have children with, and until that happens, I can wait."

"Wait?" he repeated, thinking, *For twenty-four years?*

"It's special," she said. "My heart goes along with my body. That's just the way I think it should be."

"Okay," he said, really meaning *okay* this time. The love-marriage-and-forever thing… He'd never really believed in it. He thought it was a fantasy, a fairy tale, an impossibility, but she obviously really wanted to believe it, and he didn't want to be the one to make her see it for the sham it was.

He wished, for her sake, that it wasn't a sham at all.

"Okay," she said, looking relieved and quite happy. "So, we're going to be friends?"

"Yes." He guessed so. Just friends. It would be a whole new concept for him.

"And you'll let me help you?"

"Yes."

"Good. Can you open the closet now? Or would you like me to?"

That shoved his musings right out of his head.

She knew he couldn't even open the closet? He didn't like that at all.

But he didn't feel lousy or like he was drowning anymore. Even odder, she seemed to understand perfectly why a grown man wouldn't be able to do so much as open a linen-closet door.

He looked into her eyes and saw understanding and acceptance and compassion, things he'd never really needed or expected from a woman.

How was he to know it would feel so good?

She gave him a half shy, half knowing smile and reached around him for the doorknob, which made him want to kiss her all over again, which he really wasn't supposed to do.

She had to reach way around him to get to the closet doorknob, which meant she was very, very close. He heard the click of the door latch giving, and when she started to pull away, he just couldn't let her. Both because he wanted her close to him again and because he still wasn't ready for the closet.

He slid his arms around her, holding her easily, staring down at her.

"It's all right." She brought her hands up to his face and stretched up on tiptoe. "We'll take this one step at a time, until we get it done. And I'll be here to help you."

Clean out a closet, a house, all that was left of a life.

"It's not about the closet," he admitted. "Or all the stuff. I'm not even sure what it's about." But that was a lie. He knew, could never hide from it for long, even talking to a pretty woman.

It was about what his mother had said to him.

That he didn't even know what was important in life, and now, she wasn't even here to show him or to argue with him about it or to let him show her that she was wrong, that he did know, or that he hadn't really screwed up his life.

"Jax, we don't have to do anything tonight except clean out this closet. That's it."

"Okay," he said, thinking it wasn't, thinking if he could just shove all his feelings into some dark, hidden-away place, like a closet in his mind, he'd be fine.

Why couldn't he do that and never have to face feelings like this again?

Surely there was a way to bury them for good.

Gwen let him go, reached behind him and opened that door.

He waited for everything he was trying to bury inside him to come spilling out, like water overflowing from a dam.

But nothing happened. She stepped back, tugging him by the hand, and he moved back, too, until she could open up that door.

It was kind of dark. There wasn't much light at this end of the hall. And he stared inside, as though monsters might come roaring out.

But it was just a closet.

Towels and sheets.

He was acting scared of stacks of linens.

"I think sometimes I'm going crazy," he admitted.

Gwen just smiled up at him. "Me, too."

He supposed she did.

Gwen grabbed a stack of towels and handed them to him, and then grabbed another for herself, and they started sorting towels. Nothing earth-shattering. One step at a time.

Jax couldn't believe how many towels his mother had. Every time he reached into the closet, he found more stuff.

"This is crazy," he said when they were finally done. "She probably has another linen closet as stuffed as this one."

"And we'll tackle it another day."

He held out a hand and hauled her to her feet, feeling more self-conscious with her than he ever had with a woman. He'd been about to fall apart one minute, kissing her the next, and then falling apart again.

How exactly had that happened?

"Gwen? How is this going to work between us?"

"I'm going to help you, and you're going to help me," she said, bending over and picking up a box, which she handed to him. "Another?"

"Yeah." She stacked another on top of the first. "That's it? You help me through this?"

"And you can help me, too." She picked up a box of her own and then said, "You need a place to store things to give away, and you'll probably have a lot of it."

"Back bedroom, on the right. It has the least amount of stuff in it." They both turned and headed for it. "How exactly am I going to help you?"

"By giving me something to do so I'm not alone every night," she said.

"Not enough," he complained as he set his boxes down in a corner and cleared some things out to make room for hers.

"It's a lot to me. I don't like being alone at night."

He stood there and shook his head. "Still not enough."

"Well, I'll try to think of something, okay?"

"Okay," he said. "You had dinner?"

"No."

"Me, neither. Come on. The least I can do is feed you."

Chapter Ten

Three days later, Jax was just getting out of the shower after work when he heard someone ringing the doorbell.

He picked up his watch off the edge of the sink and glanced at the time. Six-ten. He was expecting Gwen, but it was a little early for her. He heard Romeo bounding for the door and calling out a greeting, so he knew someone was there. Maybe Gwen was early.

He rubbed a bit of the water off his chest and from his hair, grabbed a pair of jeans and stepped into them.

The bell rang again. If he didn't show up there soon, she'd think he wasn't home.

"Coming," he yelled, grabbing a shirt.

Romeo was yelping happily, standing at the back door with his tail swishing back and forth. He gave Jax a look that said, *Hurry! She's here!*

He grabbed for the door, pulling on his shirt, talking to her before he had it open. "Gwen, I'm starving. How about we eat first and then—"

He broke off midsentence.

It wasn't Gwen.

It was all three of his sisters, scowling at him.

"And then what?" Katie asked, all wrapped up in one of her junior-real-estate-mogul suits, glancing pointedly at him, standing there with still wet hair and his shirt unbuttoned. "Not that I can't guess. Honestly, Jax, what is wrong with you?"

She pushed him aside and came in.

His other two sisters gave him sad, worried looks and came inside, too.

"Why did you ring the doorbell?" he asked. "You never ring the doorbell at this house."

"We weren't sure what we'd find if we just walked in," Katie said, plowing through the kitchen, into the living room and then down the hall to the bedrooms.

"What are you doing?" he asked.

"Looking to see what you and that woman have done to this house." Katie came out of the first bedroom and headed for the second.

"That woman?"

"Gwen Moss," Katie said, frowning when she didn't find any evidence of Gwen's presence.

"The whole town knows, Jax," Kim said, looking like a hurt puppy.

"Knows what?"

"That you've taken up with her. Every night this week! People have seen you all over town and coming and going from this house. Your own mother's house, Jax? The week after she died? What are you thinking?"

He gritted his teeth and managed not to yell. "Gwen's helping me clean out the house. That's it. We work, and then we usually grab something to eat. It's the least I can do for all the work she's putting in here."

Katie laughed. "You're seen with a woman for three

nights in a row, and you expect us to believe you're doing nothing but cleaning out this house?"

"Do I make a habit of lying to you, Katie? Because I don't remember ever doing that. Gwen's not like that," he said.

"Sure she's not." Katie folded her arms in front of her chest and glared at him some more.

Kathie and Kim looked even more miserable than they had at first, and Romeo was whining and cocking his head back and forth, like he just didn't understand but he was going to figure it out, one way or another.

"What is the matter with you?" Jax yelled at Katie. "Mom dies, and you suddenly decide to run my life for me? Or that everything I'm doing is wrong, and that you need to tell me about it?"

"It looks awful. You here with that woman, right after we buried Mom. What would Mom think?"

"She'd be happy that I had someone to help me through this," he said.

"Help you through this? In your usual way?"

He opened his mouth to say, no, not in the "usual" way, but he looked up and there was Gwen, standing just inside the kitchen door, taking everything in and looking horrified.

He stared at her, and then all three of his sisters stepped into the kitchen, turned and stared, too. Gwen looked like she wanted to disappear into thin air, and his sisters looked like they wanted to make her.

"I'm sorry," she said. "I knocked, but I guess nobody heard me. And…well…" She looked at Jax again, and she did, indeed, blush like crazy. "I'll just leave the four of you to this. Sorry."

"Gwen, wait," he called out.

"Jax—"

"Shut up, Katie. You've done enough already."

He took off after her. She turned and glanced at him, stalking across the deck, and walked even faster. Romeo must have thought it was some sort of game, because he bounded after Jax, overtook him and then caught up with Gwen, barking merrily and trying to get her to stop and play with him.

"Jax, would you get dressed?" she yelled back at him.

"If you'll stop and talk to me."

She stopped but didn't turn around. Romeo made even more of a ruckus until she knelt down and petted him. Jax stood in front of her, noting that she hadn't dared look above his ankles.

"Would you get back inside?" she said.

"In a minute. I didn't want you running off upset. Or mad. I wanted to apologize for my nosy, interfering sisters," he said, finally buttoning his shirt.

"Okay. You've done it. Now go home."

"I'm sorry for what they said. Don't worry. I'll set them straight."

"Fine."

"You'll come back when they're gone?" he asked, because he'd gotten used to having her around. He didn't dread the days so much, knowing he'd see her at the end of them.

"Okay. I'll be there."

"I'm really sorry, Gwen."

"It's all right. I don't really care what your sisters think of me."

"Well, I do," he said.

They were doing the stair-step thing again when he went inside, all lined up in a row from oldest to youngest. Every time they did this, it took him right back to that day their father died and Jax thinking he had to hold it together for the three of them and his mother. They'd followed him around like ducklings for months afterward, lost and scared and not knowing where else to turn, except to him and their mother.

And now there was no one but him.

He was so mad he could have spit nails one minute, and then he was ashamed of himself for yelling at them.

And he sure didn't feel like being attacked by a mob of girls. When they ganged up on him, they could be formidable. He decided it was time to divide and conquer.

He took Katie by the arm and said, "Come with me."

She came, and when the other two started to follow, he pivoted around and said, "Stay right there. I'll be back."

Katie started muttering about not liking being manhandled one bit, but he didn't care. "I could throw you over my shoulder, if you like." He'd been doing it since she was two, and she'd loved it then.

He got her outside on the deck, out of earshot of the other two, and then did a quick scan of the backyard and alley. Lucky him. No neighbors around to hear. He let Katie go, and then leaned back against the railing of the deck, looking as relaxed as he could manage. Folding his arms across his chest, he said, "Okay, lemme have it."

She looked puzzled that he'd just invite her to do that, but quickly got into the spirit of things. "What are you doing?"

"Trying to get through this as best I can."

"By picking up yet another woman, Jax?"

"I didn't pick her up. I'm not even dating her. She offered to help me clean out the house. Something *you* never offered to do. Something *Kathie and Kim* haven't offered to do. I couldn't get the three of you to take so much as a fork out of this house without bawling over it and telling stories about every meal Mom ever cooked that you ate with that particular utensil, and I can't do that, Katie. I can't have somebody crying over every object in that house and it taking us months to get rid of it all. I can't."

And of course, now she looked near tears. "I'm just not ready to let her go yet."

"Well, neither am I, but nobody listened when I said I wasn't ready. She's gone, and that fact doesn't change, whether we keep every speck of dust in that house in absolutely the same place it was when she lived here or whether we burn the place down. She'll still be gone."

"Well, you don't have to have such a good time sorting through her things."

He positively saw red at that. "I…am…not…having… a…good…time…. Got it?"

"You always manage to have a good time with a woman."

"Well, this one feels like she's saving my life, okay? I feel so miserable and so alone, I could just about choke to death on all the feelings I'm trying to stuff back inside me. And she's there. She's kind. She's patient. She understands, and I need that. I need it so much it scares me. Can you understand that?"

Katie looked skeptical. Jax had never been one to admit to needing anyone.

"I'm doing the best I can, Katie. This is it. I can't do any more. I'm thankful just to get through every day right now, and I'm sorry I don't have more to give or that I can't live up to some idea you have about how I'm supposed to grieve. But just because you don't see it or it doesn't look like what you think it should look like doesn't mean I'm not hurting, too. I am. And you've got to stop jumping me every time you get upset."

"I'm not," she said, tears starting again.

"Yeah, you are, and I've got to tell you—putting my life in order is not going to solve your problems right now."

"I'm not doing that. I never thought that—"

"Sure you did. Katie, you think it's the answer to everything. Keep things in line, exactly the way you think things should go, and nothing bad will happen. Well, it doesn't work that way."

"I never thought it did," she claimed.

"Sweetheart, you've been doing that your whole life. Ever since you were eight. The week after dad died, you reorganized the whole house. Don't you remember?" No one had been able to find anything for months.

"I just... Things were a mess."

"Yeah, they were. And if putting things in their place made you feel better, I'm fine with that. But you're not eight anymore, and you and I have been down this lousy road before."

She stood quietly in front of him, a fine trembling moving through her, tears falling freely now. He took two steps forward and pulled her into his arms.

She clung as tightly as she could and said, "I don't know what else to do."

"Well, we'll just have to find something else."

"I think I'm driving Joe crazy," she confessed.

"Yeah, well...your fiancé will understand."

"I'm not so sure. He's been understanding me for a long time, and I think he may not have any understanding left where I'm concerned."

"Sure he does. He loves you."

"I'm not so sure anymore. I think I've managed to push him away the same way I'm pushing you."

"Katie, you could never get rid of me. Never. Shove as hard as you want, it just wouldn't work. I wouldn't let you go. Not ever."

"I'm sorry," she sobbed.

"I know. I know."

He comforted her as best he could, and then he dried her eyes and sent her off to her fiancé's, to make her peace with him.

He took Kim next, who at twenty-one still tended to do most anything her older sisters wanted to do, which usually meant what Katie wanted, if Kathie wouldn't argue with her, which Kathie seldom did. All Kim really needed to hear was that he missed their mother desperately. So he hugged her and let her cry for a few minutes and then sent her on her way, feeling guilty that he didn't spend more time with her.

Kathie came outside last, and he could tell she'd been dragged along reluctantly on this little mission, because she looked as if she had serious regrets now. It wasn't her nature to argue with anyone or to cause trouble.

"Sorry about that," she said. "Really."

He shrugged it off. "I'll live."

"I know it's really hard for you," Kathie said. "And I know we probably make you crazy and always have, but… Jax, I need to ask you something."

He had a feeling he didn't like what was coming, but reluctantly, he said, "Okay. Shoot."

"All those women you've…dated?"

He raised an eyebrow at that. Kathie had never given him a hard time about that. He didn't want one now from her.

"Well—" she drew in a breath and her gaze came up to meet his "—were you ever in love with any of them?"

"I thought I might be heading in that direction a couple of times, but… No. Didn't work that way."

"You never had one that, no matter what, you just

couldn't get her out of your head? No matter how hard you tried? And I mean, really, really tried?"

"No," he said, thinking, *Did she really think she was in love?*

At twenty-four, he hoped not. She was way too naive. It would be way too easy for a guy to take advantage of her completely, because she always believed the best about everyone. He slid an arm around her, companionably, and said, "Somebody threatening to break your heart, darlin'?"

She hesitated. "Maybe. I mean, I'm trying not to let him, but...sometimes you just can't help yourself, you know?"

"I don't know. Is there some reason you know it won't work out with this guy?"

She nodded bleakly.

"He's just not a...a good guy?"

"No, he is. Really good. He's a great guy."

He'd better be, if he wanted to be with Kathie. "So, what's wrong?"

"I can't tell you."

Oh. The dreaded, *I can't tell you.*

Definitely a woman thing.

They came to him, said they needed to talk, made it sound positively dire, and then when it came down to the heart of the matter, they said, *I can't tell you.* Which with his sisters, usually meant, *I'll let you worry about it for a few days or so, and then I'll tell you.*

And other than losing their father and then their mother, they'd never run up against a problem they couldn't solve. Jax was sure they could handle this one, too.

"You can tell me," he said, because that's what he always said.

"No. Really, I can't." Which was what they always said.

"Sure you can."

"No," she cried.

"Okay. If you're sure…"

"I'm sure."

"Well, what can I do?" he tried.

"I don't know. Nothing, I guess. I mean, Mom would say that nothing was truly hopeless—"

Jax grinned. There it was. The platitude she needed at this moment. "Mom would definitely say that. So…just don't give up."

"I'm trying, but…" She sighed heavily, her bottom lip trembling and tears glistening in her eyes.

"No," he said. "No, no, no. Don't do that. Kathie, you'll figure it out. I know you will."

And she'd tell him what was wrong. He'd have it out of her before the weekend was over.

Sad tears spilled over and rolled down her cheeks.

"Ah, Kath." He didn't have a dry shoulder left to offer, but she was short enough that he could tuck her against his chest and dry her tears and even coax a smile out of her before he finally sent her on her way.

He stood there and watched her drive off, part of him thinking something bad was going on and the other part thinking she'd done something horrifying like develop a crush on a guy who'd been out all of twice with one of her friends, or something equally disastrous as that.

Women. They were so dramatic. So emotional.

He'd soothed and patted and dried more tears in the past few months than he thought he could stand, and at the moment, he felt utterly weary, utterly drained.

Then he looked up and happened to catch sight of Gwen standing in her backyard. He didn't think he'd ever been so glad to see anyone in his entire life.

* * *

Gwen saw him out on the deck with one of his sisters. At least he was fully dressed now.

She'd blushed at the way he'd looked before, and she was instantly ashamed of herself.

The man was so sad, he seemed to ache with it, and he was doing his best to hold his family together, and what was she doing?

Thinking he looked really nice fresh from the shower.

Bad, Gwen.

But he was beautiful. Like the Greek statues that had made Gwen blush when she'd gone to Europe with a church group one summer.

Bad, bad Gwen.

Jax really was amazing in every way, and she was starting to fear that her reaction to him was simply that—a reaction purely to him. And nothing was ever going to really happen between her and him.

"Gwen?"

She nearly jumped out of her own skin, looked up and there he was.

What was she going to do with him now?

Chapter Eleven

She realized with dismay that he had bare feet, wet hair and that he smelled really good. Gwen curled her bottom lip over her teeth and bit down to keep from doing or saying anything she shouldn't.

"You okay?" he asked.

She nodded. "You?"

"Yeah. I finally got the water buckets calmed down and sent them on their way."

"The water buckets?"

"My weeping sisters," he said. "You have to promise me one thing. One very important thing."

"Okay," she said.

"I'm serious. I need this promise, or I'm going to have to march back to that lonely house and lock myself away from the world until morning."

He grinned when he said it, and despite the fact that he looked bone weary, the charm shone through. It struck her that she'd never seen Jax at his ultracharming best. She'd only seen him exhausted and slammed by grief, struggling to make the best of an awful situation.

Jax at his charming best... She wasn't sure if her heart could take that.

"Well," he said. "You gonna promise?"

"What do you need me to promise?"

"That not a single tear will fall down your pretty face tonight."

She laughed. "That's it? No tears?"

"No tears."

"The water buckets were too much for you?" she guessed.

He nodded solemnly. "Promise?"

"I promise."

"Thank you," he said, looking like she'd granted him a reprieve from a firing squad. "I hate it when women cry."

"Oh, please. You're a pro at handling women's tears."

"But I hate it. I never know what to do."

"Jax, you know exactly what to do."

"What?" he asked

"You listen. You listen really well."

He shrugged. "Well, if I'm standing right there, what choice do I have?"

"You could walk away. Lots of men do. You could get mad, just because you don't know what to do. Men do that, too. They get impatient. They act like whatever's wrong really isn't that important. Or like tears are the worst thing in the world."

"They are," he said.

"Are not." Gwen laughed. He'd made her laugh about tears, when she'd shed buckets herself this past year.

"There is nothing funny about this," he said. "I grew up in a house with four women. Plus my father had four sisters and all of them had daughters. Can you imagine how many crying women have been inside that house over the years?"

"And I'm sure you took good care of them all," she said. "You have wonderful shoulders to cry on, and great arms, so you can hold a woman tight and make her feel like you can protect her from anything. You listen to her problems and you're patient and kind and... You're great with them. I should know. I've cried on your shoulder before."

He hesitated, looked away for a moment, then back at her again. So seriously, he said, "It never seems like enough."

"It's a lot. Especially when a woman's upset," she promised him. "And it's not like it's up to you to solve everyone's problems. Even if they make you feel like that sometimes."

"I want to... I like fixing things for people."

"Sure you do. And I can tell you're really good at it. But you can't fix everything. No one could expect you to. You're just a man."

A strong man. A determined one. A very good one.

She might not understand a lot about him and the way he lived his life, but she was sure that he was good to the core.

And realizing it made her like him even more.

Just what she needed.

"I promise I won't cry tonight. And I'll try not to cry tomorrow. Or the day after. Or the day after that."

He shrugged, grinning slightly. "Hey, I'm not looking for miracles here. Tonight will do."

"No, it's time I stopped. I want to. I want my life to be different. To be better. And it's all your fault."

"My fault?"

She nodded. "You helped me."

"Gwen, I didn't do anything."

"Yes, you did. You listened to me, and you cared about what happened and you told me it wasn't my fault, and you helped me to stop feeling so sorry for myself."

"All that?" He was skeptical. "No way."

"You did."

She couldn't resist anymore. She touched him. Just a hand on his arm. He pulled his arm back until they were palm to palm, and then he wrapped his fingers around hers and held on.

She closed her eyes and dipped her head down, until the top of it was resting against his chest.

"You know the best part of all?" she whispered.

"What?"

"When I'm with you, even close to you like this, I'm not afraid." She lifted her head and looked at him again. "And you can't know what that means to me, Jax. I was afraid for so long. I thought I always would be, and with you, the fear is just gone."

He looked like he just didn't understand or like he couldn't quite believe her when she said how important that was. That he didn't see what he gave to everyone around him.

A good man who didn't know he was one.

What was she supposed to do about that?

She blinked once, twice, three times, her vision blurry from strong feelings she couldn't really explain. Gratitude was part of it. Happiness was another. Wonder. A hint of fear. Not about him being close but about all that she might come to feel for him if she let this go on, and that was a whole new kind of fear for her.

"Hey," he said, coming ever closer, his hand cupping the side of her face. "You promised. No more tears tonight."

"I know," she said, her voice breaking. "Which means, I really have to go."

"No. Gwen, don't."

She thought he would have pulled her into his arms and let her cry it out if she'd let him. But she really meant it—

she wanted to be done mourning, and she didn't want to be one more woman whose life he was supposed to fix. She wanted to help him instead.

Did the man ever let anyone truly help him?

Still, she stood there caught up in the wonder of him. The soft touch of his hand at the side of her face and his other hand clasped in hers.

She wanted to bury her nose against him and let those big, strong arms of his curl around her and tuck her against him.

He had the best hands, and he treated a woman like a piece of fine china he feared he might break. She'd never understood how truly wonderful it could be or how powerful, simply to have a man touch her face or hold her tight. He made her want things she wasn't going to let herself have.

"I'm sorry. But really, I have to go," she said, and turned around and fled.

He called an hour later, sounding tentative and bewildered. "Are you okay?"

"Yes."

"What did I do, Gwen?"

"To upset me? Nothing."

"Of course I did."

"No. It wasn't you. It was just…everything. Other things," she clarified. *The way she felt about him.* All the things she couldn't begin to figure out.

It had sounded so simple at first. He made her feel better. Finally, it seemed she was better. And she was attracted to him. Maybe just him. Or maybe it was just time, and she was ready and she could get on with her life and not be afraid.

Whatever it was, she needed to know. She couldn't figure out what to do without knowing what was going on here, and if she didn't know what to do, she might just drift on for another year, wasting time and feeling sorry for herself. She couldn't let that happen.

"Let me help," he insisted, which had her thinking, *He's just the sweetest thing.*

"You do," she told him. Every day, in a dozen different ways.

"And I'm sorry about my sisters. About what they said."

"Jax, it's okay."

"They had no right to say what they did. They're just a mess over losing our mother—"

"I know, and it's okay."

"And I didn't even think about people seeing us together and talking, but I should have. People are going to think something's going on between us. Does that bother you?"

"No."

"I could try to set them straight—"

"No. Don't worry about it. People will think what they want, and some of them love to think the worst of everyone. I'm not going to stay away from you just because of what some people might say or think."

"Okay. If you're sure—"

"I am. I want to help you—"

"You are," he insisted. "Probably a lot more than I'm helping you. I don't know what I'd do without you right now, Gwen."

She frowned. It was not what she was expecting at all. She didn't want to think he was even nicer than she'd already believed. She didn't want to like him any more than she already did.

"I don't think I've ever really let myself depend on a woman like this before. Except maybe my mother," he said. When she still didn't say anything, because she had no idea what to say, he added, "Not that I think of you in any kind of motherly way."

Gwen laughed at that.

"You don't see me in any sort of fatherly way, do you?" he asked.

"No."

"Or a brotherly way?"

"No."

"Well, I'm glad we cleared that up," he said. "And I'm really glad we're not doing the sibling thing, because I really don't think I could handle having another sister right now. Of course, you're capable of cleaning out closets without weeping, and you don't recoil in horror when I mention getting rid of family heirlooms, like eggbeaters and pot holders and blenders that were made sometime during the Vietnam War, and I can't tell you how important that is to me right now."

"Your sisters didn't want you to get rid of the eggbeaters?"

"Well, you know, it's a big step and they're just not ready. Not yet."

Gwen laughed, because he'd predicted that he wouldn't even be able to get rid of a box of kitchen utensils without a fight, and he was right.

"They're horrified by the work you and I've done. I had six bags of trash in the laundry room, waiting for garbage-collection day. Katie opened them up and found dish towels at the top of one. I swear, I think she took that bag and put it in the trunk of her car so I couldn't throw it away. Do you think they need psychiatric help?"

"No, I think they just need time. You can have some time, too, you know."

"No, I have to do this now."

Some people coped with bad things by keeping as busy as they could, by trying not to even give themselves time to think, time to grieve. She suspected Jax was one of those people.

And it was going to catch up to him someday. She knew that. Gwen had tried to hide from what happened to her, to stay so quiet and so still and keep her head down so far, that no bad thing could possibly find her again.

But that sort of behavior caught up to everyone in the end.

"Say you'll keep helping me with all this stuff in the house?" Jax asked.

"I will."

As coping mechanisms went, his was at least practical. They hadn't actually gotten rid of anything, just organized and boxed. No really hard decisions had been made. They hadn't even gone into his mother's room, which poor Romeo had commandeered as his own for the time being.

"Okay," Jax said. "See you tomorrow after work?"

"Actually, I'm off tomorrow, so I'll be over in the morning, if you like."

"Yes, please."

"Tell Romeo good-night for me."

"Gwen, he's a dog. He doesn't speak English."

"Dogs are capable of understanding a number of words, and you know it. Otherwise, you couldn't train them to obey commands."

"Well, I doubt good-night is one of them."

"I bet he knows what it means when you tell him it's time to go to bed. Give it a try, and see what he does."

"This is ridiculous," he complained.

But it was all for show, she thought. The dog was growing on him. "Just do it."

"All right. All right. Let me find the dog. Romeo!" he yelled. "There he is. Romeo, time to go to bed. Yeah, bed. Go to bed, Romeo."

"What's he doing?" she asked.

"He's trotting down the hall."

"There you go. He's a good boy."

"Wait. He isn't going into the bedroom. Nope. He's heading for the back bedroom where we're storing boxes of things we've already sorted through, and he's… Hey. Wait a minute! He's in one of the boxes nosing around. Romeo!"

Gwen laughed. "What did he want?"

"I don't know. What does he ever want? It's always something. Romeo, what have you got?"

"Well?"

Jax got really quiet.

"What is it?" Gwen asked.

"One of my mother's aprons. He's trotting down the hall with an apron in his mouth. Maybe I could get him a job in a kitchen."

"A kitchen?"

"Yeah. I was thinking, if I can't get rid of him in the normal way, I might be able to find him a job. Lots of dogs work for their keep, you know?"

"No, I didn't know."

"Maybe he wants to be a chef. Romeo, cook! Cook, Romeo!"

Gwen laughed. "I don't think that plan's going to work. I've never seen a dog who cooked."

"Guess not. He's not even heading for the kitchen. He's heading into my mother's bedroom instead, and…"

The teasing sound was gone. She heard Jax grumble softly, heard the dog whine pitifully and then start to whimper, as if he was crying.

"Jax? What's wrong?"

"'I've gotta go—"

"No. Wait—"

"I'm sorry. I can't… Not right now."

"Jax?" But it was too late. He'd broken the connection.

Gwen waited all of ten seconds, worrying and imagining what might have gone wrong, telling herself they were just friends and new friends at that, and that the man deserved some privacy if he wanted it.

All he had to do was ask her to come over, if he'd wanted her to, and he hadn't. But she'd never been any good at asking for help, either, when she needed it, and she'd spent a lot of time grieving and miserably alone.

She didn't want him to have to do that.

She grabbed her sandals and the house keys and off she went. Standing at the back door to his mother's house, she hesitated, thinking she was being pushy and maybe even nosy. But she was worried, too.

She knocked softly on the screen door. The main one was open. It was a cool but comfortable night.

"Jax?" she called out.

"Back here," he answered. "In my mother's room."

She pulled open the screen door and went through the kitchen and down the hall. There was a weak light burning in his mother's room and the door, which he normally kept closed, was open.

Jax was standing with his back to the door, arms crossed and tucked against himself like his insides hurt, head down and turned away. She couldn't see the expression on his face.

Gwen went to his side, put a hand on his arm.

Romeo was in the middle of the bed lying down flat, even his snout pressed flat to the bed, and he was making his crying sound, which always broke her heart.

He'd made a nest of sorts in the middle of the bed. Gwen saw the apron he must have taken from the box in the back room. And there were a few brightly colored scarves, what looked like a nightgown, maybe a bathrobe, a towel, a dress or two.

All Jax's mother's things.

He'd gathered them all about him to sleep with him.

Gwen took a breath. "Poor baby."

She went to Romeo and kissed his snout, rubbed her nose against the top of his head and said, "I'm so sorry, sweetie."

Then she stepped back to Jax's side, slipped her hand under his arm and let her head fall against the side of his arm. He pulled his arm out from between them and slipped it around her shoulders, settling her more fully against his side.

"Is that the most pathetic thing you've ever seen?"

"He just misses her, Jax."

"He's a dog."

"But he loved her, and now he's mourning her the only way he knows. All those things probably carry a faint scent of her, and that's as close to her as he can get now."

Jax drew in a breath and let it out slow, and then she felt his head come down on the top of hers. "He's got to go."

"You don't mean that."

"Yeah, I do. I have no desire for a dog. Especially one that's constantly thinking of my mother, who's gone."

"You can't just get rid of him," she argued.

"Maybe one of my sisters will take him. Of course, they don't even want a spare set of towels. Not ready, they said. You'd think I'd have asked them if it was okay to just blow the house up, from the reaction I got to the question, *Could you use some extra towels?* My mother's towels are precious now."

"It's just going to take some time," Gwen said.

"Well, I don't want it to take all this time," he said, pulling away from her, his voice rising on every word. "I want it to be over. I want my life back. I want things to be normal. That's all I want."

Gwen sat down on the edge of the bed and stroked the dog, who started whimpering again. "Jax, normal is going to be something brand-new, and you're not going to see it overnight. Or in a few days or a few weeks or even months. Normal is something new that you have to make or that you have to find. I still haven't found it, and it's been almost a year since my life blew up."

He whirled around to face her, his face bleak. "You're telling me I'm going to feel like this for a year or more?"

"Maybe." Actually, she was starting to think the problem was that he thought he could skip the grief process all together. That he'd get through it by taking care of everyone else and holding his family together and carrying out his mother's wishes, and when that was done, he'd have his life back.

No time for thinking of what he'd lost or how everything was going to change.

"It's like trying to sprint through quicksand," she said. "You just don't get anywhere by trying to power through it. If you try, you'll just keep sinking."

"I feel like I'm definitely sinking," he admitted.

"Well, it's only been a few days," she said gently.

He threw his head back, like a man ready to shriek at the heavens. "It feels like forever already."

"I know." She remembered that part of it, time moving in slow motion, each second excruciating, each minute an eternity.

"I keep finding myself walking into a room and forgetting why I came in there. I know I had a reason, but I can't remember what it was. I pick up the phone because I need to call somebody, and in between dialing the number and the person picking up, I can't remember who I called. It's the weirdest thing. People mention doing something with me in the last few days, and I have no memory of it. It's like I'm losing my mind."

"No, just grieving. I think it's too much sometimes, and our brains just blank out. It can't process everything, and the grief is so overwhelming, we just forget," Gwen said. "It goes away. Slowly."

"I don't know how to do this," he admitted.

"Well, it's not a test. No one's giving you a grade—"

"Except my sisters. And I'm flunking."

"Well, they're just going to have to stop doing that. It's not fair." She'd tell them so if she had to.

"I'm doing the best I can, and I'm afraid it's not enough."

"You're getting through it. I know that. I have faith in you. And, I think I'm starting to have more faith in God, too. In the goodness in this world."

"I don't have that, Gwen."

"Give it time. It'll come."

She dared to look up at him then. He had his back to the wall, slumped against it, head down, arms crossed, trying to hold himself together. She knew about that, too.

She saw one tear running down his cheek.

Gwen went to him, touched her forehead to his, blinked back her own tears. She brushed his cheek with the back of her hand, and then both of her hands settled against the sides of his face.

She kissed his cheek, then his closed eyes, and then his arms came around her, catching her in a grip that was painful in its need.

Chapter Twelve

She held him until he stopped shaking.

Until, finally, he lifted his head from her shoulder and loosened the death-grip he'd had on her. Looking embarrassed and incredibly sad, he pulled himself up straight and leaned back against the wall, hands shoved into his pockets, eyes aimed somewhere at the floor.

"This is crazy," he said. "I'm thirty years old. I can take care of myself. It's not like I'm going to fall apart just because... I'm not gonna fall apart."

"No." Gwen shook her head. "But she was your mother, and you loved her dearly."

He nodded. "I did. I really did."

"I think you should tell me about her."

He frowned at her.

"I think you need to. Give it a try. What was it about her that made her so special? What will you always remember?"

"I could talk all night about that."

"Okay." Gwen shrugged. "There's no place I have to be."

"She was an amazing woman," he began. "Such spirit and so much happiness inside her, and it wasn't that life had been a breeze for her, because it wasn't. She adored my father. They got married right after she graduated from high school, had me a year later. She was only thirty-one when he died and left her with the four of us. Can you imagine being left alone with four kids to raise at that age?"

"No, I can't."

"To find a way to go on and be happy and so strong?"

"No. Here I thought I was so grown up and so capable, and then, life throws something really hard at me, and I just crumble."

"You didn't crumble," he said.

"You didn't see me. I did."

"I see you now," he said. "You can't fool me. You're tough. No doubt about it."

Gwen felt ridiculously pleased, like he'd paid her one of the highest compliments in the world. She was a tough girl, and here she was, alone at night with a man, not scared at all and not even thinking of herself, which was an amazing relief.

She grinned, and he caught sight of it and said, "What?"

"Nothing."

"I know it was something," he insisted.

"There's no way to say this and have it come out right."

"That's okay. Just say it."

"For so long, everything in my life revolved around my own problems. I was so sick of myself, I could hardly stand it, and then—Jax, it sounds so mean, and I don't want it to sound like that."

"You couldn't be mean if you tried. Now tell me. What were you thinking?"

"I was thinking, 'Wow, a guy with even more problems than me. What a relief.'"

He laughed out loud. The sound rolled though him like waves on a rough sea.

Soon, she was laughing just as loud. "I didn't mean it like that. Honest."

He shrugged. "Never thought I'd be appreciated for the problems I can bring to the table in a friendship."

They both laughed again. Romeo, from his nest on the bed, stared at them like they'd absolutely lost their minds, and then he started barking at them like he was scolding them for disturbing him while he was in mourning.

"Oh, baby. I'm sorry," Gwen said. She knelt beside the bed and rubbed the dog between the ears and tried to apologize.

He whined and put on his sad face and looked all put out.

"I know. I know," she said, giving his big furry head a hug.

"Come on." Jax stuck out a hand to her and said, "If he wants to be miserable, let him. I was planning to drag you off to an early dinner tonight, but we got sidetracked. I'm starving."

"Me, too." She held out her hand, and he helped her to her feet. "But it's late. I bet nothing's still open."

"That's okay. Let's see what we have to work with here."

They found an absolute treasure trove of desserts in the freezer. Four cakes, two pies, three flavors of ice cream and an amazing number of toppings.

"Wow. Hard to turn your back on that, isn't it?" he asked.

Gwen nodded. "Did you tell people you wanted to open a sweets shop or something?"

"No. It's from one of Mom's parties for the Bees."

Jax piled her arms full of nuts, sauce, whipped cream and a crumbled cookie mixture in a pretty, red canister, then pulled serving bowls out of one of the cabinets.

"Your mother fed sweets to bees?"

"Not *bees,* Bees. Her cancer support group. She called 'em the Bees. They mostly just laughed when I asked what it stood for. Bald, bold, beautiful babes. I've heard all those words at one point or another." He frowned. "But that couldn't be it. Not all of them had lost their hair… I don't know what the name stood for, fully, but she threw parties for them and served the most decadent things she could find. It was really hard to get some of them into eating, and they were just skin and bones. She tried to take care of them all, even when she was so sick."

"I can see her doing that."

"A few weeks before she died, one of the women in her group got the news that she was in remission, finally, and Mom insisted on having a party." He set the bowls down on the counter and dug in a drawer, coming up with spoons. "It was one of her last really good days."

Gwen emptied her arms of goodies onto the counter beside him and said, "She had a lot of good days, Jax. I know that about her from all the things everyone told me about her. Including you."

"I know."

"But it doesn't help?"

"Seems like it would, but… All that time, it just wasn't enough, you know? How is it ever enough? She was only fifty. Fifty's nothing these days. She should have had so much more." He looked up at her and frowned. "Sorry. We were doing really well for a while, weren't we?"

Gwen nodded.

"We'll get it back," he said, flipping open a carton of ice cream and scooping out a swirly mixture of chocolate, vanilla and some dark, chunky stuff. "You like this?"

"Sure," she said agreeably.

He fought until he'd managed to empty a hunk into one of those huge bowls he'd gotten out of the cabinet.

"Can't find the ice-cream scoop," he said. "I think we packed every one of them. Million memories in all three of 'em, you know? No way we can get rid of them."

She laughed. "Of course not."

He laughed harder. "Katie actually said she remembered Kim having her first taste of ice cream out of that Mickey Mouse scoop we found."

"She did not."

"I swear, she did." He was shaking with laughter again, leaning against the counter. "It was even more of a treasure than the eggbeaters. Do they even make eggbeaters anymore? I've always just used a fork."

"No, you use those little wire things. You know? Whisks! That's it. You use a whisk."

He frowned. "I thought that was a laundry detergent."

"It is, but it's an egg thing, too."

He shrugged. "Then we'll probably find six of them in a drawer, and we can recount the Cassidy-family history as told through its six whisks, three ice-cream scoops and three eggbeaters."

"I'd listen to that story." He slid a huge bowl of ice cream in front of her. "What is that?"

"Yours."

"Jax, that's enough for three people."

"No, it's not."

"That's a serving bowl. One you fill up and put on a table and pass around to everyone so they can each have some."

He shrugged. "It's a bowl. I eat lots of things out of these bowls. I could recite recollections of at least a dozen fabulous things I ate in these bowls. Cereal. Soup. Pasta. All sorts of things on all sorts of momentous occasions.

We can never get rid of these bowls. Should we even be eating out of them?"

"You eat out of that one. I'll find my own," she said, pulling out a much smaller one from the cabinet behind him.

"It's gonna go on like this for a long time, isn't it?" he asked soberly.

"Probably. But you laughed a lot tonight. We both did. It wasn't all bad."

"No. It wasn't."

They topped their ice cream outrageously, then went and sat on the front porch to eat it, because Jax said when he was younger, his family ate ice cream on the porch.

It was quiet on the street, and yet they still saw two neighbors walk by and stop to say hello. Three people in cars slowed down and waved as they went by.

"Uh-oh. My sisters are going to hear about this, too. I can practically hear the phone lines buzzing with the news that you and I are sharing ice cream on my poor dead mother's porch—"

"Jax—"

"Like she'd care," he added. "She'd love you. She'd be thrilled to see me with a woman like you."

"A woman like me? What do you mean, like me?"

"A nice woman," he said.

"Oh." *That.*

"No. I didn't mean it like that. I mean, someone who's kind and generous and not afraid to stick by someone through the tough times. Although she'd be happy that you keep me at arm's length, too, unlike most women I've known. My mother wasn't very happy with that part of my life. Thought I'd made some bad choices."

"Oh."

He laughed. "Nothing to say to that? Just a very careful, completely noncommittal *Oh?*"

"Honestly, I don't know what to say to that. I don't want to sound like I'm judging you—"

"But you are—"

"No. I mean, I'm trying not to. I don't understand the choices you've made, but then I don't really know about the choices you've made. I just know a few things I've heard and things you've told me, and I don't think it would be fair to judge your actions or your choices based on nothing but that."

"Try again, Gwen. Your voice is all but dripping with disapproval."

"Okay. How about, I'd love to understand better why you are the way you are with women." Because that might tell her how likely it was that he might change. And because she knew him better now. He was a very nice man in a lot of ways. The way he was with women didn't make sense. "I think it's got to be much more complicated than the most obvious reason—because you don't want anything but a quick, short-term relationship with anyone—"

"That's what I want," he claimed.

"Okay, if that's what you want, then why do you want only that?"

"Why should I want more?"

"Everybody wants more than that."

"You're not listening, Gwen. I just told you I don't, and I meant it."

"You may think that's the only kind of relationship you'll ever have that will work out, so those are the only kind you even try to have anymore. But you'd love to have more than that."

"I don't—"

"Jax, who wouldn't want a relationship that really works out long term?"

"That's the thing. They never really work out for long. They don't last."

"Okay. There we go. There's a reason you are the way you are with women. You don't think you have a chance of anything more than a short-term relationship, so you won't even try to have one that lasts."

"Gwen, nothing lasts."

"Of course it does."

"Name one thing that truly lasts," he challenged her.

"Your love for your mother."

"She's dead."

"But you still love her. You'll never stop loving her."

"What does the fact that I loved her get me now that she's gone? It just means it hurts even more. That I miss her even more. That life has messed things up for me and my sisters one more time. Love is no help in a situation like this."

"You don't believe that."

"Look at me," he said. "Look at what's happening right now. There's all that's left of her life inside that house. Egg-beaters and ice-cream scoops and sets of towels. Me and my sisters and the stupid, whining dog all missing her like crazy. What is that? It's nothing. I mean, what was the point? She was here. Now she's gone. She had to live through losing my father and struggling to raise me and my sisters and then this horrible, horrible disease. All of the pain and the fear and the fight she put up. You can't imagine the way she fought, and for what? To lose? What was the point in that? What's the point in any of this? Tell me, because I'd really like to know."

"I don't know," Gwen said. "I've asked myself the same thing dozens of times since… Well, you know when, and I don't know the answers. But I started to think I was figuring out some of it since I came here. Maybe someone is watching out for me…"

"I'm definitely watching out for you."

"I know—"

"But that's not what you mean?"

"No. I'm thinking that, all that time I was wondering where God was, when I was so lost and so sad, and maybe He was there all along, watching out for me. Maybe He sent people to me, to help me. Maybe…you, I thought… Well, I guess it doesn't matter what I thought."

"No," he said. "Don't do that. Don't forget who I am. Don't forget what I am. What I'm like. Because all those things you've heard about me and the other women. It's true, Gwen. All of it. I just told you myself a minute ago. Don't go thinking I'm going to change or that you're going to change me, because it won't happen. I appreciate all that you've done. Really, I do. More than I can say. But I won't lie to you. This is all there is to me. If you expect more, you're going to be disappointed."

She stood there and stared at him, her mouth hanging open, having trouble believing all he'd said and even more trouble accepting it.

"You're wrong," she said finally. "There's so much more to you. You just won't even try to have a lasting relationship with a woman, because you're afraid. That's all. You're just too scared to even try to have anything that lasts."

He thought she was going to stay and argue long and loud with him, but instead she looked surprised and then hurt and then just got up and walked away, off his porch and down the sidewalk.

Jax had the ridiculous urge to stand up and yell after her, "Am not!"

He was feeling really mature and rational at the moment.

"Gwen?" he called out instead, heading down the steps and down the sidewalk after her.

"Forget it. I'm going home."

"You don't walk home alone at this hour. You're afraid of the dark," he reminded her.

"Well, I guess it's time I got over that, too, isn't it?"

"Just gimme a minute, okay? Please?"

She kept right on walking.

He was steaming, his head kind of fuzzy. How had this gotten so out of hand so quickly? And why wouldn't she just slow down?

He was turning the corner, heading down her street when a car pulled to the curb beside him and stopped. The window on the passenger side of the SUV slid down, and filling the opening was the face of a woman with long, dark hair and pretty, green eyes.

He knew those eyes.

"Jax," she said appreciatively, her face lighting up. "Where have you been hiding? It's been ages since I saw you. And even longer since you called me. Don't think I've forgotten you were supposed to call me."

"Hey, Debbie," he said.

"Need a ride? Just hop in. I'll take you anywhere you want to go."

And she would. He had no doubt about that. Anywhere he wanted to go.

Maybe that was what he needed tonight, and even if it wasn't, it sure couldn't hurt. His life had been so full of chemo and doctors' visits and sitting up nights with his mother while her body positively ached, that he hadn't been anywhere or done anything in the longest time.

He started to ask Debbie, *Promise we don't have to talk about anything?* Because that sounded really good.

Then he glanced down the sidewalk at Gwen. She'd stopped now. She was standing under a streetlight about fifteen feet away, watching him and waiting to see what he did.

He wondered how Miss Nonjudgmental was doing right now.

It was one thing to hear about him and his women, but another thing to see it with her own eyes.

And he felt like a heel, despite the fact that he'd told her up front exactly what he was like, and she'd claimed she understood, and they really weren't anything but friends anyway. So why this should even matter that much, he didn't understand.

"Go home, Gwen. I'll watch until you're inside the house," he said, then reached out and opened up the door to Debbie's SUV.

He saw Gwen flinch, like he'd struck her, and then she called out, "You really think this is going to make all those things you're feeling just go away?"

"For a while." If that was the best he could do, he'd take it. Anything just to let go of all this for a little bit of time.

Gwen turned and walked down the sidewalk.

Jax waited and watched, standing in the doorway of the SUV.

"Trouble with the new girlfriend?" Debbie asked.

"She's not my girlfriend," Jax said. And she never would be. But she'd been kind to him, and he didn't have to do this in front of her.

He waited until she was safely inside her house, and then he climbed in the SUV beside Debbie. They'd had a nice, brief relationship about a year ago, and he hadn't seen her since.

"Thanks for waiting," he said.

"No problem," she said. "Anyplace in particular you'd like to go? I'd invite you back to my place, but I'm just visiting for the weekend, and I'm staying at my folks'...."

"Just turn right here and go halfway down the block to the little brick house with the white trim," he said.

She did, parking out front. His sisters would hear about this, too, and they'd really have a fit. Two women here, late, on the same night. He'd never hear the end of it.

"Your mom still sick?" Debbie asked as she climbed out of the car and clicked on the key to lock it.

"No. Not anymore," he said and let it go at that. She hadn't heard the news, and he was just fine with that. "Where have you been anyway?"

"Atlanta. I got an apartment with some of my friends from college, and I'm loving it." She slid her arm through his and let him lead her up the stairs and inside. In the living room, she turned and said, "Of course, I haven't met anyone there half as interesting as you."

And then she grabbed him.

He waited for those old feelings to come over him, to black out nearly everything else, but when he closed his eyes, all he saw was Gwen's face.

Jax pulled away abruptly, the woman who'd been in his arms staring at him strangely. "Are you okay?"

"Yeah."

"Is your mom or someone here?"

"No. It's just us."

"Good. I really did miss you, Jax. I'm so glad I ran into you tonight."

He was confused.

How did all of this work again?

He didn't feel anything.

She grabbed him again and he braced himself, trying to make this work, trying—

And then she screamed.

Jax jumped back, spotting Romeo at their feet.

"That thing licked my knee," Debbie complained, wiping off her leg with her hand and then holding out that hand as if it had been contaminated.

Romeo took a step forward and started licking her palm.

"Ooohhh," she cried. "Get away from me."

Romeo growled.

"Jax?" She climbed onto the sofa, like she thought Romeo might make a snack of her in the next ten seconds.

"He won't hurt you," Jax said, taking her hand to steady her and then turned to the dog. "I don't understand it. He loves women."

"Well, I'd hate to be one he disliked."

"Romeo, come on." Jax grabbed him by the collar and headed for the back door, Romeo howling all the way. Jax practically booted him out the door and slammed it in the dog's face.

Debbie was still standing on the sofa. "I hate dogs."

"Yeah, this one drives me crazy, too."

Romeo was outside scratching at the door and howling. Jax opened the door wide enough to threaten him again, not that it did any good. Romeo only howled louder.

"Is he going to keep that up?"

"Probably," Jax said, actually grateful to the dog for once. "I don't know what's wrong. He's never done this before."

"I can't stay here with that racket."

"Sure. I understand." He had to work not to grin as he hustled her to the front door.

She pouted prettily. Or maybe she thought it was pretty. "Call me?"

"Sure." He'd call, and then he'd probably make some excuse not to see her again, but he would call, at least to be nice.

She got into her car and waved cheerily. He was happy when she finally disappeared around the next corner. Romeo came trotting around the side of the house and stood by Jax's side. When Jax looked down, the dog was grinning.

"What was that about?" Jax asked.

Romeo gave Jax his best Mr. Innocent look.

"No. You knew exactly what you were doing," Jax insisted, then realized he was arguing with a dog, something that seemed to be happening more and more frequently. "What is it? You want a girl for yourself? Is that it? If you can't have one, I can't either? Because, that's just what we need—another dog running around here, and then a dozen little Romeos."

Romeo decided to ignore him. He walked up the front steps and waited by the door for Jax to let him in.

"No doubt about it," Jax said. "You have got to go."

Chapter Thirteen

Gwen did not cry.

She was too mad.

Mad at herself and at Jackson Cassidy and the world in general.

She'd started to hope. Hope that she'd be all better someday. That she could get back most of what her life had been like before *it* happened. That she could find a man to love someday and to marry and to have children with, and that life could be good, just as she always thought it would be.

And she'd entertained thoughts that that man might just be Jackson Cassidy. No matter what he'd told her about the women he liked and how little he truly wanted from them.

She thought he really just didn't know what he wanted, and that maybe she could make him realize that, and that once she did, he'd realize he wanted a relationship with her.

Her, Gwen the mouse, who was afraid of her own shadow, sometimes. I'm-saving-myself-for-marriage Gwen.

Sure.

Like *that* was going to happen.

She sat miserably in her living room, and her gaze happened to land on the angel on the mantel, but she didn't feel like sobbing out her troubles to anyone.

She wanted to yell at someone.

Mostly, she wanted to yell at God, but she'd been raised to show reverence for Him at all times. Not that she'd always managed. But she'd never yelled at Him in anger, either.

She'd cried out in fear. She'd begged Him to help her when that awful man had attacked her in that dark alley, hurting her, and she'd thought she was going to die.

But He hadn't answered her then. Or had He?

She'd felt as alone as she'd ever been in her life, and it had left her furious and completely without faith, and... Well, she couldn't yell at Him now, if she didn't even believe in Him, could she?

Gwen puzzled over it for a moment.

Of course, she shouldn't be afraid to yell at Someone she didn't even believe in, either.

Obviously, she believed something. She'd survived the last year and now, her life seemed to be getting better. She was feeling stronger and more hopeful, and it didn't seem to be anything she'd done on her own.

In fact, all along it had seemed like she was supposed to come here, like things were falling into place for her here, like maybe this was something Someone had intended for her all along.

Like God, maybe, guiding her along to a place where she could be happy and feel safe. To people who'd be nice to her and take care of her.

Of course, at the moment, things weren't going exactly as she'd hoped or expected.

Jax was furious with her and hurt, and he was off with another woman, and that made Gwen even more furious.

She wanted his arms around *her*. She wanted to be there because he realized how stupid and how scared he'd been, and he was in love with her and wanted to spend the rest of his life with her.

That's what she thought, maybe, God had put together for her, but maybe she was wrong.

I really thought it was going to be him, she prayed. *I thought I had it all figured out.*

Jax slept late and woke up groggy and grumpy to a dog scratching and barking at the back door, wanting to go out.

He let the dog out, then stood in the kitchen hating that he was still here, that he'd made so little progress in getting his life back to normal, that he still felt so lousy.

He hated that he was worried about Gwen and wanted to call her or go see her and say he was sorry, and that he couldn't give her what she wanted or make her happy.

He hated that the dog was still here, still annoying him, and that soon his sisters would be here, yelling at him and then crying, and that he felt completely inadequate to deal with them or anything else today.

And then he decided to go running until he dropped.

He changed into his running clothes and shoes, grabbed a house key, a bottle of water and Romeo's leash, and off they went.

He must have looked really bad, because the first three people he saw that morning all asked if he was okay. Not in that polite way people had of inquiring about someone's well-being, but in a way that told him they really wanted to say, *You look terrible. What's wrong?*

He mumbled something he hoped they couldn't quite make out and kept running. He and Romeo made it into the park, crossed Falls Creek on one of the footbridges, tried not to even look at the flower shop where Gwen worked and headed toward the eastern edge of town. Without meaning to, he ended up near one of the last places he wanted to go—the cemetery.

He hadn't been there since the funeral.

Romeo barked happily and took off through the cemetery gates.

"Hey," Jax shouted. "Get back here."

But Romeo just kept right on running.

Jax should have had him on the leash, but the dog loved to run, and he was usually very well behaved. He knew if he wasn't, he'd stay shackled to Jax.

"Romeo, stop," Jax tried.

Nothing.

And if Jax didn't know better, he'd say the dog was heading right for Jax's mother's grave.

Jax stood there, sweating and breathing hard, thinking he could just let the stupid dog go. But if anything happened to him, his mother would… Well, she wouldn't do anything, because she was well and truly gone.

So it shouldn't matter to her what happened to her precious dog.

But it mattered to Jax. She'd asked him to take care of the dog, and that didn't include letting him run loose all over town.

Groaning aloud to let go of some of his frustrations, Jax set off after the dog. Sure enough, he was right there by Jax's mother's grave.

It didn't even have a headstone yet, and the groundskeepers had removed the flowers that had been there at the funeral. They'd patted down the ground, so that Jax had to look to find the spot where they'd put her.

But there it was, and Romeo was lying on top of the

freshly packed mound of earth, looking as happy as he had lying on her bed next to her before she died. He had a huge grin on his face, and he was panting, his tongue hanging out, and making the most ridiculous noises. Little grunts and whines, almost as if he was talking to her.

The dog looked up and saw Jax and barked happily, as if to say, *Look! I found her!*

Jax slowly came closer, and Romeo licked his hand and then trotted happily around the grave, before plopping down on top of it again, as though he could happily stay there for the rest of his life.

Jax planted himself at the base of a big old oak tree fifteen feet away. He backed up to it and then slid down, letting the weight of the tree support him on his way down, and then he sat on the ground and fought in vain to hold his emotions in check.

They bubbled inside of him, swelled like a growing thing, threatened to choke him when he tried to hold them back and then to smother him when he finally set them free.

It was a physical ache, a physical pressure that he simply didn't know how to fight. Tears fell down his face. He let his head fall back against the tree and looked up through its branches to the lazy blue of a brand-new morning's sky. The sun was up, but still low enough in the sky that it held a pinkish glow, as did the horizon line.

A brand-new day.

Would it be as lousy as the last one?

"I can't do this," he said, to no one at all.

Romeo whined and lifted his head, as if to ask if Jax was talking to him.

Jax laughed. He was either talking to a dog or his dead mother or a God he didn't believe in. He wasn't sure which idea was worse.

"I can't," he said again, deciding it would have to be his mother. "Really, I'm sorry, but I can't."

Can't, what? she'd say. He could almost hear her.

Closing his eyes tightly, tears streaming down his face, he said, "I can't do this. I can't deal with this. I don't know how to be here without you."

They'd had a lot of conversations before she died. Late at night, the lights turned down, no one around but him and her. She hadn't been afraid to talk about dying or what she believed would happen afterward or what she thought her son needed to do.

He knew exactly what she'd say to him right now.

You can do this. You just don't realize it yet. It's too close now. It hurts too much.

"That's it. It hurts too much. I'm not strong enough. I have all these things I have to do and all these people depending on me, and I can't handle it. I'm going to let you down. It's probably the most important thing you've ever asked of me, and I'm going to let you down."

No, darling. You're not. You're going to be just fine, and your sisters are, too. It's just going to take some time. And I don't expect you to fix everything. In fact, the most important thing I need for you to do is to look after yourself. Everything else will fall into place the way it's supposed to. You'll see.

"I don't see how anything is going to work out. I don't have that kind of blind faith that you do—"

It's not blind. I know exactly what I believe in. Life taught me what's real and what isn't. What's important and what isn't.

"But it hasn't taught me. Or maybe it tried, and I just didn't get it, and I know I let you down with that. I know I disappointed you so badly—"

"Jax?"

He scrambled upright, breathing hard, expecting... He didn't know what he expected, but it was just a friend of his mother's from church.

"Mrs. Myers?"

"Yes, dear. Come to visit your mother?" she asked, as if it was perfectly normal to be trying to talk to her at her grave.

"Yes," he said.

"Me, too. I miss talking to her, so I come here sometimes and just talk."

"You do?"

"Of course. I decided, why not? It makes me feel closer to her, even though she's gone."

"That's...uhhh..." Weird, he thought, but he really didn't care anymore. He missed her too much to care if it was weird to want to talk to her still.

Of course, his mother had claimed, after his father died, that there had been times when she'd just know what he'd think about something, what he would have said to her, if he'd still been there, and that she'd taken comfort in knowing.

So, maybe it wasn't all that weird.

"Now, I know you miss her, dear, but is something else going on? You seem so troubled."

"I'm...uhhh." What to say?

"You know she loved you," Mrs. Meyers said. "That she was so proud of you—"

"No," he said, shaking his head.

"Of course she was."

"No. Really. She was disappointed in me. She told me so, right before she died."

"Oh, Jax, that's the most ridiculous thing I've ever heard—"

"She said it. I was there. It was the last thing
to me."

"She may have been disappointed in a few parts of your
life, and I'm sure you can imagine what those were. But
those are just pieces of who you are, not the sum and total
of you. That, she loved. No question. She'd be disappointed
if you ever believed otherwise—"

"Mrs. Myers—"

"She would think she'd been a bad mother to you, if
she'd died without you knowing how much she loved you
and how proud she was of you."

Could that be true? He wanted it to be true, wanted it
desperately.

"I don't know what to do without her," he said.

"None of us do, yet. It's too soon. We're still looking
up and thinking she's going to be there. It'll just take some
time. Don't you worry. Just try to take care of yourself. The
rest will work out."

"I don't think I believe that," he confessed.

"Well, it will. And you know what your mother would
have said, dear? She'd have said, If you don't believe yet,
it's because life hasn't taught you to believe yet. Those are
life lessons, dear. She was a firm believer in the fact that
God gives us every lesson we need to learn, whenever
we're ready for it."

"But she knew I didn't believe that."

"It doesn't matter. She believed it, and she trusted Him
to take care of you. And He will. I don't have any doubts
about that, and one day, you won't either. You're going to
be just fine."

"I'm nowhere near being fine. I'm falling apart."

"You're sad and missing her, and, as for the rest of it,

you're a work in progress, dear. No one expects you to be perfect."

"I'd settle for not being miserable."

"And one day you won't be. You have so much time, Jax, and so many people who love you. You'll have days that are filled with nothing but joy, and you'll have hard times, but you'll get through them. You're going to be fine. I promise."

Jax sat there for a long time after the woman was gone, feeling sad but not so horrible anymore, as he fought to believe the things his mother's friend had said.

Romeo was still there, sprawled on top of the grave, grinning and happy as could be. He came over and nudged Jax's side. Jax unhooked the bottle, took a few long swallows and then gave the rest to the dog. Romeo opened up his mouth wide and Jax squirted the water in. Kids loved that little trick, and Romeo loved showing off.

Romeo finished his water and went and plopped back down on the grave, content as could be.

Jax thought about all the things he needed to take care of, but didn't want to, and then he thought of Gwen.

You'd have liked her, Mom. She's as kindhearted as you were.

And she probably couldn't stand him right now.

And he was back to trying to talk to his dead mother about it.

"Okay," Jax said, getting to his feet and trying to figure out what to do next. He picked up the water bottle, picked up Romeo's leash, because he was afraid he was going to need it.

"Gonna go quietly?" he asked the dog. "Or do I need to restrain you and drag you out of here?"

Romeo whined and put his head down flat against the ground, as if he liked it just fine where he was.

"Knew it," Jax said.

He got the leash attached to Romeo's collar, and then they played tug-of-war all the way to the cemetery entrance. Jax won. Barely. Romeo cried all the way. It was pathetic. Really. Jax barely managed not to shed a tear.

"Maybe they need a guard dog," Jax said. "Maybe one of the groundskeepers could hire you, and you could live there, with what's left of her. That would be a great job for you."

The dog would be happy, and Jax wouldn't have to fool with him anymore. He could go talk to his mother and the dog anytime he wanted to.

Jax, you really are losing it, he told himself.

He looked up and realized he and Romeo weren't far from his mother's attorney's office, and he decided it was time to have another little chat with Alicia. He walked into her office with his shirt still damp with sweat, smelling awful, and Romeo beside him.

"Sorry," Jax said to her secretary, who he thought was the younger sister of a girl he'd dated about five years ago. "We didn't exactly plan this, but I really need to talk to Alicia."

Romeo set about charming the lawyer's secretary until she agreed that he could sit there beside her while Jax talked to her boss. The dog could be useful at times. Jax walked into Alicia's office and told himself to try not to sound too crazy if he could help it.

"Jax?" She seemed amused, and he hadn't even said a word. "What can I do for you?"

"Why did my mother do this? Why did she leave everything up to me?"

"I don't know."

"Alicia, she didn't leave things like this up in the air. She spent a day digging through her financial records, sorting them into piles by year and labeling them all so we could find everything once she was gone. She did that on a day when we didn't think she should have even gotten out of bed. She didn't take a pain pill, when she was in a lot of pain, so she'd be clearheaded enough to sort through a bunch of papers. This is not the kind of woman who just didn't get around to making a real will."

"Her will is perfectly real and valid, I assure you."

"I'm not arguing legalities!" Jax yelled. "I'm just trying to make some sense of it, and it's not like I can go ask her. Why did she do it? She must have had a reason."

"If she did, she didn't share it with me."

"Did you ask?"

To which Alicia said nothing.

"So you did ask." Jax could do this. He interrogated people for a living. "What did she say when you asked?"

"That's between me and her. She was my client—"

"And I'm her son, and she's dead. You can't assert attorney-client privilege."

"I can and I am. We're not in a court of law, Jax."

Jax swore softly. "Don't you understand how hard this is for me? To live in that house? To be surrounded by all her things and know that I'm stuck there, to make all those decisions about everything that's left of her life? I don't know if I can do that."

"I'm sorry. I know it's hard."

"Why won't you help me understand this?" he begged.

"I'm trying. You think she was trying to tell you something by asking you to take care of things for her? Well, I do, too," Alicia admitted. "But she didn't tell me what it was."

"Okay," he said, thoroughly defeated, worried he might break down right there in Alicia's office. "I don't know if I can do this," he repeated.

"You can."

She was actually pretty nice about the whole thing, especially since he'd barged in here like a madman, screaming and making demands.

He apologized three times and then left. Romeo was eating out of the secretary's hand—literally—when Jax walked out of the office.

"What a sweet thing," she said. "I think he's hungry."

"I'm sure he is. We got a little carried away this morning with our run." Jax looked back at the woman, thinking, *Why not?* "I don't suppose you'd like to have a dog, would you?"

"I have three," she said. "My husband swears the next dog I bring home, he's leaving."

Three dogs? Poor guy. Jax thanked her for taking care of Romeo and they left.

He didn't want to go home. All three of his sisters were probably there. Debbie would probably call him because he hadn't called her like he promised, and if he tried to see Gwen, she'd likely ignore him. He was hungry and Romeo was probably starving. That seemed like the most pressing need.

They found a hot-dog vendor on the edge of the park. He pulled a twenty out of his pocket, and he and Romeo each had a hot dog and a bottled water. As Jax guzzled his down, he found himself facing the flower shop, wondering what he could possibly do to make Gwen not hate him so much.

Flowers were always an option.

Women loved that.

He knew. He'd sent a lot of flowers in his day, for reasons much less substantial than this. And Gwen wasn't in the shop. She'd told him last night that she didn't have to go in until noon.

Why not? he decided. *Nothing to lose.*

"Come on, Romeo. Let's give it our best shot."

Maybe nobody ever sent flowers to a woman who worked in a florist shop. Maybe she'd think the whole idea kind of funny or at least worth a smile.

Romeo was all too glad to go to the flower shop.

They walked in, and there was no one out front, so Jax rang the bell at the front desk, trying to figure out whether to have the flowers delivered or to work up his courage and take them to her door himself. He really wasn't sure.

"Be right there," someone called out from the back room.

And he knew that voice.

He walked behind the counter and into the stockroom, and there was Gwen.

Chapter Fourteen

She stopped short when she saw him. There was no yelling. No tears. Nothing. He appreciated that very much.

"Thought you weren't on until noon," he said.

"I wasn't supposed to be, but Margie didn't feel well this morning. I told her I'd cover for her. And I know you didn't come looking for me, so... What can I do for the two of you?"

She waited, not looking happy, not looking like anything Jax could identify easily. He didn't understand.

"Flowers for someone?" she suggested.

And then he got it. She thought he'd come into her flower shop to order flowers for Debbie.

"She didn't stay, Gwen. Nothing happened."

"Okay. Does she still get flowers?"

Her voice was cautiously even, her face carefully blank. He didn't know what to make of it. He was used to women's tears, to ones with a temper, to having to soothe them and try to make everything better for them. But he didn't know what to do with Gwen.

"You're not going to yell at me?" he asked.

"No."

"Why not?"

"Why would I?"

"I wasn't very nice to you last night. I hurt your feelings. And I never should have taken off with Debbie in front of you."

"Were you honest with me, Jax? When you told me how you feel about me and women in general?"

"Yes," he said.

"Then you weren't being mean. You were being honest, and I needed to hear it. It's better, in the long run. You were right. I had no right to start thinking the things I was. None of it was your fault."

"I think it was. You were kind to me, and I hurt you."

"Not intentionally. Maybe not until you got into that car. You didn't have to do that in front of me, but it's not that you didn't have the right. Because there's really nothing between us, right?"

Yeah, right.

He'd messed up big-time.

"It was like a reflex. Like an old habit," he tried.

"Reflex?"

"Finding someone to come home with me for a night or two."

"Oh." She laughed. "And to think, some people think of a reflex as the thing that makes their knee jerk when the doctor hits it with a little hammer."

Yeah. He deserved that.

"I just wanted to forget everything for a while. And as hard as it is for someone like you to understand, that's one of the ways I forget. That's my favorite way to forget, actually. "

"Okay," she said, "but there's more to it than that."

"Yeah. Probably. Want to help me figure out why else I treat women that way?"

"Not while you're still doing it."

"That's fair. What if I don't do it? While you and I are… Well… What *are* we doing, Gwen?"

"I don't know. What are we doing?"

"I'm just trying to get through the day. One after another. That's it. That's all I can manage right now. I think a better question is, what can I do for you? Because this just can't be about you helping me. I'm not that selfish. Thoughtless, maybe. Sometimes. Like last night. But not selfish. At least I hope not. So, what's in this for you?"

"I need a friend like you. And I don't want to be afraid of men for the rest of my life. That's really important to me, and I thought for a while I would be. But…I feel comfortable with you."

Jax frowned. There was comfortable, and then there was *comfortable*. He was either flattered, or his overinflated ego was bruised. He wasn't sure which.

And he needed to know.

So he came to her, very, very slowly, put his hands on her arms, up near her shoulders. She tensed and went still. He eased closer, until he was a breath away, and waited to see how she reacted. "Comfortable…like an old shoe?"

She took a breath and wouldn't meet his eyes. "Not exactly."

So there was some man-woman stuff going on. She felt it, too, and at the moment he was selfish enough to want her to, even if he didn't know what to do about it.

He came closer, leaning down until his cheek was pressed against hers. He was careful not to let any other parts of their bodies touch, just hold her loosely and stand there, cheek-to-cheek.

He'd never taken the time to realize just how nice that could be. She had the softest skin, and she smelled like a half a dozen different things. Flowers, soap, sunshine, nerves. He thought he detected them all.

He nudged his nose against her ear, heard her suck in a quick breath.

He was feeling very comfortable now, and yet he wasn't. If he was lucky, she felt exactly the way he did.

What was he going to do about that?

Other than wish he could stay just like this. But he was the kind of man who picked up a woman to forget what happened on a lousy day, and she wanted someone to put a wedding ring on her finger.

So if he really wanted to be her friend, he had to want what was best for her—to find someone to love. But he wasn't sure if he was a good enough guy to do that.

Maybe he wasn't so nice after all.

"I was actually thinking," she said, "since nothing's really going to happen between us, because of the way you are and the way I am, that…maybe, you could be… Well—"

"Go ahead. Tell me. I can take it."

"You could be like…a practice guy for me. To see if we could be friends without me being afraid."

Okay.

He definitely wasn't that nice of a guy.

Jax stepped back, let his hands drop to his sides. He'd asked, and she'd told him. He shook his head and tried to work up a smile, not really succeeding.

"Would that be too much to ask?" she tried. "I mean, it's kind of like that already, isn't it?"

"For you to get comfortable enough with the idea of being around a man, all so that you could leave me and go find another one?" He grimaced as he said it.

"I want to. Someday. I want a husband and children, and I know that's not what you want, and it's okay. I mean, we both know what we want, right? And it's completely opposite things. So nobody's going to get hurt, right?"

"Yeah, right. How'd you feel last night when you saw me get in the car with Debbie?"

"I didn't have any right to feel that way, Jax. I know that."

"How'd you feel?"

"I felt a lot of different things."

"Like you wanted to pull me out of that car? Call me an idiot? Those kinds of things?"

"Yes," she admitted.

He nodded. "Good."

"No, Jax. It's not good—"

"Because when I got her back to my mother's house, and that woman grabbed me, I closed my eyes and do you know what I saw?"

"No," she whispered.

"I saw your face," he admitted. "And I realized that what I wanted, more than anything, was for her to be you."

She blinked up at him, like she was trying to comprehend how big the universe truly was or why a pair of socks could go into the wash and only one of them make it out of the dryer, or some other great mystery of the world.

"Well, that's not going to work," she said finally.

"Tell me about it."

"You're just not yourself right now, Jax. Everything's all messed up. That's all it is. You'll get over it."

"Maybe," he admitted. "But I fall asleep dreaming about you, and I wake up dreaming about you."

In his dreams, he didn't have to put a wedding ring on her finger. She never even asked for one. He supposed, if he dreamed long enough, he'd walk away from her, the way he did from all the others, and she wouldn't even get her feelings hurt.

Jax's perfect world.

He walked away. Nobody got hurt. And nothing ever, ever lasted.

"Well…maybe you've just never met a woman you couldn't have," Gwen said. "Did you think about that?"

"Yeah. I did. And don't let this get around town, but there actually are women I've been interested in before that I've never had. I didn't react this way to them."

"How did you react to them?"

"I got bored and decided they weren't worth the trouble and walked away. No big deal. I think you're worth a lot of trouble, Gwen."

"But I'm still never going to be the kind of woman you want, the kind who'll be with you for a while and then walk away. So, we just don't have anything to offer each other, do we?"

"I don't know. Maybe it's time I learned to just be friends with a woman."

"Can you do that?"

"I can try. I mean it, Gwen. I'll really try. I hated it this morning when I woke up and thought I might not get to see you again."

"I didn't want to not see you, either," she admitted.

"I have a lot of people in my life who need so many things from me, and I try to give them all they need. But I realized in the last few months that I didn't have anybody who was thinking about what I needed. I mean, my sisters, if I went to them and said I was in trouble and that I needed something from them…they'd move heaven and earth to give it to me. But I don't say things like that to them. *I've* always tried to take care of *them*."

"I think you need to say it to them. Everybody needs someone sometimes, Jax."

"So, we have a deal? I practice the friendship thing with you," he said. "And you practice your getting-comfort-able-being-around-a-man thing on me?"

She frowned. "It sounds…perfectly reasonable and simple, but I've learned, things aren't simple with you."

"So I'll work on it. I'll simplify. What do you say? Friends?"

She frowned at him again. "You really dream about me?"

"Yes," he said, sounding more irritated than he intended. "You like that idea, do you?"

She shrugged helplessly. "I shouldn't."

And then he had her in his arms, with things that felt like little, sparkly bubbles bouncing around inside of him.

They worked together that night when Gwen got off work, and then he walked her home and kissed her in the shadows of her front porch, then held open the door for her and waited until she was safely locked inside.

Then he went home and dreamed of her again.

On Monday, he reported back to work, managed to accept everyone's condolences with some bit of grace and gratitude, he hoped, and was genuinely glad to be back at work.

His sisters called, one by one, and without jumping him, still managed to find out that, yes, he had been seen with Gwen Moss. But he shut them up fast by asking when they were going to come over and look through their mother's things, to see if there was anything they wanted to keep, and he didn't even feel that guilty about it.

They really needed to come to the house and start figuring out what keepsakes they wanted.

On Tuesday, he was still in a good mood, despite the fact that that morning, on their run, Romeo had whined and fussed and growled, until Jax had given in and run through the cemetery with the dog, stopping for a little visit to his mother's grave.

He didn't fall asleep, and he didn't hear any voices, thankfully.

On Wednesday, Gwen had an idea for something to do with some of his mother's stuff. Her cancer support group—the Bees. One of the things they did was help people get the things they needed to cope with the disease, and they'd probably be happy to have his mother's scarf collection and her hats and even the wigs she'd tried and despised. Plus all the medical equipment they'd bought to help her through the last few months.

Jax had told her she was absolutely brilliant. Not only would it clear out a bunch of stuff, but it would be helping people his mother adored. It would have made her very, very happy.

There was no place to go with his relationship with Gwen, but he didn't care. She was the only one he wanted to be with, the only one he wanted to touch and kiss.

And something had to give.

He wasn't sure if it would be him or her.

But he didn't see how this could go on much longer.

On Saturday, he pulled a three-to-eleven shift, and in the middle of it, he and his partner got called to a motel near the interstate, to a young woman who'd been roughed up by a guy she'd gone out with a few times and then decided to meet at that motel.

She'd liked him at first, she said. She'd trusted him, never thinking he would really hurt her. But when he got her into that motel room and she'd wanted to leave, he'd gotten mad and scared her half to death, before the man in the next room had heard her scream and started pounding on the door and called the police.

The guy had run off before Jax and his partner arrived, and the young woman had been so distraught, they hadn't been willing to leave her to go chase him.

She'd been roughed up pretty badly, and no matter how hard she tried, she just couldn't stop shaking.

Jax had talked to her in a voice as soothing as possible, had held her hand, and he'd sat in the back seat of the car with her as they'd driven her to the hospital to be checked out. She'd let him put his arm around her in the emergency room as she'd waited for the doctor to see her, and she'd sobbed her heart out with her face buried against his shoulder, but in all that time she hadn't stopped shaking. Not once.

And all he'd been able to think of was Gwen.

He'd called her from the hospital as soon as he could get to a phone, to make sure she was okay, and told her to be sure her doors were locked, because they still hadn't caught the guy. But they had ID'd him, and his grandmother lived not far from Gwen.

And there was really no reason to think, after attacking one woman that night, he'd ever go after another, particularly a complete stranger like Gwen.

But reason was not playing a big part in Jax's actions that night.

He'd never been able to reason with Gwen anyway. Their entire involvement made absolutely no sense, and yet he kept seeing her.

So why would logic come into play in something like this?

He'd stayed with the girl until the emergency-room doctor decided to admit her and her parents arrived. And the minute he was off duty, he'd headed straight to Gwen's.

He called from his car when he was five minutes away, saying, "Tell me you are still up, because I'm coming over."

"I'm still up, because you're coming over," she repeated.

"Good."

She laughed. "I was making fun of the way you just announced you were coming and that I'd better be ready, Jax, not agreeing with you."

"Too bad. I'm coming over anyway."

"Is something wrong?" she asked.

"Yes. I need to see you. I'm two minutes from your front door."

"Well, okay. That's all you had to say."

"That I was two minutes away?" he asked, puzzled.

"No, that you needed me."

He groaned and tried not to think about how true those words were, not just that night but every night. Every night now, he wanted to be with her, in whatever way she'd let him, and when he'd seen that girl tonight, seen how shaken she was, how scared, how alone…

All he could think of was Gwen.

It had seemed like it took him three days to get to her afterward, not a matter of hours. He didn't draw an easy breath until he was inside her aunt's house and he had her in his arms.

She opened the door, he barreled in, pushed the door closed behind him and had just grabbed her in the kind of hold that had her protesting that he was making it difficult for her to breathe.

"Sorry," he said, loosening his arms instantly.

"Jax, what happened?"

"Bad call," he said. "It happens sometimes." Although truth was, while he'd answered bad calls and had trouble dealing with what he'd found, he'd never been this anxious for his job to be over and to get home to someone and hang on to her like this.

Gwen's arms came around him, and she snuggled against him, and then he realized she wasn't the one who was trembling.

"Want to tell me about it?" she asked.

"If I can hold you while I do it."

"Of course. Whatever you need."

He made himself comfortable on the couch, and then pulled her to his side, and when he had her head tucked against his chest and his arms locked around her, he started to talk.

"It was a girl. Early twenties actually, but…just a girl, and a guy had roughed her up pretty good and scared her half to death, and when I looked at her and listened to her story, all I could think of was you," he said. "And we didn't catch the guy yet, and…I just got scared for you. I mean, I know he's not going to be out looking for some other woman to hurt. It wasn't that kind of attack. He'd gone out with that girl a few times, and it's… Well, there are guys who attack women they date and those who grab strangers off the street. One or the other. So it didn't… Well, I don't want you to be scared of this guy. I just…I needed to be with you and know were okay."

"Well, I'm fine," she said, turning her face to his chest. *Well, he wasn't.*

There was still a fine trembling moving through his body in little waves. His hands against her back were shaking, and when he closed his eyes now, he saw that girl with her bumps and bruises superimposed over Gwen's face.

"He really hurt her." He took a long breath. "Gwen, with you, when it was over…"

"I had a broken wrist, three broken ribs, one of which punctured one of my lungs, and the cut on my neck, and an assortment of bruises. Mostly from when he dragged me into the alley. There was gravel and some glass and I don't even know what on the pavement. He dragged me and then kind of sat on me, to cut my clothes off... My back was a mess. It's still... I don't know. I haven't looked in a while. Actually, the truth is, I haven't thought of it that much in a while."

"Can I see your back? Please?"

She hesitated. "It was a really ugly sight at first. I know it's not that bad now, but—"

"Please," he said.

"Okay."

He eased off the couch. On his knees, kneeling beside it, he reached over her to turn on the light on the coffee table, and turned her so that she was lying facedown on the cushions.

She had on a pair of pajamas, and he just slid his hands under her top and slowly inched it up a bit.

With his fingertips, he felt a series of slight bumps and swells along her lower back, especially on her right side. *Gravel, dug into her back.* There were a few deeper gouges here and there. *Rocks, maybe glass.*

He bent over her and touched his lips to one of the gouges and then another and another. He had tears on his face, and they'd fallen onto her back, and she probably knew he was crying but he didn't care.

"I wish I'd been there," he said. "I mean, most of all, I wish it had never happened, Gwen, but..."

"I know." She rolled onto her back, pulling down her top at the same time, then folded an arm behind her head like a pillow and stared at him.

He sat back on his heels, practically kneeling in front

of her, and looked her in the eye when he said, "But if it had to happen, I wish I'd been with you after it happened."

"Me, too."

"When I was trying to help that girl tonight, I kept thinking, if this was Gwen, what would she have needed in this moment? And that's what I tried to give that girl."

"I'm sure you were great with her."

"No. I tried, but no matter what I did, it just wasn't enough. I hate that. I keep thinking, there's gotta be something I can do, and sometimes there just isn't."

"Like with your sisters sometimes?"

"Uh-huh."

"And your mother, in the end?"

"Yeah. Like that."

He bent his head down until his forehead was resting against the sofa cushion, the top of his head pressed against her. She rolled onto her side and he felt her hand in his hair, closed his eyes and thought, *Just hold me, Gwen. I need to have your hands on me, so I don't feel so alone.*

"You know, it seems like a whole lot of people expect you to be able to make things better for them, even to fix things completely, and one of the things I love about you..."

Gwen went silent.

What exactly had she just said?

Jax felt as if his mind was racing back and forth between the scene with that girl and what he could now imagine all too clearly that Gwen had gone through, and he couldn't quite keep up with the conversation.

"One of the things I love about you," she rushed on, "is...that you... Well, that you try so hard to make things better for so many people. But you can't do that, Jax."

He cocked his head ever so slightly to the left and bit back the first words he thought of saying. *Love? Huh?*

He tried to say something that he worried came out something like, *Bllluuub, blluuub, bluuub?*

But maybe it was more like, Why not? Gwen acted like he'd said, *Why not?*

"Because you're just one person, and like it or not, you're only human," she claimed. "You can't take on the whole world alone and expect to win that battle."

"I don't have to win for the whole world. I just want to win for the people I love." There it was. That dangerous word again. "I mean, if you can't do that, what kind of man are you?"

What kind indeed?

"Just a man," she told him. "A very good one in so many ways."

"It's not enough. It just doesn't seem right. People get hurt. They die. Things you count on disappear. What is that?"

"It's life. It's all this stuff that keeps happening and shaking us up and scaring us. But it's the stuff that's wonderful, too."

"What do you suppose the chances are that it's all going to balance out in the end?"

"If you'd asked me a year ago or six months ago or even six weeks ago, I'd have said I thought the scales were tipped hopelessly against us. But I don't believe that anymore, and you don't, either. You're just in one of those really bad places where we all end up sometimes."

"I want out," he said. "How do you get out?"

"I don't know exactly. I just know that I feel better. Being here, in this town. Being around the people here. Being with you, I feel stronger and not so afraid and more hopeful, and I think I'm going to be okay. And part of that is your fault. You made me better."

"I didn't do anything, Gwen."

"Yes, you did. I was in a really awful place, and you came along and it was like you shined a little light into this deep dark hole I'd fallen into and held out your hand. All of a sudden I thought, *Wow. There's a way out. Maybe I should start climbing.* You did that. For me. And I want to do that for you. Do you think you could tell me how?"

He shook his head.

"Well, I guess I'll just have to figure it out so I can help you, too."

He was quiet for a long time, his brain still kind of muddled. But he did know one thing for certain, and finally, he got it out.

"When that man attacked you, if I'd been there last year... If you and I had been...like we are now...I would have stood by you, Gwen."

"I know that."

"I don't run when things get hard. I've wanted to, from a lot of things. But I don't let myself."

"I know."

"If anything ever happens to you again, I'll be there."

Chapter Fifteen

He said it like a vow, like something that might as well be carved in stone. He meant it. If she ever woke up in a hospital again, all battered and bruised and scared out of her mind, all she had to do was call, and he'd be there. He wouldn't judge her. He wouldn't question her. He wouldn't tell her to snap out of it or that it wasn't that bad.

He'd just be there, and he was solid gold.

The man might be a lousy marriage prospect, but as friendship and strength and steadfastness went, he was a rock.

Her rock.

And he was exhausted and very, very sad and beating himself up because he couldn't do more for everyone around him.

Time for her to take care of him.

Gwen sat up, and he looked up at her. "What?"

"I bet you didn't stop working all night. Did you ever eat? I could make you some soup or a sandwich."

"Then I'd have to move, and I don't want to."

Truthfully, Gwen didn't want to move, either. There was something about just being here with him that was special.

It could be so sweet, it nearly made her cry. It could take away her fears. Take her completely out of her own life and her own troubles and set her down in a place where it felt like nothing bad or sad could touch her. It could make her feel so lazy and content that she never wanted to move. Tonight was like that. Healing, soothing, so sweet.

She wanted forever with him. As much as he kept insisting he couldn't give her that, the way he treated her had her thinking he was wrong about that. That he could give her everything she'd ever wanted.

Jax went to sleep.

Gwen found a quilt in the linen closet and covered him up, then kissed him softly on the forehead and sat down on the floor by the sofa, close but not touching him at all, not wanting him to be alone right now.

She feared she was already in love with him.

And what was she supposed to do about that?

About loving Mr.-Never-Stayed-With-Any-One-Woman-For-Long?

She wasn't going to be another in the long line of women who'd been his and then had to stand there and watch him walk away, taking a big piece of her heart with him. But he swore he didn't have anything else to offer her or anyone.

It would take a miracle, wouldn't it, for her to have his heart and for him to want hers?

Still, things changed all the time.

Just in the last year, she'd changed so much. She felt both weaker and stronger. Sad and yet proud to have survived everything that had happened in the last year. Angry and yet…she was such a different person now. Looking back, she felt like she'd been such a child before, clueless about so many things, and now…

Now she'd found Jax.

One of the things I love about you...

She'd really said that to him?

Gwen's breath caught in her throat.

And what had he said?

Something about doing battle for those he loved?

She'd known already that he would.

That he needed to win those battles for those he loved?

She'd known that, too.

That he counted her among those he loved?

He hadn't said that. He'd said he'd stand by her. She'd known that about him already, too, and she believed it with all her heart.

Gwen took a breath, watching the seconds tick by on the clock. It was late and she decided it would really be a great thing to be able to stop time. She'd stay right here with him, nervous and hopeful and giddy and silly in that way girls were when they first caught a hint of how special this thing called love might be.

She wasn't a girl. She was innocent, but she wasn't naive.

And she really didn't want to get hurt.

Oh, Gwen. You know this is crazy. You know life can really, really hurt.

Jax stirred, shifting and then going completely still. Cautiously, he opened one eye, then the other, and frowned at her.

She grinned back.

He blinked once, then again, then reached out and tugged on a few strands of her hair.

"Ouch," she said.

He looked even more puzzled. "You're real?"

She nodded and said, "Hi," as if she'd watched him sleep all the time.

"Hi?" He frowned yet again. "What time is it?"

"Late. You have to go."

"You mean, I slept here with you, and I was so exhausted, I don't remember a thing about it?"

She grinned. "I mean that you slept here, on my couch, and I sat here on the floor waiting for you to wake up."

"Oh." He sounded disappointed.

"Sorry. I probably should have sent you home earlier, but you seemed exhausted."

"If I were a better man, I'd be sorry, too, but honestly, Gwen, I'm not." He settled more comfortably back into the cushions, as if he weren't going anywhere anytime soon, and asked, "So I don't guess you'd let me stay?"

"You know I won't," she said, thinking it was no surprise she might well be falling in love with him.

He nodded, too. Even something as simple as that and something as innocent as him sleeping on her couch, he could make seem dangerous in some way. She was really in trouble here.

"Sorry about earlier," he said.

"Why?"

"Showing up here the way I did, being such a mess. Everything."

"I'm not sorry about that. I'm glad you came to me." That seemed to trouble him more than anything they'd mentioned before. "Was it so hard to let yourself come here and tell me about your bad night?"

"No, it was way too easy," he said.

She couldn't help it. She grinned.

Jax frowned, a little, frosty look coming into his eyes.

Uh-oh.

It was like she could see him replaying the conversation from earlier in his head, could see how uneasy it left him.

"Feel like you're choking all of a sudden?" she asked, because she did.

He raised an eyebrow at that and stared at her. "What?"

"Or like something big and heavy has settled on your chest and maybe it's trying to work its way up your windpipe, so it's hard to talk?"

"I'm finding it not so easy to talk," he admitted.

Part of her wanted very much to talk about it, and part of her just wanted to let it live inside of her for a time, while she examined it from every angle, analyzed it half to death in hopes of understanding exactly what it was. This thing that seemed to grow with every passing day and take on a life of its own.

Was that love?

"Jax…" She took a breath and wished she had been in love before with a very skittish man, so that maybe she'd know how to handle this. "About what I said earlier…"

"Yeah?"

"I wasn't making some grand declaration of love, you know."

"Okay."

"I just… I don't know what that was exactly," she said. "One minute we were talking, and you were so upset, and then…it just slipped out. I don't even know how I really feel about you, okay?"

And that was true, wasn't it?

"Okay," he said again.

"I mean, there are all kinds of love," she said, stumbling on. It was like a downhill train, once she got started. The words just kept rolling out. "I mean, I have a blue sweater that I think is absolutely beautiful and so comfortable and I feel great every time I wear it, and if somebody asked, I'd say I loved that blue sweater."

"Sure," he said, like he had a blue sweater, too.

"And I love all kinds of flowers," she said. "Because of the way they smell or the way they make me feel when I stare at them."

"Me, too," he agreed.

"I love cheap ice-cream sandwiches from that little cart in the middle of the park—"

"Oh, yeah. Those are great."

"And the fresh smell of rain sometimes and gold and red leaves falling off the trees in autumn. I love all kinds of things."

"Exactly."

This wasn't getting any better, she feared, and kept talking. "There are a lot of things I love about your dog, even, so for me to say there are things I love about you—"

"I'm right up there with the dog?" he asked, finally looking like he wasn't choking on something.

She grinned, at last hitting on something he understood, something that didn't scare him.

"I don't know," she said. "What am I to you?"

"I don't know, Gwen."

"Then you can be my blue sweater or the dog, and I'll be one more person you want to take care of. I'm sure that list is a mile long. Let's not get crazy about this, okay?"

He waited a long, long time, thought and thought and thought before finally saying, "Okay." Like he wasn't at all sure it was.

"I honestly don't know what I feel right now, Jax. I wouldn't lie to you about that."

He sat up, tilted her head ever so slightly toward his with a fingertip to her chin, brushed a kiss across her cheek and said, "All right. Thanks for letting me rest for a bit."

"You're welcome."

"I guess I need to go." Jax frowned. "Romeo's probably ready to eat my shoe by now."

He got to his feet. Gwen stepped back, thinking it was best to give him some room. He turned for the door, and she followed him to it. He stepped through, and took her hand and tugged her closer.

His arms came up to cup her elbows in a loose embrace, and then he took one hand and guided her head down to his chest. His lips brushed against the side of her face and then the top of her head.

"Tonight was… It was nice, Gwen. Really nice. And I don't know exactly what's going on here, either. But you're not just one person on a long, long list to me."

He didn't look at her again, just let her go, turned around and walked away.

Gwen had to be at work at nine, so she headed straight to bed for a few hours of sleep. She made it to work, barely on time. She slipped inside the store just as the owner, Joanie, flipped the sign on the front door from Closed to Open.

"Sorry," she said, heading into the back room to grab a clean, green apron, the store uniform, and put it on.

Joanie followed her. "Interesting night?"

"What?" Gwen asked, turning around.

"Oh, honey. Come on."

Gwen blushed as if she were twelve and someone had just told the cutest guy in her class that she liked him. That's what it felt like—kind of silly, and there were more of those little bubbles inside of her and heat flooding her cheeks. She could do nothing but stammer in trying to respond to Joanie's question.

"Oh, yeah. And you look so good."

"I do?" Gwen glanced down at herself. Jeans, that blue sweater she'd told Jax about, the green apron. She'd barely had time to shower and pull back her hair into a ponytail and run out the door.

"You look happy, Gwen. You're smiling. You're blushing. You're not wearing mouse brown. You've even been humming at work. If I didn't know better, I'd say you must be happy. Very, very happy."

"Oh. I guess…I am. I mean, nothing's really happened. I…I'm just getting to know someone, and it's not like it's any big serious thing. It might be. But…I don't know yet."

"Sweetie, if he does this to you when nothing's really happened, it's serious. Seriously good." Joanie beamed at her. "I was afraid you were going to hide in that shell of yours forever and never come out. But look at you now."

"I feel alive again."

"Now, that's a man for you."

Gwen thought she must have grinned foolishly for the rest of the day. Life was indeed very good.

Business was steady. The customers were all happy. Some days were like that in a flower shop. Joyous. Some were awful and full of flowers for sick people or for funerals. This was a good day.

The only sad arrangement she had was for a woman at the hospital, a get-well, cheer-her-up thing that Gwen took extra care with because she wanted everyone to feel good that day.

"I'm going to drop that by on my way home," Joanie said. "It's for my neighbors', James and Brenda Farmer's, niece, Amy. Somebody beat her up something awful, a guy she'd gone out with a couple of times. Poor thing."

"Last night?" Gwen asked.

Joanie nodded. "Do you know her?"

"No, I just…heard about it." Gwen made her decision in a split second. "I could drop off the flowers at the hospital if you like. I'm done here, and…well, she might need someone to talk to, and I…well, you know. I've been there."

"You sure you want to do that?" Joanie asked.

"Yes. I do." Maybe she could help. Someone had come to talk to her in the hospital, someone with a victims' resources group, and it had been reassuring to have someone say, *I know how awful it was,* when the person actually did know. So few people did.

Joanie gave her the card with Amy's name and room number on it, and Gwen set off before she could get nervous and change her mind. She could do this.

Amy was on the fourth floor, a room in the far corner. Gwen stood outside the door, taking a fortifying breath, about to go in, when she peered around the corner and saw Jax standing by the girl's bedside, talking quietly to her and squeezing her hand.

He must have sensed that someone else was there, because he looked up and saw her. The girl on the bed, her face battered and bruised, did too.

"Gwen?"

"Hi." She stepped inside and looked from him to the girl. "Sorry. I didn't mean to interrupt. Didn't know anyone was here. I was just bringing some flowers for Amy."

Amy Farmer looked lost, as if she was holding on to Jax's hand for dear life. Gwen didn't blame her. She knew how reassuring it was to hang on to him.

"I can come back," Gwen said.

"No. It's okay. We're done," Jax said, then looked down at the girl. "Unless you have any more questions?"

"No," she said in a little-girl voice, hardly above a whisper.

Gwen remembered that, too. Being scared to make a sound. *Poor baby.*

"Okay. Anything happens. Anything you remember, just call me," Jax said, looking like a man able to leap tall buildings in a single bound and generally protect the world around him from anything. Amy looked at him as if she believed it, as if a major case of hero worship was developing, and Gwen couldn't blame her for that, either.

Jax told her to call if she had any questions or if anything came up, and then turned to Gwen. "You have a minute?"

"Sure." She let him take her by the arm and lead her outside. "Be right back," she told Amy.

They got out into the hall, just outside the room, Gwen with her back to the wall and Jax standing in front of her, one hand propped on the wall beside her head, close but not too close.

Gwen's heart didn't seem to care. It started thudding away as if he had her pinned to the wall.

"Hi," she said, grinning at him.

"You look…different," he said.

"That's what Joanie said," Gwen told him. "Do you date a lot of women you meet through your job?"

"What?" he whispered.

She smiled again. "Just a guess." Jax, gorgeous as he was, and in full protection mode on top of that, would be impossible to resist.

He frowned at her. "What's happened to you?"

"I think…I'm happy," she said in the same way she might announce she was taking off on a trip around the world or something.

She thought Jax might get scared, thinking about that treacherous L-word again. But he didn't. He looked surprised and thoughtful.

"This is you happy?"

She nodded. "Like it?"

"Yeah, I do. I don't suppose you'd change your mind about the rules for our relationship?"

"Sure. Buy the ring and get down on one knee."

She managed to keep a straight face until he looked honestly worried, and then she started giggling, a sound she quickly stifled with a hand over her mouth. "Sorry. I have no business doing that outside that poor girl's room. I just…I am happy. Thank you."

And then she rose on her toes and kissed him softly.

"See you tonight?" she asked.

"You'll see me." He made it sound like an event fraught with opportunity, then added, "Hey, don't they have dogs coming into hospitals these days. You know—therapy dogs? I was thinking maybe I could get Romeo a job here. You know, cheer people up. He could do that."

"Sure," Gwen said. "He'd be a natural. I bet if you went down to personnel, they'd have an application and everything. You're counting on the position coming with room and board, right?"

"Absolutely."

"You're going to admit that you like that dog one day," Gwen told him.

He just grinned and waved before walking away.

Gwen stood there and watched him go, like a lovesick puppy.

She was in so much trouble.

And then she remembered why she was here.

The girl.

Gwen was supposed to make her feel better, if she could, not stand here and giggle and grin outside this room. She wiped the smile off her face and then walked into the room.

The girl gaped at her. "Is he yours?"

"Not exactly," Gwen said.

"Oh. Okay. It's just that… He's so wonderful."

"I know," Gwen said.

"Last night I was so scared, and he just started talking to me in that quiet, soothing voice of his, and he held my hand, and I think I cried on his shoulder, too." Amy paused and looked worried. "Not that…I mean, it's not anything for you to be jealous of. I just—"

"Oh, sweetie, I understand. He has the best shoulders. I've cried on them, too. And it's his job to take care of people like you and to make you feel safe."

"He's really good at it," Amy said.

"Yes, he is." Gwen held out the flowers. "These are for you. From your aunt and uncle. There's a card."

Amy took the card, and Gwen set the flowers on the table by her bed. "Thank you."

"Do you feel like having some company?"

"Sure."

She looked and sounded like such a little girl. Her sad face was a mess, and she didn't look as though she weighed a hundred pounds, even. It would be so easy to hurt her.

"Jax told me what happened," Gwen said. "Not your name or anything. I didn't know that until I made up the flowers and my boss told me what had happened to the person who was getting them. Then I just put two and two together, and thought you must be the one he'd taken care of last night, and I thought… Well, I offered to deliver the flowers because I thought you might need someone to talk to. Amy, this time last year, I was right where you are now."

"Somebody attacked you, too?"

"Yes."

"Someone you knew?"

"No. Someone just grabbed me on the street and pulled me into a dark alley. I'd never seen him before."

"I knew this guy," she explained. "We'd been out a few times, and we were supposed to go to the movies, and he said he'd forgotten his wallet back in his motel room. I wasn't even really worried. He seemed like such a nice guy. A nice normal guy. And I just walked right into that room with him."

"That doesn't give him the right to do what he did to you," Gwen said. "It doesn't matter if you knew him, if you went somewhere willingly with him or if he was a complete stranger."

"I know that. I think. I just feel so stupid—"

"I did, too," Gwen said.

"But you didn't do anything."

"I was walking down the street alone after dark—"

"But you didn't know what was going to happen."

"Neither did you, Amy. It wasn't your fault. You may not believe it now, but please try to remember it. Because, someday, I bet you will be able to believe it, too. You need to believe it if you're going to get better."

Amy started to cry. "I don't think I'm ever going to get better."

"I know." Gwen took her hand and held it. "I didn't think I would, either."

Amy sniffled and wiped away tears with one hand. The other remained in Gwen's. "Every time I close my eyes, I see it happen again. And when I actually fall asleep, it's even worse, because it's like I'm right back there."

"And it'll be like that for a while. But not forever."

She sniffled again, then nodded. "I hope not. I don't know what I'd do if it always felt this bad."

"It won't."

"The minister of my church came by, and he sa[id] have to have faith, that if I do, everything will be ok[ay], but I don't know if I believe that. Or maybe I just don't have enough faith."

"Neither did I," Gwen confided.

Amy almost smiled. "And then my godmother came in right after him, and she said faith isn't something we're born with or something we can just decide to believe in. She says it's a soul lesson we have to learn, and that the learning doesn't come easy. That it comes in times like these."

Gwen considered that for a moment and then said, "I guess I'm still learning that one."

"Me, too. She said you just have to ask for the help you need, and you'll get it. I'm not sure if I believe that, either, but I guess it couldn't hurt to try. And now that I think about it, I was feeling really alone today, like nobody really understood what I was going through, and then Jax showed up and then you. And I feel a little better."

"Good," Gwen said. "I could come back if you like. Or I could leave you my phone number just in case, and you could call me. Would you like that?"

"Yes. Please."

Gwen wrote her name and number on the card Jax had left for Amy, gave the girl a little hug and promised to be back soon.

She was home, showered and dressed and ready to leave the house that night, when she stopped in the middle of her living room and realized that the TV wasn't on, to drown out other noises that might frighten her. That she didn't need the TV because she was humming.

Humming.

And grinning for all she was worth.

Gwen had to sit down, had to take a minute to absorb what was going on inside her. She was so happy. She felt so much stronger, more capable, more confident. She hadn't forgotten what happened, but she had dealt with it, gotten past it.

She really, really hadn't been sure she'd ever make it this far, that she'd ever be healed or feel safe again.

The feeling of safety had come first, and it had come in Jax's arms, but it was like the feeling had sunk into her skin, and it was hers now. She felt safe again, and it was so wonderful.

She flashed back to something Amy had told her.

You just have to ask for what you need.

Gwen hadn't had much faith in anything the past year. Not herself. Not in God. Oh, she'd made some tentative steps back toward Him. She'd been going to church and paying attention and trying to puzzle things out. But it wasn't like she'd opened up her heart to Him again.

Of course, that hadn't stopped her from asking Him for help, and one of the main things she'd asked for was to feel safe again.

And now that she thought about it—the things she'd so desperately needed and how they seemed to have been delivered to her, just in a way she hadn't recognized at first, and how much better she felt, how much stronger, how much safer….

If she were a woman with more faith, she'd have to wonder if He hadn't heard her prayers.

And sent Jax to her.

Chapter Sixteen

As soon as he got off work that evening, Jax ran back to his mother's grave and took the dog with him.

Romeo was as happy as he had been when Jax's mother dropped a T-bone steak on the ground at a family cookout a year ago, and Romeo snagged it faster than anyone could even blink.

"That good, huh?" Jax asked.

Romeo lay on top of Jax's mother's grave, grinning and sticking his nose up into the breeze. He really liked a good breeze to ruffle his fur.

Jax sat with his back against the tree once again, looking out over the town and then back to the spot where they'd buried his mother.

"What am I supposed to do with her?" he said.

Romeo answered with a puzzled bark.

"Not you, Romeo. Just lie there."

Jax closed his eyes and didn't even take a second to think about how foolish he felt, except to hope that no one came along and caught him looking like he was talking to the dog. He just had to think about this, and he really wanted to talk to his mother, and so he figured, why not?

"She looked so happy today, Mom. She was just glowing and so pretty. I mean, I know you think that's all I care about—how a woman looks—but that's not true. I promise. And with Gwen, it wasn't about that at all at first. It was about how sad she was and that I was so sad, and that she listened to me and she understood."

Not a bad start, my darling. That was what she'd say.

"Last night, she said there are things she loves about me. Me and the dog, she claimed, but she didn't say it like that. Not until she started worrying about me getting scared, and I guess, me running away. I can't run away from her, but I don't want to hurt her, either, and you know me—and love—you know I don't believe in that."

Jax, just because you don't believe in it doesn't mean that love doesn't exist. You're not the final authority on everything in this world, my darling. She'd said that to him so many times. That his opinion wasn't the absolute truth, just his opinion.

"Okay. I know that. I didn't mean it that way. I just… She's been through so much, and I don't want to hurt her."

That part was easy, as far as his mother was concerned. She'd say, *Then don't.*

Jax frowned. It wasn't quite that easy. In one of those last nights he'd spent sitting up with his mother, he'd argued that even with the best of intentions, people hurt each other. Look at everything that had happened to his family, everything they'd lost, their father and soon to be, their mother.

His mother hadn't bought into that for a second.

Jax. Do you honestly believe that the only things that exist in this entire universe are things you can see or touch or understand?

"I don't know what I believe anymore," he'd said.

Well, let me try and help you. Try not to be so afraid. Wonderful things do happen. They happen all the time, Jax. You just think too much. Sometimes you worry too much. And considering what you've been through—losing your father so young and with me dying, you trying so hard to take care of your sisters—I can understand that. Experiences like that change us. They mark us. They change the way we see the world. They distort things in our minds sometimes, and we have to work to let go of those fears and to see things as they really are.

"I see things just fine," he'd insisted.

No, you still see things through the eyes of an eleven-year-old boy who lost his father and decided it was dangerous to ever love anyone else, because you might lose those new people, too.

"I'm not eleven years old," he'd argued.

I didn't say you were. I said you still see things with his eyes at times and you feel with his battered heart.

"You're saying I'm damaged. Beyond repair, I guess."

I'm saying things have happened to you in your life that have made you believe ideas that aren't necessarily true, and it's time to unlearn those lessons.

"Mom—"

I'm sorry, darling. If I could do this for you, I would. But you'll figure it out. I promise. Just remember that I'll love you always.

"Mom!" He could tell she'd been drifting off again, afraid it might be the last time.

And take good care of my dog.

The conversation ran out. No more words of wisdom that he remembered from right there at the end of her life came to mind.

Jax sat there for a long time afterward, staring up at the

sky, wondering where she was and what was beyond that big, blue sky.

Mom? Is that you? Are you there?

But no one answered.

Gwen came over that night, and they worked on gathering the things of his mother's that they thought the Bees could use. Jax was quiet, still mulling over what had happened at the cemetery. Gwen was quiet, too, and looking at him in an odd way.

Not an I-think-I-love-you-but-I'm-not-going-to-tell-you way.

Jax knew that look.

He'd been on the receiving end of that one a lot. It practically gave him hives because it always meant it was time to move on.

But Gwen wasn't looking at him like that. She was sitting on the floor putting pretty scarves in one box, hats in another, and every time she thought he wasn't looking at her, she was staring at him. As if he had grown three heads or something.

What was that about?

Was the whole world just getting weird?

Romeo, now that he'd snatched a hat for his nest on Jax's mother's bed, was sprawled out on the floor in front of the fireplace as though he was supervising and congratulating himself on a job well done.

Which reminded Jax... "Gwen, did you think anymore about getting a dog?"

"I...uh... No. I forgot."

And then she went back to staring at him as unobtrusively as possible.

What in the world?

He had an urge to ask her if she believed people died but didn't really die. If she had any dead relatives she'd talked to. *Kind of.* But she already seemed to think he had three heads or something, and the subject was just too weird to bring up.

I kind of...talked to my mother today.

Oh, really? How nice for you.

No, he wouldn't do that.

He dug something else out of a drawer in his mother's spare bedroom and then realized Gwen wasn't staring at him so oddly anymore. She was staring at what was in his hand.

He looked down and frowned at the flesh-colored pouch. "It's my mother's extra breast."

"Huh?" Gwen asked.

"One of the fake ones. They cut off one because of the cancer, and she had these things for a while, to sort of...even things out. But they kept falling out of her clothes." He started to laugh, then stopped. "She was at a funeral for one of the first ladies she met in the Bees, and everybody was bawling, they missed that woman so much. My mother spoke at the graveside service on behalf of the group, and as she was walking back to her seat, her fake breast fell out and rolled along behind her. People had the oddest looks on their faces. They didn't really know what it was, except for all the women who'd had cancer, and they all just cracked up, right there at the funeral. My mother said it was just like Grace McGraw to give them one last great laugh."

Gwen laughed until she cried. Jax did, too. Gwen wiped his tears away, and he wiped away hers.

Romeo looked like he wanted in on the joke, too, and then he came and snatched the fake breast out of Jax's hand and trotted off to his nest with it.

Which only made Jax and Gwen laugh harder.

He ended up sitting on the floor with his arms around Gwen, and her looking up at him.

"You're starting to feel better," she said.

"Yeah, I am."

"It's okay to feel better. Your mother would want that."

"I know she would," he agreed, and then he didn't care if she did think he was weird. He asked, "Do you think, when people die, that's it? They're gone for good?"

Gwen made a face. That was certainly an odd turn in the conversation. "You mean, do I believe in ghosts?"

"Not exactly."

"You mean, do I believe in God and because of Him we never really die?"

"Not…exactly."

"Want to tell me what you mean?" she tried.

It was Jax's turn to make a face, as if he was in pain, as if he'd stubbed his toe or something. Except he was sitting down.

"Want to tell me why you've been looking at me like I've grown three heads?" he asked.

Gwen was silent for a long time. "Not exactly."

"Okay," he said.

"No, it's not okay. You tell me your thing first. Just say it. It can't be any odder than what I'm going to tell you."

He squeezed his eyes shut, as though he just couldn't face forcing out the words, and finally said, "I go to my mother's grave, and it's like…she talks to me… I mean, I don't hear her voice or anything. It's like I connect with her in some way. I either remember something she said that I need in that moment, or one day, one of her friends showed up and said some things. It's like my mother's still here, like she is helping me."

Then he opened his eyes and stared at her.

"Okay." Gwen did nothing else but nod.

He could almost see the questions running through her mind, a million of them. *He talked to his dead mother?*

"Your turn," he insisted. "Tell me yours."

"Okay. I haven't exactly been on speaking terms with God for the past year—since I was attacked—but I did grumble at Him from time to time, when I was really mad and frustrated. I asked Him for something. Always the same thing. I asked if I could just have one person who understood and cared and who I felt safe with. And I really hadn't thought that much about it lately until I was talking to Amy today, and something she said made me think that… Well, that maybe God sent me you."

Jax thought this must have been how she felt when he confessed to having conversations with his dead mother. She thought God had sent her someone like him?

"Oh," he said, feeling more articulate with every passing moment.

"So… Your mother talks to you, kind of?"

Jax nodded. This was going so well. He was so glad he'd started it.

"Well, it's a little weird, but I guess I believe that's possible.

"Thank you." Jax felt better. "I needed to hear that."

"So, you want to know if I think she's gone from the world as you and I know it, but not really gone, and that somehow she's able to try to help you by communicating with you now?"

"Yeah. I guess so."

"Well, I used to dream about my grandfather after he died. I really missed him, and sometimes when I was really lonely or really sad, I'd dream about him, and it was like he was just there, hanging out with me, and it made me feel better. Just like having you in my life has made me feel so much better. I really needed you, Jax. And I think you needed me, and you need to hear some things from your mother. Despite all the bad things that happen that we don't understand and that don't seem fair at all, things we blame God for... What if they're not His fault, and He's still around and even if He's not stopping all the awful things, He's still helping us through them."

"Why not just stop them from happening?"

"I don't know," she cried. "I wish I did. It would be so much easier to believe if I understood that part, but I don't. I just know that despite how mad I've been and how hurt I've been and despite the fact that I turned my back on Him, He's still around, and I think He's helping me in really important ways. I don't feel alone anymore. I feel like, if anything rotten happens, someone's going to be around to help me through it, whether it's Him or someone He sent to me. And it looks like He's doing the same thing for you."

"You believe this thing that's happening at the cemetery is my mother getting to me somehow, helping me? Because God's helping her do that or He's helping me? Even though He took her away from me for reasons I will never understand."

"What if He didn't take her away from you?"

"She's gone, isn't she? He's all-powerful, all-knowing. He can do anything, and she's gone, and if He wanted to, He could have stopped it."

"Okay, so you believe in Him, you just don't like the way He runs the world?"

"Not mine," Jax said, then groaned. "I don't know what I believe anymore. I thought I did, and now I just don't know. Life is crazy. I don't understand it at all. I hate that she's gone, but then, sometimes, when I really need her, it's like she's there with me."

"And I think that's God. Helping us. He can't fix everything, and I don't know why, but He does what He can to help us when we really need it."

"That doesn't make any sense, Gwen."

"You're the one who thinks your mother's talking to you, despite the fact that she's dead. Maybe it's God speaking to you in a voice you understand and trust. *Hers.* Does it really matter? You need help, and it's there for you."

"I don't believe that."

"I do," she said. "I wasn't quite sure of it until right now, but I do. You're sad and lonely and confused, and God's helping you, and you're getting through this. You're going to be okay. I'm going to be okay, too."

"I didn't think you had that kind of faith."

"My grandfather said faith isn't something you either have or you don't. It's a lesson life teaches you. It's something that's inside of us all, from the time we're created, and it just takes a while for us to recognize it and acknowledge it, for life to show it to us. I think I finally got it."

"I don't have it," he claimed.

"Give it time, Jax. Look around you. See if you can't find things going on right now that point to the fact that Someone is watching over you and helping you, and ask yourself who that is."

"It's my mother—"

"Okay. And how is it that she's able to?"

"So, that's it? I'm either going crazy or there is a God?" He laughed softly, wearily.

"Is that so hard for you to believe? I mean, wouldn't it be kind of silly if we were all just here living our lives, and then we were gone. Alive one day and dead the next? What would be the point in that? Just to be here for a while and then disappear into nothing? I don't believe that. I have to believe that we're here for some reason, that there's some point to our lives. Do you really think there's no point to our lives?"

Gwen thought she had him there, that he'd admit she was right and that would open up the door to him considering all sorts of other things, things that could include staying with her.

"I don't know," he said. "I mean, I lost my father when I was eleven. What was the point in that?"

"I don't know."

"Why take him away from all of us? He was a good man. He had my mother, who loved him like crazy, and me and three little girls. Kim wasn't even two. Why would Someone take him from us all, when there are all sorts of horrible people in the world still here, walking around?"

"I don't know that, either. But the way you're making it sound—you at least believe someone's in charge, making all these things happen."

"If there is, He took my father from me, and now He's got my mother, and I'm not happy with Him. And Gwen, you have got to know, I'm sure not the kind of man who'd be the answer to any woman's prayers."

"Why not? You're a good man."

"I've never stayed with a woman for more than three months in my entire life."

"Why?"

"It wouldn't last much longer than that anyway," he insisted.

"Why?"

"Because things like that don't last," he said as if he were the ultimate authority on that for the entire universe.

"Sure they do."

"I already had this conversation with my dead mother today," he said.

"And she didn't buy this theory of yours any more than I do, right?"

"What does that have to do with anything?"

"Did you ever meet a woman you wanted to stay with for more than three months, anyway?" she tried, deciding to change tactics.

"No," he admitted.

"Well, maybe that's changed. Did you even think of that?" It would have to change if he was going to be the answer to her prayers. "I feel safe with you. Do you know what that means to me? How wonderful it is? I didn't think I'd ever feel safe again, especially not with a man, and now, here you are."

"But I won't stay. I don't know how. What about that?"

"I don't know. I didn't say I believed without a doubt that you're the answer to my prayers. I'm just…considering the possibility. That's all. Just like I'm considering the possibility that your mother talks to you somehow. You believe that. Why can't you at least consider the other?"

"I don't know," he said. "I feel like I don't know anything anymore."

"Well, I think I'm starting to figure some things out, so maybe I can help you. You've helped me. A lot. Just try to let me help you in return. And don't get all upset about the answer-to-my-prayers thing. Or the fact that I love you and my blue sweater and the dog. Just wait and see what happens. You never know, Jax. Things might just work out perfectly."

He frowned at her. "You really need to get a dog."

"What does the dog have to do with anything?" she yelled.

"It has to do with you feeling safe."

"I feel safe with you."

"Well, I'm not always around, and someday I might not be around at all—"

"You're going to run away?"

"I didn't say that."

Her voice got louder. She couldn't help it. "You're going to get spooked and run away."

"Hey, I could get hit by a truck tomorrow. I could get shot. I could get cancer. All sorts of things could happen so that I wouldn't be here to look out for you. Get a dog."

Gwen didn't get it, didn't see why this could possibly be so important to him. But she loved him, probably not kind-of, probably all-the-way, stupidly-and-blindly-on-faith loved him, and it wasn't so much to ask—that she get a dog.

If it was that important to him, she could do it.

"Okay," she agreed. "I'll get a dog."

There were all sorts of dogs.

Gwen bought a book that listed hundreds of different kinds, and that was just the purebreds, which said nothing about the infinite variety of mixed breeds.

She spent her lunch break sitting in the park studying all the dogs there. She talked to a woman walking a Great Dane. It was as big as a horse. Gwen didn't think she needed a horselike dog. She noticed that the littler the dogs were, the more noise they tended to make, as if they were trying to convince the entire world that they were big dogs and not to be messed with, or else. She didn't really need a dog with attitude. Some of them looked big and playful, and some pranced along with their noses in the air, like miniature princesses who didn't want to get their paws dirty in the grass.

She pulled out her cell phone, as she sat on a park bench, to call Jax, and when he answered, said, "What kind of dog is Romeo?"

"Australian shepherd," Jax said.

"Are they all so pretty?"

"He doesn't think anyone is as pretty as he is, but yeah, they tend to be pretty dogs. But you don't pick a dog because he's pretty," Jax said. "I mean, I guess you could, if that's important to you. But you're looking for some other qualities in an animal, right?"

"Sure." She wanted one who'd be a good friend. One who was sweet. Cuddly would be good. She liked cuddling a lot with Romeo, and she'd decided cuddling was something a woman couldn't have too much of. Life was too short and too hard.

She wanted a friendly dog, one who greeted the world with a smile, because she'd frowned too much in the past year. Intelligence would be good. Playful. Funny. A woman couldn't laugh too much, either.

"So…you have any ideas?" Jax asked.

"I think I'll make a list."

"Oh… Okay."

He sounded like he wasn't sure that was a good idea. How could making a list be a bad thing?

"It's a big decision," she said. "I want to get the right one."

"Sure you do."

"Jax, did something happen?"

"No. What do you mean?"

"You sound funny." He could be nervous about her thinking he was a gift from God. Or about her loving him. Or about any number of things. She really hoped he didn't go out with another woman just to see how that worked for him. She'd been seriously annoyed with him over that.

"I'm fine," he insisted.

"Okay. I think I have to get back to work."

"Don't worry about the dog thing. I'll help you find just the right one," he promised.

"Okay."

"See you about six?"

"Sure."

And then he was gone. Gwen stared at a golden Lab playing Frisbee with a twenty-something-year-old guy. The dog could jump so high in the air and twist his body every which way to catch the thing. Then he trotted back to his owner with the Frisbee in his mouth.

Gwen considered adding *athletic* and *good paw/eye coordination* to her list, but then decided those weren't really important to her. *Playful* was enough.

She gathered up the remains of her lunch—chicken salad and fruit from a nearby deli—and tossed it in a trash can, then walked back to the flower shop.

Along the way she passed a lady who wanted to come into the shop that week—time to place the final order for the flowers for her daughter's wedding. They'd finally agreed on a color scheme.

"That's wonderful, Mrs. Lee. I'll call you as soon as I get back and have the appointment book in front of me." Her daughter still had another year of college to go, and the parents were not happy about the timing of the wedding, but the daughter seemed to be and promised she'd finish her degree. Gwen had played referee the first time the mother and daughter had come in.

Then she ran into Mrs. Castle, whose daughter had just had a baby, a girl, seven pounds, nine ounces, named Anne Marie. Gwen knew because she'd made the flower arrangement Mrs. Castle had taken to the hospital the day before.

"Good morning, Mrs. Castle," Gwen said.

"Morning, dear."

"How's the baby?"

"Just beautiful. I'm on my way to the drugstore to pick up the first photos of her."

"That's great. Come by the shop and show them to us."

"I will," she promised.

Gwen grinned all the way back to the shop.

Joanie was behind the counter when she arrived, helping Brian Wright, one of their regulars, select something from the stock of flowers in the big vases out front.

Gwen knew just what he was saying, that he wanted something different, something bold and unusual. He always said that. His girlfriend, Janie Ross, thought he was too predictable, too set in his ways, and she'd been resisting all efforts he made to get her to marry him.

He kept thinking flowers were the answer.

Gwen greeted them both, and Joanie said, "Gwen, you'll never guess what happened."

Brian was absolutely beaming at her, which was all she needed to see to know. "Janie said yes?" she guessed.

"Yes. Finally!"

"That's terrific."

And she still got flowers? Even better.

"Now, when it comes time to plan the wedding," Joanie said, "you bring her to us, and we'll make sure she has the most beautiful flowers this town has ever seen, okay?"

"Yes, ma'am," he said.

Gwen was still grinning when she got into the back room. Good for him. She hoped they'd be very happy, hoped she'd be making bouquets for their first anniversary and their tenth and even their twentieth.

Why shouldn't she? She liked it here, and Joanie was great, like a second mother to her, or an indulgent aunt.

Putting on her apron, Gwen went over to the worktable and picked up an order that needed filling. Table arrangements for Mr. and Mrs. Covington's surprise anniversary party, thrown by their four children. The couple had been together for forty years, and it had Gwen thinking about how being in the shop made her so much a part of people's lives. The best and the worst, but still a part of everyone.

The town was great. People knew each other and were so friendly. She was starting to feel a part of something here.

Even the sad occasions, she didn't mind so much anymore. People told her their troubles and about the tragedies in their lives, and she listened and tried to make them feel better.

It had given her a stronger sense of the way life went, that good and bad came to everyone, and life went on.

She'd learned a lot in the past year.

She took a bundle of greenery from the big cooler in back, which she'd use as a base for the table arrangements, and set them down on her worktable. When she turned around to grab the tulips, Joanie was staring at her.

"What?" Gwen asked.

"You were humming again."

Gwen just grinned.

Joanie came over and gave her a big hug, and when she went to pull away, Gwen noticed that her boss had tears in her eyes.

"What?" Gwen asked.

"Oh, honey. You were so sad when you came here. I've been so worried. And now, to see you like this… Well, I'm just so happy." And then Joanie started to cry.

Gwen nearly did, too.

"You're really happy now, aren't you?" Joanie asked.

"Yes. I am."

"And the Farmers' niece said you were so nice to her and so helpful yesterday when you talked to her. She felt so much better, said you seemed so strong and so sure of yourself. She just wished she could be half as strong as you."

"She's going to be fine. She seemed so much more together than I was right after I was attacked. I'll have to go back and see her and tell her so."

"And things are going well, with you and Jax?"

"I think so. I mean, I know he's not entirely comfortable with everything, but I think he really cares about me, and he's such a great guy." Gwen worked up her courage and said, "I think I'm in love with him. I just couldn't help myself."

Joanie looked worried then. "He tends to have that effect on women. But I think losing his mother changed him."

"Me, too," Gwen said.

"And he couldn't keep going the way he has been with women. All men have to grow up sometime. I guess anything is possible."

"Right," Gwen said. She figured, if nothing else, she could wait him out. Wait for him not to be so afraid of loving someone, not so afraid that it wouldn't last, that nothing did. He had to get over that idea sooner or later.

Gwen just hoped it was sooner.

"One more thing," Gwen said. "I'm thinking of getting a dog, but I don't know how to pick one."

"Well, in my experience, the best ones find you."

"What do you mean?"

"They just show up under your nose. It's like they know who they need in their lives and who needs them, and they pick you."

"Oh." Gwen hadn't thought of that.

But later that night, as she was getting ready to go see Jax, she happened to glance up at her angel on the mantel and thought of her idea that maybe, just maybe, God had been listening to her after all and that He'd sent Jax to her, to help them both through their troubles and maybe the rest of their lives.

She stood in the middle of her living room, realizing she was humming and that Jax was waiting and that she wasn't afraid, that life did indeed seem very, very good, and she offered up a heartfelt prayer of thanks to God for looking out for her the past year and said she was sorry for being so mad at Him and for blaming Him for the attack.

And, if it's not too much trouble, could you send me a dog?

Chapter Seventeen

Gwen went to church that Sunday morning feeling as though she was coming home in so many ways, and tears of joy and relief and gratitude fell down her cheeks through much of the service.

The woman sitting next to her put her arm around Gwen and asked if she was okay. The woman on her other side kept handing her tissues. People were staring, and she was managing to smile through her tears.

It was a kind little church, welcoming, supportive, understanding, encouraging…everything Gwen thought a house of God should be, and the people around her that day opened their hearts to her, fussed over her, patted her back, even kissed her cheek. All of that had been right there waiting for her the whole time she'd been in Magnolia Falls. All she'd had to do was open her eyes and her heart to it.

She stood outside in the bright spring sunshine chatting with more people, waiting until the crowd drifted away, and then slipped back into the empty church and sat down in the third pew and cried some more.

It was as if the remnants of every hurt she'd experienced in the last year was pouring out of her, leaving her body once and for all, like a burden she didn't have to carry anymore, a weight that had been lifted off of her.

She closed her eyes and said a simple prayer.

Thank You for taking care of me, even when I didn't know You were there. Even when I was mad at You because I didn't think You were there. And thank you for bringing me to this nice, little town, and for all the people here who've been so kind to me. Especially Jax.

A part of her wanted to ask if she could keep Jax forever, but that seemed a bit too much to ask, considering all God had done for her recently. Gwen didn't want to seem greedy.

And then she thought of something else she should be asking for.

Please help me to help him.

The next day, Gwen was outside emptying a can of flower cuttings into the flower shop's composting bin when she heard a really odd sound coming from somewhere down the alley.

She shook out the bin to make sure it was empty and then lowered it to the ground, frowning as she surveyed the alley, wondering what that sound might have been. She wouldn't have been surprised to see a cat crawl out from behind one of the Dumpsters or come around a corner of a building. But there was nothing. Maybe she'd imagined the whole thing.

She turned to go back inside, and then she heard it again.

Maybe not a cat. Maybe something else.

Whatever it was, it made a pitiful sound. Something like poor Romeo when his heart was broken, missing Jax's mother.

Gwen crept down the alley. It was broad daylight, near noon, in fact, nothing sinister about this place at all. She walked past the craft shop next door, past the sporting goods store, and came to the back of the little café where she often got a sandwich for her lunch.

"Hello?" she called out, and something mewed in response.

Gwen hunched down on her heels and looked along the ground below two cars and then the Dumpster. Nothing.

"Where are you?" she tried.

Mew. There it was again.

She walked around the cars, around the Dumpster, all along the back of the café. Still nothing.

The only place she hadn't looked was inside the Dumpster. *Oooh.* Although she supposed if something was hungry enough, a restaurant Dumpster was the place to be.

She stood up on her toes and peered over the side, wrinkling up her nose from the smell. It was awful. She didn't want to think of what was in there, besides her mewing thing.

And then, as she was watching, something moved beneath the pile of rubble.

"Ahhh." It startled her and she jumped back.

The smell really was horrendous. She had to force herself to look in there again. Something was definitely there, below a pile of vegetable trimmings and other things she really didn't want to know about.

"Come here, baby," Gwen said. "Come on."

Then she heard a little roar.

Okay.

She tried climbing on the outside of the Dumpster so she could get a better view, but that wasn't working. She needed a ladder. And some gloves. She ran back to the flower shop, burst in the back door and yelled for Joanie.

"There's something in Charlie's Café's Dumpster!"

"What do you mean, something?" Joanie said.

"I don't know. A cat maybe." Gwen grimaced. "I can see it wriggling around under this morning's garbage, but it wouldn't come out when I called to it."

"Okay. We'll take the broom. Maybe we can move some stuff around with the handle."

"And the stepladder. And gloves," Gwen said, grabbing the broom because it was the first item she found.

They ran back down the alley as fast as they could, given what they were carrying. Gwen climbed up the stepladder, then Joanie handed her the broom.

"Here, kitty," she said, thinking to get a fix on its position.

It made the little roaring sound again.

"I don't blame you, baby. I'd be mad, too, if someone threw veggie scraps on top of me." Gwen poked tentatively here and there with the broom handle, moving things around as best she could and hitting nothing at first.

"There," Joanie said, pointing to the far corner. "I think something moved under there."

Gwen shifted the ladder to the right and then started poking through garbage again. Something yelped, and she jerked back, nearly falling off the stepladder. By the time she'd climbed back up again, she could see a gray, furry thing wriggling in the corner. A big, gray, furry thing.

It was either the biggest cat she'd ever seen or...

"It's a dog!" she cried, then frowned at it. "Isn't it?"

"Maybe," Joanie said. She was standing on tiptoe and could barely see over the side of the Dumpster.

The thing inside was kind of gray, with some light brown hair, some dark brown hair, but really long, long hair, matted badly in spots, and she wasn't even sure at first if it had a face or where its face might be. But then she realized one little speck of black off to the right of the furry blob was either its nose or one eye.

"Auurrrrff," it whined, turning toward Gwen.

Yes, that was definitely a nose. It shook off the worst of the veggies and then bounded over the top of the garbage heap and came to side of the Dumpster where Gwen was. Then it lifted itself up on its hind paws like it was trying to climb out and get to her.

"Oh, yuck," Joanie said. "It smells."

"I know." Gwen frowned down into the little face looking so eagerly at her. All that bouncing around had cleared a bit of the fur from its face, and she could see parts of two big black eyes staring back at her and a little twitching nose, a tiny black mouth.

"Ruuufff!"

"Okay, so it knows it's a dog at least," Joanie said, then looked at Gwen. "Are you going to lift it out of there?"

Gwen made a face. Was that mustard in its fur? Or something even more disgusting?

"Ruuufff!" the thing said, wagging its tail like crazy.

"Okay, okay," Gwen said. "Just give me a minute."

She gave Joanie the broom and then took off her pretty Petal Pushers apron, thinking to wrap the dog in it until they could wash it off.

The dog needed no more than that as encouragement. It scrambled up the side of the Dumpster and launched itself into Gwen's arms, landing against her chest, its stench increasing steadily the closer it came.

Then it started licking her cheek.

"Ooohhh," Gwen yelled.

Joanie laughed.

The dog barked excitedly.

"I think it likes you," Joanie said.

Gwen wrapped it up as best she could in the apron, something the dog didn't appreciate in the least, then looked down at what had been one of her favorite white shirts.

"Don't even think about it," Joanie said. "We'll just run back to the shop and throw the dog in one of the big sinks in the back, and if we have to, we'll hose you down."

Joanie was laughing then.

Gwen was, too.

The dog was licking her again.

"No, no, no," she said. "Not that. Please?"

"Aaarrrf!" it said, wiping its nose on her shirt.

"Come on," Joanie said. "I always keep a change of clothes at the shop, just in case I make a mess of what I'm wearing."

They hurried back to the flower shop and put the dog in the big metal sink in back, which the animal did not appreciate in the least. It whined pitifully and begged to get out.

"Don't worry," Gwen said. "We're going to make it all better. You'll come out smelling like a rose."

Because they had rose-scented soap. It was either use that or take the time to go to the supermarket and get doggie shampoo. She didn't think she or Joanie could stand to be in the same room with the dog for the time it would take to go get doggie shampoo, and they couldn't leave the creature alone.

Joanie came out of her office with a clean shirt for Gwen and told her to go change, and Gwen did, grateful not to have to spend another second in her soiled shirt. When she came back, Joanie had soaked the dog and starting soaping up its smelly, matted fur.

"This is so disgusting," Joanie said.

The dog looked like it had shrunk to half its previous size now that its fur was wet. The poor thing howled and made sad eyes at Gwen, the kind that said it felt horribly betrayed by this bath. As if a sinkful of clean water was worse than a Dumpster.

"Oh, it's probably starving, if it was desperate enough to hop in the Dumpster," Gwen said.

"I have a ham sandwich in my purse. We can feed her that."

"It's a her?" Gwen asked.

"Yes. I checked. No tag. No collar." Joanie grinned. "I told you the best dogs find us."

Gwen grinned, too. "I bet she's really cute when she's clean and her fur's trimmed."

She couldn't wait to introduce this pretty baby to Jax and Romeo.

They called the county animal shelter. No one had reported the dog missing. Checked the lost-and-found ads in the newspaper. Nothing there, either.

And the dog had obviously been on the streets for a while, given the condition of her coat. Joanie said to run an ad in the lost-and-found for a week, and they'd left information at the shelter about the dog, in case anyone was looking for it. And if no one claimed her by then, to consider the dog hers. Gwen thought that sounded like a good plan.

After two baths with rose-scented soap and then another two, later in the day, with doggie shampoo, the animal didn't smell too bad, although she was spitting mad about the four baths.

"I suppose that is a bit much in any one day," Gwen admitted.

She'd bought a collar, a leash, a brush and dog food when she'd gone to the market to grab the shampoo. The dog wasn't gray, as she'd first thought, just really, really dirty. She was actually a beautiful white with light and dark highlights and long, pretty, corkscrew curls.

"I used to want hair just like yours," she told the dog, as they walked home that evening.

The dog, still damp from her baths, looked skeptical.

"Really, I did. I thought life would be glorious if only I had corkscrew curls. Of course, we're going to have to get you a good trim. But don't worry. After the Dumpster anything's going to be a step up. Even another bath and a trip to the dog groomer's."

The dog frowned up at Gwen and cocked her head the way Romeo did when he didn't understand.

"Maybe we'll just let that part be a surprise, okay?"

And off they went quite happily.

Jax called as Gwen was getting ready to leave for his mother's house that evening, and she said, "I was just coming over. I have a surprise for you."

"What kind of surprise?"

"A good one. No…a great one. I can't wait for you to see it."

"See what?"

"The surprise. I can't tell you. Then it wouldn't be a surprise," she reasoned.

She took another few minutes to fuss over the dog. She'd dried her hair with a blow-dryer, worried that the dog had been wet all day and might catch cold—if dogs caught colds—and the blow-dryer had left the poor dog's excessive fur all puffed up. She seemed to know she looked even funnier now than she had covered with Dumpster goo.

Gwen brushed the dog's fur as best she could, was tempted to cut out the worst of the matted knots, but Joanie said she really should let the dog groomer do it, and they did have an appointment for the next day. But she wanted her to be so pretty for Jax and Romeo.

"We'll wow 'em tomorrow," Gwen promised. "For now, I think this is the best we can do."

She snapped the leash back on and off they went. The dog pranced down the alley, head held high, and Gwen hummed.

Life was very, very good.

Jax had had one of those days. The Bees had come and talked about Jax's mother fondly and cried copious tears, then began hauling away stuff when his sister Katie showed up. She looked horrified as she saw boxes and boxes of stuff being hauled out of the house, barely acknowledged the Bees' greetings and then got Jax off into a corner alone.

"They're taking her stuff? You're just getting rid of her things without a word to me and Kim and Kathie?"

"Yes," he said defiantly.

Katie sputtered and stammered, finally managing to get out, "How can you be so mean about this?"

"I'm not being mean. It's not mean to give away wigs that she hated and scarves that she only put on because her head was bare and got cold, and a cane she hated using, her bedpan. Do you really want her bedpan, Katie?"

Which made his sister start to cry.

Great.

"She was generous with everything she ever had, and she loved these women. Some of them are going bald and won't be able to afford a wig of their own or the other stuff they need. She'd want them to have it, Katie. You know that."

"I do."

"Then why are you yelling at me for doing something she'd do herself if she was here."

"I just miss her so much," Katie cried.

"So do I. But she's not here in this stuff. There might be little parts of her or at least good memories of her in some other things in this house, and they're still here. You can take any of it you like. But you can't ask me to stay here indefinitely, surrounded by all her things. It's too hard for me. And we don't want to leave the house empty for any length of time, especially with all of her belongings still in it. And we sure can't sell the place or rent it with all these things in it. So the stuff has to go."

"I know," she admitted.

"I'm doing the best I can, and I need for you to either help me or let me do it. But I can't take arguing with you about all of it. I can't."

She frowned. "But…you can do anything."

She slayed him with that and stood there blinking back tears, looking as if she could crumble at any moment, his poor, controlling sister.

"Okay," she admitted. "I guess I know you really can't do everything. I guess I've just always believed you could. That you and Mom both could."

"And now both of us have failed you?" he said. Their mother by dying. Jax by not handling it as well as his sisters thought he should.

"I'm not being fair to you. I know that. And I just keep doing it," she cried. "I don't know why. I can't seem to stop myself."

"It's probably easier to be mad at me than to think about how much you miss Mom."

"Kind of," she admitted. "But…I think the real problem is, I feel like I should be taking care of this, and I can't. I can't do what you're doing, and I feel like I'm failing everyone, too, by not being able to do this."

Jax hugged her tightly. "You don't have to do it, Katie. I will."

Maybe that's why his mother had left the job to him— because she knew he and Katie were her best bets for getting this done, and she knew it would be too much for Katie. So she gave the job to Jax.

"I'm sorry," she said, squeezing him tight. "I'm going to stop yelling. I promise."

"Thank you."

She eased away from him and looked around sadly. "I know she's not here. It just still feels like her space. I can hear her voice here. I can see her in the rooms of this house. The bathroom and the bedroom smell of her perfume and the lotion she used on her skin. I'm afraid when those things are gone, it'll be like losing her all over again."

"Okay." Jax took her by the hand and tugged her along behind him. He led her into the bathroom down the hall and found their mother's favorite perfume and handed it to Katie. "Take this."

"All right," she said.

"The lotion she liked is in the bedroom. Take that, too."

"I will."

"You're actually going to take something from this house?" he asked.

Katie nodded sadly, and Jax grinned at her.

"Thank you. That helps a lot. How 'bout an eggbeater just loaded with family memories?"

Katie bent her head, touching her forehead to Jax's shoulder. "I'm sorry. I'm just not ready for the eggbeater yet, but I'll try. I promise"

"That's my girl." He gave her another quick hug.

"I love you, Jax."

"I love you, too."

A few more sniffles and a few more hugs, and Katie left. So did the Bees. Jax glanced at the clock on the wall, wanting Gwen.

She was a creature of habit, and he knew her routines. She should have been here by now. He didn't like it that she wasn't, didn't like how uneasy it made him that she wasn't here.

What am I going to do with her, Mom? I can't keep her. It would never work. What I have to give her would never be enough to make her happy.

Romeo came trotting into the kitchen, staring oddly at Jax. Had he been talking out loud? Romeo cocked his head to the right and whined, then went to the door.

"Gwen?" Jax called out on his way to the door. He pulled it open, and there she was, getting ready to knock. "It's about time."

"I was busy," she said, Romeo all over her as he greeted her.

"Romeo, what's the matter with you? She doesn't want to be pawed at and jumped on. Off."

Romeo whined and tried to get outside.

"You just went," Jax said.

"No, let him out for a minute. Remember I told you I had a surprise?"

"It's outside?"

Gwen nodded, looking very happy with herself. She stepped back onto the deck and Romeo took off, running down the three steps to the backyard and disappearing to the right.

Jax stepped out more slowly and looked around. "Okay. Where is it?"

Romeo went, "Wooofff!" in his big, deep voice, and then something answered, something with a high-pitched, squeaky, surprised "Aaarff."

Jax stopped where he was and said, "Gwen? What is that?"

Her grin got even bigger. "My surprise. Come and see."

She took his hand and led him down to the yard, where, off to the right, tied to one of the posts of the deck, was… something.

Jax scowled at it, thinking this had to be a trick of the fading light. "What is it? Some kind of deranged sheep?"

"No!" Gwen yelled.

Jax took a step closer. It was either really fat or really puffy and mostly white, a little more than half the size of Romeo, and Romeo seemed leery of the thing, but excited, too. He was sniffing and keeping his distance for now. Jax didn't blame him.

"Aaarff!" the thing said, sounding more like what he feared it was.

"I know she doesn't look like much now, but we fished her out of a Dumpster behind Charlie's Café. Believe me, she looks better than she did when we found her. And she has an appointment at the dog groomer's tomorrow."

"The dog groomer's?" Jax repeated. "Gwen, that is not a dog."

"Of course it's a dog."

"No. Romeo is a dog. He's big and loud, and if he needed to, he could sink his teeth into a bad guy and get him to run like crazy, which is what you need. That thing… Does it even have a face?" All he saw was fur.

"Of course she has a face. She has a pretty face. Her bangs are just too long. Here. Look at her."

Gwen pulled a hunk of fur back and there, indeed, was

what looked like two, dark eyes, a nose and a tiny mouth about the size of a cat's.

Romeo perked up right away at that and started panting. It seemed he'd figured out it was a girl.

Jax couldn't believe it. "That might as well be a stuffed toy for all the good it could do you. Or a giant cotton ball."

"Stop it," Gwen said, covering the dog's ears with her hands.

Romeo turned to him and growled, too.

That thing she called a dog looked like it might be grinning stupidly, as if Jax had just said something nice about it.

"What's it going to do if someone breaks in to your house?" Jax tried. "Tell a joke and hope while the guy's laughing, you can run away?"

Gwen gaped at him. "How can you be so mean?"

Romeo growled at Jax again. Apparently, he liked the thing.

The giant cotton ball nearly purred as Gwen scratched its chest.

"I'm being practical," Jax insisted. "You need a dog who can protect you."

"Petunia will do that."

"Pehh— What?"

"Her name is Petunia."

Romeo woofed again, swished his tail back and forth and licked the thing in the face.

"Yes," Gwen crooned and petted him. "At least *you* like her." Then she scowled at Jax, her expression almost as annoyed as the dog's.

"You cannot be serious," he said, feeling his whole plan unravel. All he had to do was get rid of the stupid dog.

"She was in the Dumpster, trying to keep herself fed—"

"Gwen, it doesn't look like she's been missing any meals—"

"She just needs a trim. Her fur got even puffier when I blew it dry—"

"You blew the dog's hair dry?"

"What's wrong with that? She was all wet, and I didn't want her to catch cold."

"She's a dog!"

"I thought you said she wasn't a dog?" Gwen reminded him.

"I did. You know what I mean."

"No, I don't. She was lost and trying to take care of herself as best she could, and someone had dumped vegetable cuttings on her and garbage, and I found her, and Joanie and I cleaned her up. She doesn't have a collar or a tag, and no one seems to be looking for her. And she's sweet—"

"You don't need sweet—"

"Yes, I do. She's funny and silly and happy and sweet, and I need all that in my life. I need it a lot."

"You need a watchdog more," Jax said.

"I've been just fine without a watchdog for nearly a year now."

"Gwen, you said you wanted to feel safe, remember?"

"Yes. I feel safe with you."

Jax took it like a hundred-pound weight had just landed on his chest. Landed hard. Life was really hard. It had taught him that, if it had taught him nothing else.

"What if I'm not around?"

"Tired of me already?" she asked. "Or just scared?"

"I'm not scared," he lied, knowing it for the lie it was the moment he said it. But he still didn't take it back. He stood there and tried to look like he'd meant every word and like he wasn't about to break her heart, something he'd sworn he'd never do.

"Decided I'm just too much trouble after all?" she suggested, giving him another out if he wanted it.

"No," he said, leaving himself nowhere to go, at least not that he saw.

"Then what's the problem?"

"The dog," he said. "Both of them."

Gwen looked down at her feet. The fur ball she claimed was a dog was sitting there, happily wagging its cotton-ball tail while Romeo licked its hair-covered face, like he was either admiring it or trying to give it a bath. *Stupid dog.*

"They look perfectly happy to me," Gwen said. "You're the only one who seems to be having a problem, Jax. What's the problem?"

"I just thought… It seemed like the perfect answer…"

"What did?"

"That you'd take the dog."

"I did take the dog. She's right here."

"Not that. Not her. That you'd take Romeo." He just blurted it out. "I thought you'd take Romeo."

Chapter Eighteen

Gwen gaped at him. "All this time you were with me because you thought I'd take Romeo off your hands?"

"Why not?" he said. "It makes perfect sense. You like him. You fuss over him the way my mother did. He likes you, and he gets stupid sometimes, but he's big and he's trained to protect people. If anyone ever tried to break in to your house, Romeo would handle it."

"That's what all this has been? You trying to get rid of your poor mother's dog?"

"All what?"

"You know what, Jackson Cassidy, you rat. Don't stand here and act like nothing happened. Like you didn't do anything to make me think something was happening between us, and if I think there was, I must be crazy. Don't you dare try that with me."

"Gwen, I—"

"You swore you didn't lie to women. Don't start now."

"I'm not lying," he claimed, dog that he was.

"I helped you, didn't I?"

"Of course you did."

"I mean, I haven't let a lot of people lean on me. I usually do the leaning. So I can't be sure… But I thought I was doing that for you, and I thought it was important."

"You were. It was."

"I held on to you when you were so mad and so sad your whole body was trembling. I listened to everything you had to say, didn't I?"

"Yes."

"And I cleaned and sorted boxes full of a really sweet, dead woman's stuff—"

"And I'm grateful for that.

"But you expect me to believe that all that time all you really wanted was for me to take your mother's dog off your hands? So you can get on with dismantling your mother's life and go back to the lousy life you had before she died? Is that what you're claiming you want?"

"There was nothing lousy about my life before," he told her.

"Oh, right. Nothing like finding a new girl every few months or so. Never getting too attached to them. Never risking anything like love. You were doing just fine."

"I was," he said.

"Liar."

"Gwen—"

"Coward."

"I never wanted to hurt you," he tried.

"Well, I want to hurt you. Right now. I want to grab you and shake some sense into you and make you be honest with yourself and with me. I wish I was the kind of woman who could scream at you and hurt you and then just walk away, but I can't do that. Because I don't believe you for one second when you say this was all about me taking that dog."

"It wasn't. Not really. It was just…in the beginning. That was all. The beginning."

"And then what?" she asked.

"And then things got all complicated, and I shouldn't have let it. I mean, I told you, Gwen. I told you it wouldn't last. You know it won't."

"No, I don't know that," she said. "I know it won't last unless some things inside you change in a very fundamental way—"

"Oh, yeah. Just like a woman. Always wanting to change a man."

"No, I don't. I never cared enough about any man before to want to change him."

"But you want to change me?"

"You need to change, Jax. You need to change the way you think about life and about love. About faith and about God."

"I don't have any faith left, and I don't believe in a God who'd take so much away from me."

"You believe in your mother and that she still exists somewhere. You believe she's helping you in some way. You told me so yourself."

"Yeah, well. What does that mean? I felt like I could talk to my father, too, after he died."

"And you got through it. You've gotten through everything life's ever thrown at you. You'll get through this, too."

"I am getting through it."

"By getting rid of me? By pushing everyone away from you? That's not living, Jax."

"I'm getting through it the best way I know how."

"Well, it's time you found a better way," Gwen said.

"You need to think about what's important. What means something. What lasts."

"Nothing lasts," he said.

"Jax, your mother's still here. Everything you feel for her. All the love she has for you—it hasn't gone anywhere. All the memories you have of her. Everything she's taught you. None of that ends. She's still helping you, even now. You know that. You're just afraid to admit it to yourself."

"Fine," he said. "I'm a coward. I won't argue that with you."

"I didn't mean it. I was just angry. I wanted to hurt you, and I'm sorry for that. But I'm not trying to hurt you now. I'm trying to help."

"By wanting me to love you? To try to build a life with you? How is that going to help?" he cried. "I already told you—it won't last. Nothing does."

"So you're never going to let anyone else be important to you, except your sisters? And why is that? Why is it okay to love your sisters?"

"How could I not? They're my sisters."

"A lot of people manage not to love their siblings at all. So that can't be the reason, although I think I know what it is."

"Fine," he said. "Tell me why I love my sisters."

"Because it was too late. By the time life started teaching you not to let anyone get too close and that nothing really lasts—not even love—you were eleven, and you already loved them too much to ever pull away from them."

Jax didn't like hearing that at all. He didn't think it was true, but all the same, he hated hearing it. It made it hard for him to breathe.

"You must be terrified of losing them, too," Gwen said.

He took that like a kick in the chest. "Don't say that."

"It's true. You'll lose them one day, or they'll lose you—"

"And this is supposed to be helping me?"

"I'm just saying that you can't wall yourself off from life. You can try all you want to protect yourself, and bad things still get to you. Do you think you're safer by only loving three people than you could be by loving four? Is that the way you think it works?"

"I have no idea how anything works," he confessed.

"You should come spend the day with me at the flower shop. I think you can learn everything you need to know about life in a flower shop. To think, I just took the job because it's the first one I heard of when I moved here, and it turned out to be exactly what I needed. There's so much pain in the world and so much joy, and it all comes through the shop. New babies. Weddings. Anniversaries. Celebrations. Love. Illness. Funerals. It's all there. Everybody gets all of those in their lives, day after day, Jax, don't you see that?

"I see that the bad outweighs the good by a long shot."

"That's not true."

"It is for me."

"Your mother knew better. She would have known what to say—"

"Gwen, the truth is…" That he couldn't hide from it anymore. There was nowhere left to hide. Life was just too lousy. "The truth is that I was a disappointment to my mother."

"No."

"She told me so. It was the last thing she said to me. That she was disappointed in me and the way I was living my life."

"She didn't mean it. She couldn't have…."

"Oh, yeah," he said bitterly. "She did."

"Jax—"

"No," he said sharply enough that she flinched. He backed up, took a breath and said, "I'm sorry. She said it, okay? She said it. And that's something I never wanted another living soul to hear, but… There it is. That's how she felt, and if I disappointed her… Well, I'd say I'm bound to disappoint everybody who ever gets close to me."

"I know that's not true."

"Gwen, please just stop—"

"I can't. Because I think this is your big chance. People do change. They grow and they learn, and they change. You can do that, and if you do, we can be together."

"We can't," he insisted.

"We can. I think you want that. More than that, I think you need it. I think you need me, maybe even more than I need you. And I think we're here together, in this moment, with these things that are going on in your life and mine, because right now is your big chance."

"A chance for what?"

"For you to figure out some things. For your life to get better. Right now. You just have to stop being so afraid, and you have to think with your heart instead of your head. Ask yourself what you believe in your heart. Not what your head tells you is true, but what your heart tells you is possible. What's real?"

"I know what's real."

"You and I together—that's real. Your mother trying to help you? That's real, too. God is helping us both even now. That's real. All those feelings inside you that are telling you you're tired of being alone and scared and angry, and the need you have to love someone, someone who will stand beside you through the really bad times and the good ones— those feelings are real. They're already inside of you. You don't have to go looking for them. You don't need some brilliant bit of illumination or to twist yourself into a whole different person or anything like that. You just have to accept what you already know, deep down in your heart. You're a good person, and you know how to love people. You know how important it is to have people you love in your life. You just have to let me be one of those people."

"No—"

"I love you, Jax. I think you love me, too. And it scares me, but I need it. I need you. And I think you need me, and I think this is what you want. Please don't run away from this just because you're scared or because you've been knocked around by life one too many times and it hurt so bad you could hardly stand it."

"I can't stand it," he said. "I can't lose anyone else I love."

"I hope you can," she said. "Because you're about to lose me."

And then she untied her dog's leash, turned and walked away, poor little Petunia following after her.

Jax stood there like a statue.

Romeo barked like a fool and then started whining and jumping up and down, as if this was disaster in the making.

Take it like a man, Romeo.

Of course he didn't. He was a dog, and he didn't know better than to fall madly and completely in love.

Stupid dog.

Gwen had said Jax was scared to love the dog. He didn't love the dog. The dog made him crazy. His mother hadn't known what she was talking about when she'd claimed the dog and Jax were alike in so many ways.

Look at the fool thing now, running off to chase Gwen and that silly white powder puff, then turning and running back to Jax. He had to feel sorry for the dog. Back and forth he went, more agitated each time he did it.

Jax stood there and felt like he was dying.

Yeah, he was so much better off than the dog.

Then Gwen turned around and marched back to him, both dogs following her. He braced himself as best he could and thought of his boast about not loving her, about not being able to stand to lose one more person he loved. If he didn't love her, why did it feel like he was dying?

"Did you mean it about me taking Romeo?" she asked.

"What?" She'd come back to talk about the dog?

"Is that what you really want? For me to take your mother's dog? Because if you're never going to let yourself love him, he'd be better off with me."

That's what she was thinking about as she'd walked away from him? *The dog?*

"Fine," she said. "Give him to me."

Jax gaped at her.

He couldn't believe she'd come back for the dog.

"Fine. Romeo, go with Gwen."

Romeo grinned like a fool and ran to her side, licking what looked like the cotton ball's ear.

"Come on, you two," Gwen said as she turned and walked away from him once again.

Gwen got home and sat on her couch, intending to feel very sorry for herself and maybe even cry. But Petunia seemed quite concerned about Gwen. She climbed into her lap, whimpering and looking worried and trying to help. Romeo sat on the floor beside them both, whimpering and looking worried, too. It was so sweet.

"It's okay," Gwen said, not convincing either of them that it was. "I'll be okay. Really."

She hugged Petunia to her chest and then leaned over and kissed Romeo's pretty head. It wasn't like she was going to fall apart. Not the way she had after the attack. She was stronger now, and she had two, beautiful, kind-hearted dogs to comfort her.

Romeo hopped up onto the couch and then plopped down against her, his warm, furry side pressed against her leg. He moaned like a man who'd had a hard day, and then put his head on her knee and looked at her with big, sad eyes. Petunia wriggled her little mess of a tail and licked Gwen in the face.

Gwen tried not to think about where the dog's mouth had been and to take it as the gesture of comfort she was sure Petunia meant it to be.

"Tomorrow we get you a toothbrush," she said, and held the little dog tighter.

Okay, if she wasn't going to fall apart, what was she going to do? Visit Amy in the hospital. She'd promised that she would. And a nice lady from the Victims' Rights Council had called Gwen about volunteering with the organization. They'd sent someone to call on Amy, and she'd mentioned Gwen's visit, and the group thought Gwen would be great at calling on other people who'd been attacked and whose lives were a mess. She had a little experience, and it seems she was in demand.

So she'd do that, too. No one should have to feel alone after going through something like being attacked, and there was something very powerful about having someone tell you that you were going to get through it. That they knew because they'd been exactly where you'd been.

At least, that's what the victims' rights lady had told Gwen, and it sounded true to her.

So Gwen would make pretty bunches of flowers for people to celebrate all the different, wonderful days of their lives and to brighten up their last days. She'd take care of her dogs, fix up her house and do some volunteer work for the victims' rights group and go back to her nice church, full of kind, loving people, and thank God for all she had in her life that was good, and she'd be okay.

She'd probably spend some time waiting for Jax to come to his senses, hoping that he would, but that probably couldn't be helped.

Later that night, when she tried to say a little prayer to help her through this, all she could manage was to think of Jax and whisper miserably, "I thought I had it all figured out."

They got through the day without getting too emotional, but when it came time to settle down for the night, Romeo was restless. He wandered through the house sniffing everything as he went, and then he started whimpering.

Gwen was in bed already, Petunia curled at her feet, something Gwen wasn't up to fighting about. Besides, her feet always got cold at night, and Petunia was really warm. And it was her first night. And she'd been stuck in a Dumpster. They were all entitled to whatever comfort they could find together.

But Romeo would not settle down, and he seemed to be looking for something.

"Do you want your bed?" Gwen asked him, the next time he came into her room and whined.

"Aaarff!" he said.

"Okay." Gwen got up, grabbed a robe and stuck her feet into her sneakers, got Petunia's leash on her, and off the three of them went, up the alley.

She knocked on Jax's back door, and when he flung it open and shouted, "What?" before he'd ever even seen them, she said, "Romeo needs his bed."

"What?" Jax repeated.

Romeo slid past them both and trotted off down the hall.

"His bed," Gwen said. "I think he misses it, and he still misses your mother. I thought if we took the comforter off her bed and the stuff he piled on it, he'd be happy."

Jax looked like he was ready to argue about that, like he had a million things he wanted to say, and Gwen felt like she was back in high school making stupid excuses to see a boy who'd just broken up with her. Thinking that the sight of her would make him immediately regret his decision and claim undying love for her right there on the spot.

Did people ever outgrow doing stupid things in the name of love?

She closed her eyes and said, "Can we just try it? With the comforter and stuff of your mother's at my house?"

"Sure." Jax gave in, and off they went down the hall.

Romeo was in the bedroom looking from Jax to the bed, to Gwen and Petunia, obviously not sure what to do.

"Don't worry," Gwen said to Romeo. "We'll fix it."

She wrapped everything in the comforter and picked it up, barely managing to hang on to it and Petunia's leash.

Jax stood in the doorway watching them all, probably waiting for Gwen to yell at him again, which she wasn't going to do.

She was going to walk right back out of here, unless he asked her not to, which he would not do. Still, there had to be something….

"Gwen? What I said the other night? If you're ever in trouble? If you ever need me, I'll help? I meant that."

She glared at him. "Careful. That sounds an awful lot like a promise that could last, and you don't believe in anything that lasts, remember?"

To which he said nothing, just shoved his hands deep into his pockets and stood there.

"Okay, guys," she said to the dogs. "That's it. Let's go."

Jax opened the back door for them all and watched as they went outside and took off down the alley.

He didn't say another word.

Jax woke, disoriented and grumpy, to the sound of someone pounding on the back door the next morning.

He winced as sunlight hit him square in the eye as he looked at the bedside clock and saw that it was half past ten. Not surprising, since he'd stayed up until sometime after 3:00 a.m., unable to sleep and frantically sorting some of his mother's things into piles to keep and to throw away.

The pounding came again.

"Coming," he yelled, rolling out of bed, pulling on his jeans and a T-shirt.

He pulled his shirt on as he opened the door with his other hand and found his sister Kim standing there.

"Why didn't you just let yourself in?" he asked, backing up so that she could.

She hesitated in the doorway. "I wasn't sure if you'd be alone."

Jax jerked the shirt into place and tried not to glare at her. "I am most definitely alone." And he intended to stay that way for a while.

Women. They were so much trouble.

"Well, I wasn't sure that you would be, so I knocked. Were you drinking last night?"

"No, I didn't." He'd thought about that, too, but drinking wasn't going to get him out of this house and on with his miserable life, and that's what he wanted more than anything. To get on with his life. So he'd sorted things and thrown things away instead of having a few beers.

"Well, you sound grumpy enough that it seemed like a good guess," Kim said. "Is everyone in this family upset right now?"

"I'm not upset," he claimed, ridiculous as that was.

"No, you're always this sweet to me," she said, all-too-familiar tears filling her eyes.

"No. Don't you dare. No more crying women in this house. I'm making a new rule. If you cry, you can't come in. Dry eyes only in this house."

Kim sniffled and looked greatly offended. "I didn't come to cry to you about anything. I came to tell you there's something wrong with Katie and Kathie. That's all."

"Of course there is." Jax tried hard to find some scrap of patience to say, "Mom just died. We're all a mess."

"Something other than that," Kim claimed.

"How could you tell? You mean they're even more of a mess than before?"

"Yes."

Great.

"And you want me to fix it?" he asked.

She gave him a look that said, *Of course. That's what you do.*

He wondered what else could have possibly upset them more than their mother dying. What could even register on top of that? He couldn't imagine anything.

"Did they have a fight?" he tried.

"No."

"They're speaking to each other?"

"Yes. Not much. But…they're not doing the silent-treatment thing."

Jax really hated the silent-treatment thing. His sisters had it down to an art form.

"They're just being weird," Kim said.

Jax fought the urge to say, *Yeah? They're women.*

He was in a truly foul mood.

He opened his mouth to say, *Okay, I'll talk to them,* but what came out was, "You know, they're just going to have to handle it themselves. Or you can handle it. Because I can't."

Kim gave him that same look Gwen had, way back when she'd decided he'd either grown three heads or was some kind of gift from God, which turned out to be really, really funny, hadn't it?

Of course, Kim hadn't been in on the joke. She just gave him a funny look and asked, "What do you mean?"

"I can't do it," Jax said again. "I can't fix anything else this week. I'm way over my limit. It may be a month before I can fix one more thing."

"But you always make things better," Kim said.

"I know." And he felt as low as a snake, saying this to her. Next thing he knew, he was close to crying himself. He'd have to kick himself out of the house. "I just can't handle one more thing, Kimmie. I'm sorry. That's just the way it is right now."

Kim put her hand on his forehead. "Are you sick?"

"No," he said, stepping back, so that her hand fell away. She still looked as if she just didn't understand. "But—"

"I'm not in the best shape myself, okay? She was my mother, too."

"I know that, but—"

"I can't be the one who copes with everything right now." Someone else would have to be elected to the position. He couldn't fill it anymore. He was failing everyone. His mother. His sisters. Gwen. Even the stupid dog. Although Romeo was better off with Gwen. No doubt about that.

"Did something happen?" Kim tried.

"Yeah. I reached the limit of what I can do."

He stood back and waited for that to sink in. Kim looked even more worried than she had when she'd shown up at the door. No doubt, the moment she left, she'd be on the phone to both her sisters, calling for an urgent family conference, here, to figure out what was wrong with Jax.

Great.

He could tell all three of them how inadequate he was to handle this.

And he'd promised his mother he'd take care of them and everything else.

"I'm sorry," he told her, and pulled her into his arms.

"No, I'm sorry," she tried. "You always take care of us, and it's not fair. It's just…the way it's always been. I thought you could handle anything."

"So did I," he admitted.

"Are you sure nothing else happened?"

"Oh, I don't know. I broke Gwen's heart. She's in love with me, when I told her not to dare do that, and instead of loving her in return, I gave her the dog."

"You gave her Romeo?" It sounded like she thought he'd admitted to murdering someone. "But…he's Mom's dog."

"And Mom's not here. Don't worry. Gwen loves him, and he makes an absolute fool of himself over her. They'll be very happy together."

Without Jax.

Was it really going to work that way?

"She even got another dog. A girl dog. Looks like a fat marshmallow. Romeo was licking her nose last night before they left. He probably thinks they're going to have a doggie wedding or something."

"So the dog's ready to commit to one woman but you're not?" Kim claimed.

Jax scowled. "That isn't funny."

"I don't think so, either. I think it's sad."

"You don't even like Gwen," Jax reminded her.

"I don't know her. I can't dislike her if I don't even know her."

"All three of you disliked her without even knowing her. Remember?"

"Well, obviously we weren't being fair to her. She brought those nice flowers for Mom's funeral and made that really nice casserole, and she seems to have made you feel better through all this. Jax, I could learn to like anyone who could help you through this. So, you broke her heart?"

"Yeah."

"Are you ever going to quit doing that?"

"I don't know," he said.

"I want you to be happy. You don't really think you're going to be happy if you're all alone, do you?"

"Beats the alternative," he claimed.

"Does it, really? Because you sure don't look very happy this morning. And it seemed like, while she was with you, she made you happy. Why don't you call her and tell her you made a mistake? Ask her to give you another chance?"

"She doesn't want to fool around, Kimmie. She wants everything. The ring. The minister. Happily-ever-after and all that. We all know what garbage that is."

"I think that's exactly what you need," she claimed. "You need someone who loves you and is going to stand by you, even when things get really scary and really hard.

Is she someone who'd be there for you when things got really scary?"

"Not after what I said to her last night," Jax admitted.

"Well, you could always apologize. Tell her you're a fool. Tell her you're a man, and that you were wrong. She'll understand that."

"I could say that, and she'd probably forgive me. But even if we got back together, what's the point? It wouldn't last, Kim."

"How do you know that?"

"How do I know that? What do you mean, how do I know that? You're my sister. We lived the same life. We know nothing lasts."

"I don't know that," she claimed.

Jax took a breath, ready to argue. He knew he was right about this. "You know it."

"You mean because of what happened to Mom and Dad?"

"Yes."

"Jax, I get angry, and I don't understand things. I have questions that I don't think will ever be answered to my satisfaction. But I don't believe nothing good will ever come to me in life. I don't believe I won't ever have anything good that lasts. Is that what you honestly and truly believe?"

He planned to say yes, but she didn't give him the time.

"You can't really believe that," she said, putting her hand on his arm and staring up at him as if she were six and some kid down the block had just told her the tooth fairy didn't exist.

I do, he thought. *Really, I do, and I'm right.*

"Jax, you're supposed to be so much smarter than the rest of us."

Well, maybe I'm not.

He was in for a family meeting to end all family meetings, he feared. He could just hear them now.

You wouldn't believe what he told me. And he meant it. Really. I could see it in his eyes. He believes this. He's more of a mess than any of us ever realized.

Again, he remembered that he'd promised his mother he'd take care of the three of them.

He didn't know what to say. He didn't want to lie, and he sure didn't want to admit the truth of the matter.

"I have to go," he said.

"Jax—"

"Lock up, okay? I really have to go."

He slipped on his shoes and walked out the door.

Chapter Nineteen

It was like having a posse after him. His sisters would be after him, and he didn't want to get caught. And he probably knew from the beginning where he was going, but he didn't even want to admit it to himself. Gwen had called him a coward, and she was right.

He went to his mother's grave, couldn't help but think Romeo would have liked to come. He'd have to remember to tell Gwen to take him to the cemetery every now and then.

It took a long time, walking there instead of running, but he wasn't in any particular hurry. He was afraid of what would happen when he arrived.

All too soon, he found himself staring down at the grave, hands shoved into his pockets, a serious frown across his face, his heart pounding.

"I messed it all up," he began, then stared off into the sky, hearing nothing in return. "Mother, you can't quit on me now. All those times I wasn't sure what was going on or what I believed in, and you were there. I need you now. You're not done with me yet."

Nothing.

He swore softly, then sat down at the foot of the grave, staring at the blank spot where the headstone would go once it was finished. And then he found that wasn't close enough, and he stretched out on his back in the grass beside where she was, stretched out his hand toward her so that, if she was there, they could have been holding hands.

He'd held her hands a lot in the end. They'd gotten so cold.

"God, I miss her." He said the closest thing he'd come to a prayer in ages. "So much."

He didn't know what to do. He was ready to give up when he heard someone behind him and turned around, really hoping miracles did exist, that his mother was right behind him ready to explain everything to him.

Instead, he found Alicia.

He scrambled to his feet, wondering how much she'd heard and how he might explain, but before he could say a thing, she held out her hand. In it was a distinctive, cream-colored envelope he recognized right away.

His mother's pretty stationery.

She was one of the only people he knew who still sent hand-written notes, when the whole world had long ago turned to e-mail for just about everything.

"I think it's time I gave you this," Alicia said.

Jax was afraid to even take it. He turned his head to the right, stared off toward town and said, "You've been holding out on me all this time?"

Alicia shrugged. "Your mother asked me to. She thought it would take you some time to be ready to hear what she wanted to say."

"And you think I'm ready?" Truly, he wasn't sure he was.

"Well, Mrs. Myers said you seemed like you were in pretty bad shape when you went charging by her house. She lives right across the street. Didn't you know?"

Jax shook his head.

"Well, she does. She told me about seeing you here sometimes, and… Well, I don't know. Today seemed like the day. When she called me and told me you were here and seemed upset… I hope this is the right day. Your mother loved you very much, Jax."

"I know. Flaws and all, she loved me."

"I don't think she thought of you as flawed. A little confused sometimes, but not flawed."

"I am. You know that. I wish I could be the kind of man she wanted me to be," he admitted. "Her and Gwen and my sisters. The kind of man they need me to be, but I'm blowing it. I'm failing at everything, and my mother… My mother's just gone."

"That reminds me. When she handed me this, she also wanted me to tell you that you're not the final authority on what does and doesn't exist in this world, much as you'd like to think you are."

"She said that?" He knew she had. It sounded just like her.

Alicia nodded. "And that she loved you and your sisters and would be watching over you, always. Here."

Alicia held the envelope out to him again.

He finally took it, in a hand that was shaking. Alicia kissed him softly on the cheek and said, "You'll be okay."

And then she walked away, leaving him there.

Jax sat back down, heart pounding, afraid to open the envelope, afraid of what was inside.

But his mother hadn't deserted him, even now. He still had all the words of wisdom she'd given him over the years and friends of hers who were watching over him and his sisters and Gwen and maybe even God, and he had this letter from her.

I'll never really leave you, she'd told him one day near the end. It seemed she'd truly meant it.

He opened up the letter, found that it wasn't even written in his mother's handwriting. There was a little note in the corner saying that she'd been too weak to get it all down and the pastor at her church had written it for her, one day in the hospital, that if Jax had any questions, the minister would be happy to talk to him about anything in the letter.

Great, mom. You found a way to get me to talk to the man after all. Should have known you'd be able to manage even that.

Jax closed his eyes, bracing himself, looking for strength, wanting all the answers to all the questions he had to be found in this one letter. What were the chances of that happening?

And yet, so far, whenever he'd really needed help, he'd gotten it from somewhere. Who was arranging that, he wondered? Who was taking care of him now?

He knew what his mother would say. She'd say it was God.

He still didn't know how he felt about that.

And he was stalling on the letter.

Finally, he unfolded it and began to read.

My dearest Jax,

It's early in the morning, and you just left. I still had things I wanted to say to you, but I was just too tired, so I asked Reverend Paulson to help me with this letter, and I'm going to give it to Alicia to hold for you because I'm sure there's a better chance that you'll be seeing her about the will and everything than going to my church, at least right away.

He grinned. Right about that, Mom.

You said something last night that I just couldn't let go of. You said nothing important really lasts. That's just one of the silliest things you've ever said to me, and I always thought you were my reasonable child. Don't disappoint me now, Jax.

No! No! No! Not that. Not that he'd disappointed her!

Not that I could ever truly be disappointed in you, my darling. You've tried so hard, and you've been so strong, especially since we lost your father. I'm afraid I may have let myself lean on you too much and not taken care of you well enough through that, because now you seem to believe that you can't count on anything good to truly last for you, and that's just not true, darling.

Sometimes, things happen to us that we don't really understand, and we get strange ideas about life, like two and two somehow make five.

Math? She was going to give him a math lesson?

You think because you loved me and your father and you lost us both, that nothing good in life will ever really last? That people you let yourself love and count on will always disappoint you? Jax, that's your two-and-two-makes-five. It probably made you feel safe to think like that for a while, because it meant you knew how to protect yourself, by trying not to love anyone else. But you're not eleven anymore. You're a grown man. A wonderful man.

And I want you to have everything life has to offer, especially someone to love with all your heart. I know you'll find that someday.

"I think I have, Mom. She's a good woman," he said. "I mean, good down to the core, and she's stronger than she knows. She's been so alone and scared, but she kept going, and she believes in me. I'm not sure I deserve her, but I need her, and... Oh, I hurt her. I really hurt her."

And when you do, I don't want to hear anything about this silly two-and-two-makes-five thing or love not lasting or nothing good ever lasting. None of that. Let yourself believe in what you already feel, what you already know deep, down inside. There's nothing wrong with you. There's nothing you need to change. There's no reason to feel bad. You're just fine, and I love you very much. I'm so proud of you.

He was almost to the end, and he didn't want it to end. "Mom—"

And don't forget Romeo. He'll be lonely, and he'll need someone to love, too.

That was it. There was another note from her minister, saying that she'd fallen asleep, that the man wished Jax well and was ready to talk, anytime Jax needed to.

Petunia looked absolutely adorable.

Romeo lay at her feet gazing up at her adoringly, in the reception area at the dog groomer's.

She swished her pretty bouncy, curly tail, all pristine and white, with a sweet little, pink, curly ribbon tied around it and fanning out against her back, kind of like her tail was part of a bow on a Christmas present.

She had a matching pink collar with little rhinestones glittering on it, and her fur had been trimmed up tightly against her body—she wasn't fat at all, just furry when they'd found her. Around her face her pretty hair fluffed out in something like a wild, curly halo. They'd trimmed her bangs, so that Gwen could see her beautiful, dark eyes and her little button nose, her tiny mouth, which was hanging open, her little pink tongue showing as she beamed up at Gwen.

She'd been studiously ignoring Romeo, who was all but drooling.

"That's the way, darling," Gwen said. "Let him wonder a bit how you feel about him. He'll appreciate you more that way."

Not that Gwen was a big advocate of playing silly games with men. She was just feeling a bit raw this morning. Nothing like telling a man you loved him for the very first time in your life, and having him admit what he really wanted was for you to take his mother's dog off his hands.

Not that she believed he really meant that, either, but she figured she was entitled to be a little mad about it, at least for a while.

She scooped Petunia up off the floor, tipped the lady at the dog-grooming shop very, very well, and let them all fuss over pretty Petunia a moment more. Romeo didn't seem to know what to make of it. They thought Petunia was even more beautiful than he was?

Gwen grinned. "It'll be good for you in the end, Romeo. Trust me on this."

At least the dogs' love life was going to work out. Gwen could tell. She figured any little, furry girl who'd survived a restaurant Dumpster and come out of it sweet and gorgeous deserved the love and admiration of a dog like Romeo.

"Way to go, darling," she told Petunia and kissed her face.

Petunia beamed up at her. Romeo seemed a bit jealous, but he'd just have to get used to that.

"It's going to be a whole new world, Romeo," she told him.

The dog groomers grinned as if they understood perfectly and believed completely in canine love. Honestly, Romeo was more comfortable in showing his feelings than Jax was.

Gwen frowned, thinking, *Do I really want the man that much? Do I need him that much? Do I really, really love him?*

Yes, she did.

She'd just have to wait until he came to his senses, and she had some measure of faith that he would. Maybe she'd go have a talk with his mother, and then she'd just love both her dogs and try not to be so sad.

Faith, as her aunt would have said. If we knew, absolutely, that everything would all work out in the end, we wouldn't need that thing called faith.

Jax went back to the house, and there were his sisters, waiting for him, looking as if they'd come for an intervention of sorts. He walked in the door and they all came up to him and started talking at once.

"Did you really give away the dog?"

"Are you done with that woman? Because she didn't seem all that bad."

"You really should let us take care of you for a while, Jax. You always take care of us, and it's just not right."

"Stop!" he said. "Just take a breath and give me a minute here. Everybody sit and try to calm down."

He walked into the living room and sat, and they followed him, quite obediently. He was surprised. They must really be up to something if they were willing to feign cooperation with him. Must be to catch him off guard all the more.

Okay, Mom. What now? He'd forgotten to ask about the girls.

"I'm okay." That was his opening line. They stared back at him, biting their tongues, barely managing not to contradict him. "I mean, I'm not quite okay. Not all the way. But I'm better. I've been talking to Mom, and…"

Too late, he remembered what was weird about that.

Their looks got even more curious.

"I mean," he jumped in, miraculously before the three of them did, "I've been trying to think of what she'd say at a time like this…." Not bad. Keep going. He could weather that little slip. And then, a brainstorm… "Actually, I remember a lot of what she did say when Dad died, and mostly, it was that we still had each other, and we would love each other and lean on each other and get through anything that came along. And that's what we did. It worked then. It's going to work this time. I mean, things are bound to be a little crazy at first. It was then, too. But things get better. It just seems like they never will sometimes, but then they always do. I mean, what has life thrown at us that we couldn't handle? Nothing. We're still here. We're together. We'll take care of each other. We'll be okay."

He thought he'd done a pretty good job of selling that little pep talk, and he had meant it. He was starting to believe, despite everything, that they would be okay. Sad sometimes, mad at others, maybe not quite ever understanding, but okay.

"She said she'd watch out for us," he said.

"And you believe that? Really?" Katie asked.

"Yes," he said, hoping they'd all forgotten about the little conversation with her that he'd mentioned by accident.

"You do?" Kim asked.

More certain this time, he said, "Yes."

"I didn't think you really believed in things like that," Kathie said.

"Well…Mom said I don't have to believe in something for it to be true." He grinned. "She said I'm not the final authority on what exists and what doesn't in the world. She said she was proud of all of us, and that she loved us and that she'd be watching out for us. I know better than to argue with her. All of us do. She always managed to bring us around to her way of thinking, one way or another."

Oh, yeah. Why would he think she'd give that up just because she was no longer alive and well on planet Earth? He should have known better.

"You're sure you're okay?" Kathie asked.

"I'm sure."

"And you really got rid of the dog?"

"Just temporarily." At least, he hoped so.

"And Gwen?"

"I'm not done with Gwen." He just had to convince her to give him another chance.

Relieved, his sisters calmed down. They talked some more, and eventually, they got up and did the group-hug thing. There were no more tears, thank goodness, but they did express more dismay over the progress he'd made in cleaning out their mother's house and how everything was changing. Why did everything have to keep changing? Why couldn't things just stay the same for a while?

His sisters got caught up in something else for a moment, and when they weren't looking, he sneaked eggbeaters and ice-cream scoops into their purses. And when Kim left, for once, she didn't go through the garbage bags full of stuff, stacked neatly near the back porch, to save them from being carted away.

This definitely looked like progress.

When he was alone, his first thought was to rush over to Gwen's and beg her to forgive him and to find a way to convince her it was possible for a man to change completely and that she could trust that, could trust her heart to him.

He wasn't averse to making a sincere apology to a woman when he was wrong, and he was capable of admitting he was wrong. He just wasn't a man who'd ever had his heart on the line when he had to go say he was wrong and beg for forgiveness.

He hadn't ever needed so much to make a woman believe he was sincere and that he was actually capable of change, and to convince her that he now knew what he wanted, when it was so different from what he'd always wanted before.

How was he supposed to do that?

Got any ideas, Mom?

He stood there in the kitchen trying to juggle big, wooden spoons that were sticking out of a box of things to put in the estate sale. When the Bees had been here, and he'd tried to pawn some more stuff off on them, they'd told him to have a giant garage sale, and he'd offered them the profits from the sale, if they'd handle it. They'd happily agreed. But he still had to get everything sorted.

The keeper pile was still way too big.

When it came right down to it, there just wasn't much a person left on this earth that truly mattered, once they were gone.

There was stuff…. Looking around his mother's house, it was mostly just stuff. Oh, there were pictures and home movies he and his sisters would keep and always treasure, a few little things here and there that brought up a wonderful memory of her, and some things that had been his father's that meant something to him. But mostly, it was just things she'd accumulated that, without her, didn't really mean anything.

Why she'd left him this dreary job…

Oh, Mom.

One of the wooden spoons landed with a solid smack against his forehead. Another bounced across the floor. He actually caught the third.

Suddenly he knew exactly why his mother had left him this dismal little task. He couldn't believe it had taken him this long to figure it out.

She was smiling now, from wherever she was watching him, and he was certain she was watching.

Thanks, Mom. I love you.

He wasn't quite sure how he should approach the other person he needed to be thanking.

Oh, his mother had taken them to church from the time they were born. And there'd been a time when he'd just accepted everything he heard there without questioning it, when he'd said his prayers at night and tried to be good, the way he thought God wanted kids to be.

And then he'd grown up and kind of drifted away from the church and from God, when he hadn't really believed in anything and had blamed a lot of things on God, at the same time he was questioning whether God even existed.

Pretty funny, now that he thought about it—blaming things on Someone he claimed didn't even exist.

Sorry about that. That seemed as good a way to begin as any. His mother had always claimed prayers weren't anything except having a little talk with God. That the only important thing was to be honest and open up your heart.

Just that? Jax thought. *And he'd always been so good at that.*

He was going to need some help here. That seemed like a good thing to add next.

I really don't know what I'm doing here. And I feel like I've been so stupid.... So lost. And I can see now that You've been right there the whole time, waiting for me to figure this all out, and taking care of me and my family anyway....

Jax still didn't know why his father had to go away when he was so young or why his mother had to leave, too, but he knew something else that seemed even more important now.

He realized that he didn't have to have all the answers to those questions in order to believe. One didn't seem to have a lot to do with the other anymore.

The important thing was that he'd never really lost his parents, and he'd never really been alone. He never would be.

That was what he believed without any doubts at all.

Just the way he believed that one of the greatest gifts God had ever brought him was a woman named Gwendolyn Moss.

Jax grinned.

I don't think I deserve her, but I sure am grateful to have her in my life.

Assuming that she'd forgive him for the misery he'd put her through, including claiming all he'd wanted her for was to have someone to take his mother's dog.

But she would forgive him. She had to.

When Jax finally came up with a plan and worked up his nerve to carry it out, he headed down the alley and found Romeo in Gwen's backyard, sitting at Petunia's feet, gazing up at her like a lovesick puppy. Jax couldn't be sure, but it looked as if he was licking Petunia's feet.

Jax shook his head and grinned. "How the mighty have fallen, huh, Romeo?"

He unlatched the gate and walked into the backyard. Petunia, all prettied up and trimmed and beribboned, gave him a smugly superior glance and then studiously ignored him, in favor of surveying the back porch.

"Okay, that kind of girl, are you? One who holds a grudge? Guess I can't blame you. I wasn't very nice to you."

Jax heard footsteps and turned to the right and there was Gwen, coming around the side of the house with her arms wrapped around a big potted plant of some sort.

He went to her, took it from her and said, "Need some help?"

"Maybe." She looked at him in much the same way Petunia had. Did the dog's name really have to be Petunia? Surely there was something they could do about that.

"I work cheap," he offered. "And I'm good at hauling around big, heavy things, digging in the dirt, pulling weeds, whatever you need."

"You came here to work in my yard?"

"No, I came here because I thought I might talk you into taking a walk with me." He took a breath and remembered the dogs, then made himself add, "You and the dogs."

"That's why you came to see me? Because you wanted company on a walk?"

"No. I came because I finally figured out some things, and I want to tell you about them at a certain place, a place that's special to me."

"Oh."

She didn't seem like she was getting ready to yell at him or anything. That was a plus. He figured she was entitled. She looked hurt and worried, and he'd probably made her cry, something he just hated, but it seemed she was at least going to hear him out.

"Come with me," he said. "I'll beg if I have to."

Okay, now she looked like she might cry.

"Don't do that. Please," he said, reaching for her so he could maybe stop those tears. He held her chin in his hand as she dipped her head down, and the moisture in her eyes glistened ominously.

He moved closer, settling her against him, easing his arms around her.

Curious how the whole world seemed to shift gently and unerringly into place as he did that.

He felt that he was coming home. Coming home to Gwen. She laid her head against his shoulder, and her hands clutched at his sides, like she was afraid he was going to slip away from her at any minute, and she didn't want him to go.

"I'm not running away from you," he said. "Even if you do try to get rid of me."

"Really?" she muttered, snuggling against him, her forehead pressed against the side of his neck.

"Promise." He kissed her forehead, stood there and let himself absorb the wonderful feel of her in his arms, things seeming more right with his world than he'd ever thought they could be again. "I missed you."

"I missed you, too."

"I can be really stupid sometimes, Gwen."

She laughed at that. "That's what your sisters said."

"My sisters?"

She nodded. "They came to see me."

"To tell you I could be really stupid sometimes?"

"To tell me they thought they should get to know me better because they thought their brother was a mess over me. They were very nice," she claimed, then looked vulnerable again. "I didn't know if they were reading you right or not."

He gave her a gentle kiss, fought the urge to prolong it. First, they had some things to settle.

"How 'bout we walk and have a little talk?"

"Sure." She managed to smile. "Just let me get Petunia's leash."

Miss Petunia perked right up at the sound of her name. A silly grin came across her furry face and she practically bounced after Gwen. Romeo trotted off after her, shooting Jax a haughty look that seemed to say, *I understand women so much better than you do.*

"She'll tear your heart out, Romeo," he called out after the dog.

Gwen was back outside a moment later. "What was that?"

"Just a little friendly advice for the dog."

Gwen looked skeptical but snapped on Petunia's leash, ready to go. The little dog started yelping with excitement. Romeo did, too.

"They just love me, don't they?" Jax said as they took off down the alley, Gwen holding Petunia's leash, the dogs dancing around Jax and Gwen as they walked.

"Somehow, I don't think you're the big attraction for them," Gwen claimed.

"No, really. They're crazy about me. I just have one little... Well, it's not a problem. Just a question. Where did you come up with the name Petunia?"

"They're her favorite flower," Gwen said with a completely straight face.

Jax grinned. "You mean, she came out of the Dumpster with a list of her likes and dislikes?"

"No. We were in the flower shop cleaning her up, and it just seemed like a dog found behind a flower shop—"

"You said you found her in the Dumpster behind the café," he reminded her as he steered her and the parade of pooches down Maple Street and toward the park.

"Well, what was I supposed to do with that? I wasn't going to name her Cheeseburger or BLT. We saved her and took her to the flower shop to clean her up, and it just seemed like a flower name would be appropriate, and there are lots of good flower names for little girls."

"Petunia?"

"Well, there was Lily, Rose, Fern, Daisy. I really liked Daisy. But Petunia kept running up to the petunias in the big vases out front and playing hide-and-seek behind them. And if that isn't a clear indication that she wanted to be named Petunia, I don't know what is."

"Rrruuuf!" Petunia said.

"See, she likes it," Gwen said.

"Great."

"Do you have a problem with that?"

"No. Not at all." Petunia? He could just see him, another day, when they were in the same park, yelling, *Petunia, get over here right now.* Sure. That would work. "It's just kind of…girlie." That was the best argument he could make.

"Well, she's a girl. A very pretty girl."

"Yes, she is."

The walk was a pleasant one. They must have passed a dozen different people they knew. It seemed everywhere someone was waving and smiling and looking generally pleased with the world.

Miss Petunia did a dainty little tail-swishing strut, and Romeo, her slave for life, followed in what seemed to be complete joy and awe of her. Every now and then he glanced back at Jax and Gwen with a big stupid grin on his face that seemed to say, *Isn't she the greatest? Isn't life grand!*

Jax wondered if he had the same stupid grin on his face. He had a feeling he did.

He and Gwen and the dogs turned into the park and down one of the footpaths to the falls. Romeo, excited by the water, finally forgot about Petunia long enough to give an excited yelp, looking from the water to Jax and back to the water.

"No, Romeo. No swimming today."

He whined his disappointment.

"He swims?" Gwen asked.

"Loves it. Loves going down the falls, too."

"Romeo bodysurfs the falls?"

"Sure. It's tradition. You can't be an official Magnolia Falls resident without doing the falls."

"I guess that means you have?"

"About a million times. The best ones are after a big rain—"

She grimaced. "Don't tell me. Don't."

"I guess that means you've never gone over the falls?"

"No."

"Gwen?" He shook his head. "This is serious. We're going to have to do something about that."

"Not today we're not."

"Okay. Not today. But come summer, you and me, right here."

"We're going to be here? Together? In the summer?"

He nodded.

"That would be more than your three-month limit."

"Yeah. I guess we need to talk about that." They'd reached one of the little stone benches beside the falls, under the biggest, oldest tree, and he said, "Sit with me. It's nice here."

Gwen sat on one side of the bench. Jax was just getting comfortable beside her when her dog jumped up on the bench and plopped down between them. She turned to Jax and gave him a grin and then jumped up onto his lap, put her front paws on his chest and tried to lick him in the face.

Gwen laughed.

Romeo started whining pitifully, like a man who'd just had his heart broken by the love of his life.

Petunia panted happily in Jax's face and swished her tail.

"Friendly dog," Jax said, holding her back just enough to keep her from giving him a puppy kiss.

"I thought all women reacted to you this way," Gwen said.

He made a face at her, and she just laughed and finally called off her dog. Petunia pouted prettily and finally settled down, planting herself firmly between them, her chin resting on Jax's knee. Romeo looked like he felt horribly betrayed and abandoned, but finally quieted.

It wasn't exactly the quiet, private, maybe even romantic moment Jax had envisioned, but they'd just have to make do.

"I figured out what my mother was trying to teach me by leaving me to handle everything with her estate," he began.

"What?"

"That all those things we leave behind, once we're done with this world, don't really matter at all. Except for the people we have loved and the memories we have left of them. The rest of it's just stuff, and most of it doesn't mean a thing. That's what she wanted me to get. What was important. What really mattered."

"I'm glad you got it."

"Yeah. I can see it so clearly now, I can't believe it took me so long to get it. She found a way to show me what I needed to know, even on her deathbed. Even after she was gone. But then, that's the kind of woman she was." Jax put his arm around Gwen and used his other hand to turn her face to his. "She really would have loved you."

Gwen looked scared but hopeful.

"I love you, too. And not in the same way I love your blue sweater. I mean, the sweater's nice. The way you look in it is very nice. But you're not a blue sweater to me."

"You're not exactly a blue sweater to me, either," she admitted. "I tried to make you just a blue sweater, but…it was too late, I couldn't help myself."

"Me, neither. It was way too late, almost from the very beginning. I love you, and that's not something I've ever said to any woman before. I mean it, Gwen. Do you believe that?"

She took a breath and then closed her eyes, as she might have done if she was trying to convince herself to step off the edge of a cliff or go over the falls with him on a day when the water was roaring.

"I believe it," she said.

Good. That gave him the courage to keep going. "I need you."

"I need you, too, Jax."

"I think you're my gift. Not the other way around." He kissed her softly, to the tune of the dogs making confused, whining sounds. How was that for romance? He grinned down at her and said, "You know what happened here about thirty-three years ago?"

"No."

"My father proposed to my mother. Under this same tree," he said, gathering up his courage. "I think you're going to have to marry me, Gwen. I don't think anything else will do."

She looked scared for a moment, then hopeful, then happy. "Mr. I'll-Never-Get-Married, Never-Love-Some-one? Mr. Nothing-Ever-Really-Lasts?"

"Yeah. Like I said, I was stupid. Or maybe I was just waiting for you. I can make that promise, Gwen. I wouldn't say the words to you if I didn't believe them. I want you beside me forever, and I want it to be the way it was for my mother and father, and if anything ever happens to one of us... His name was the last thing my mother said. His face was the last thing she saw. She said he was waiting for her, wherever she was going. He was going to take her there, and she was going to be with him again. She died with a smile on her face and his name on her lips. I thought it was the morphine talking, but now...I believe it. I believe he was there, that he was waiting for her, that they're together again. And it scares me to think of loving you that much and of what might happen. But when I try to weigh the fear against how much I need you, how much I want you beside me... The fear isn't nearly as strong as the love, as how much I need you, how much I think we can have together."

There. He'd gotten it all out. He stopped to take a breath and try to gauge her reaction. From the smile on her face, it seemed this was going well.

"So," he dared to ask, "what do you think?"

"I don't know."

"What do you mean, you don't know?"

"Well..." She grinned at him. "There's a lot to living together. A lot of things to work out. Compatibility things."

"That's okay. You'll be with me, and everything will be just fine. More than fine. I promise. What else?"

"Your sisters didn't like me very much before," she mentioned.

"Give 'em time to get to know you better. They will."

"But—"

"They'd do anything for me. Most women would, remember?"

"Yeah. About that—"

"No. It's okay. I'll take care of it."

"How? Do you honestly think you can give up being charming?"

"The thing about Cassidy men is that once they fall in love, that's it. They're done. Ask anyone. What else?"

"Well…"

"Gwen?"

"It's just that—"

"What?"

"You know I have two dogs, don't you?"

"Yeah, I noticed."

"And you were really mean to Petunia yesterday."

"I was." He looked down at the fur ball with what he hoped was a let's-make-peace smile and said, "Sorry, Petunia."

She stuck her nose in the air and looked away, dismissing him completely. Romeo was sitting at her feet, a sickly hopeful look on his pathetic face, and she was ignoring him, too. Jax fought the urge to remind her, *You were living in a Dumpster yesterday, sweet thing. Remember?*

"You get me, you get the dogs," Gwen said. "And you have to be nice to them. Very nice to them."

"Yeah, I kind of knew that."

"It was such a great plan you had, dumping Romeo on me, thinking you could get rid of us both."

"Yeah. Great plan. I was miserable."

"Me, too," Gwen admitted. "You deserve to live with two dogs instead of one for that little stunt."

"I know." Jax grinned even wider. "Is that a yes?"

"I think that's a yes."

He kissed her soundly, then grinned some more. "Hey, you know what my mother would be doing if she were here right now?"

"No, what?"

"Laughing. She'd have said she knew all along that all I needed was a little faith and someone like you."

* * * * *

RUTH AXTELL
MORREN

WILD ROSE

An outcast all her life, Geneva Patterson endured
the cruel taunts of the New Haven townspeople in
solitude—until Caleb Phelps came to the small
Maine town. Once a respected sea captain, he'd
been wrongly accused of a shameful crime and
now held only pain in his eyes. Through
God's grace, Geneva and Caleb try to
find redemption and love.

Available wherever paperbacks are sold.

Steeple
Hill®

MOLLY NOBLE BULL

THE WINTER PEARL

In 1888 Honor McCall escapes her cruel uncle and starts
a new life. Finding a home with a handsome young minister
is more than she deserves and Honor must finally come
to terms with the love she feels for the minister and
truth she hides from him.

"The Winter Pearl is a jewel of a novel."
—Diane Noble, award-winning author of *Phoebe*

Available wherever paperbacks are sold.

Delve into the first novel for Steeple Hill by

SHELLEY BATES

GROUNDS TO BELIEVE

Ross Malcolm's mission is to protect children. Meeting Julia McNeill, a woman whose nephew has fallen prey to a secretive sect, finds Ross wanting to teach Julia the truth of God's love despite his disdain of her lifestyle.

As Julia's actions unleash a dangerous chain of events, Ross must save three lives from the evil that threatens them.

Available wherever paperbacks are sold.

Steeple Hill®

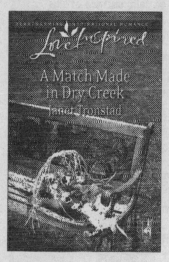

REQUEST YOUR FREE BOOKS!

2 FREE INSPIRATIONAL NOVELS
PLUS 2
FREE
MYSTERY GIFTS

Love Inspired

YES! Please send me 2 FREE Love Inspired® novels and my 2 FREE mystery gifts. After receiving them, if I don't wish to receive any more books, I can return the shipping statement marked "cancel." If I don't cancel, I will receive 4 brand-new novels every month and be billed just $3.99 per book in the U.S., or $4.74 per book in Canada, plus 25¢ shipping and handling per book and applicable taxes, if any*. That's a savings of 20% off the cover price! I understand that accepting the 2 free books and gifts places me under no obligation to buy anything. I can always return a shipment and cancel at any time. Even if I never buy another book from Steeple Hill, the two free books and gifts are mine to keep forever.

113 IDN EF26 313 IDN EF27

Name	(PLEASE PRINT)	
Address		Apt. #
City	State/Prov.	Zip/Postal Code

Signature (if under 18, a parent or guardian must sign)

Order online at www.LoveInspiredBooks.com

Or mail to Steeple Hill Reader Service™:

IN U.S.A.: P.O. Box 1867, Buffalo, NY 14240-1867
IN CANADA: P.O. Box 609, Fort Erie, Ontario L2A 5X3

Not valid to current Love Inspired subscribers.

Want to try two free books from another series?
Call 1-800-873-8635 or visit www.morefreebooks.com

* Terms and prices subject to change without notice. NY residents add applicable sales tax. Canadian residents will be charged applicable provincial taxes and GST. This offer is limited to one order per household. All orders subject to approval. Credit or debit balances in a customer's account(s) may be offset by any other outstanding balance owed by or to the customer. Please allow 4 to 6 weeks for delivery.

Your Privacy: Steeple Hill is committed to protecting your privacy. Our Privacy Policy is available online at www.eHarlequin.com or upon request from the Reader Service. From time to time we make our lists of customers available to reputable firms who may have a product or service of interest to you. If you would prefer we not share your name and address, please check here. ☐

LIREG07